HOUSE OF STONE

Rene D. Schultz

PRAISE FOR
HOUSE OF STONE

The very best thing about Rene D. Schultz's books is the way she keeps you so entertained with her amazing storylines while at the same time opening your eyes to some very real world problems and headlines.
Open up that first page and be swept away with the tides of love and loss, floods and earthquakes, weddings and funerals so well written that it feels as if you're actually there until you turn that last page and realize it's over and it was only a book after all.
~Shelby Sutton, reviewer

With a compassionate touch, Ms. Schultz also weaves in social issues and their aftermath, including homelessness, addiction, and abandoned children.
~Jada Ryker, reviewer

The characters are so well developed and so real that you can picture the events of the story actually taking place in real life or to someone that you know. I am already looking forward to the next

book that Rene writes, as I know before reading it that it will be amazing and another one to try to choose from as my favorite. Thanks for these amazing books and keep writing as I need more!!
~Stephenee Carsten, reviewer

It's so well written, and it really is a book you cannot put it down, as with all of Rene's books. Rene's passion for writing shines down on her characters and makes them jump out of the page at you.
~Amanda Jayne Bonsell, reviewer

If you want to read a book that will evoke the feelings of friendship, love, suspense, & tears of joy & sadness, House of Stone is your book. The four orphans from Bishop Street are drawn together again in Rene Schultz's sequel. The suspense starts in the first chapter continuing throughout the book in the form of a hostage situation, a flood & an earthquake. You will be transported through the story by the authors realistic portrayal of her characters, both old & new. They will become your friends as they embark in their many adventures in LA, North Dakota, Mexico & Honduras.
I would recommend this book to anyone who loves a great story with realistic characters & story line. Even though there were several new characters added they fit in very well. I didn't want the book to end but I believe there is more story to tell.
~Leslie Beebe, reviewer

This second book had me gasping in places. I literally could feel my heart pounding, the event that happened was awful, I am not going to tell you. But it had me wondering if Maggie was alive. Did

she make it? ... The characters are as solid and stone, they are rocks to each other, they are bold like boulders, unmoveable and unstoppable.... I just want you to know how this book made me FEEL. This author Rene Schultz brings out emotions in me that aren't easily displayed. There were times when I was biting my nails, times when I was crying buckets and times when I was scared. Each character has now got a place in my heart, as as this lovely unique author, Rene Schultz.
~Sue Ward, reviewer

The author has done an amazing job pulling you into the story. I cried in several spots, so have tissues handy. This book is truly an emotional roller coaster. It does leave us on a cliffhanger, but a good one! Can't wait for the next book. If you are looking for an uplifting, emotional read this is for you.
~Lauren Alumbaugh, reviewer

A NOTE FROM THE AUTHOR

WHEN I STARTED DOWN MY YELLOW BRICK ROAD OF writing, I never thought I would be where I am today. Bishop Street was a figment of my imagination; friends to hang out with on quiet evenings. For a year Maggie, Elizabeth, Lucy, and Randolph sat in my writing room, weaving their story. When it was done, like with most authors, it became very painful and sad to say goodbye to them. Since Bishop Street's release, readers and reviewers have been sending me notes asking for a sequel. And so, one quiet evening when I was pondering another book, my fingers touched the keyboard and never stopped until I gave everyone what they wanted—HOUSE OF STONE—the SEQUEL to Bishop Street. Being back with the orphans was like reminiscing with old friends, as they continued to lead me on their action-filled journey.

Maggie, Elizabeth, Lucy, Randolph, and Damon are back, challenging themselves to let go of the past. Still fused together by the immeasurable power of friendship—they will never let anything get between them again. Not tests of courage nor willingness to change; not overwhelming love and happiness; not a life-threatening flood that nearly destroys North Bend; or the Honduran earthquake that takes thousands of lives and leaves them searching for Maggie. Unexpectedly, their lives will all change forever....

Dedicated to my children:
Brett and Kelly -- Lisa and Todd

Always remember:
"Unity is strength...when there is teamwork and collaboration, wonderful things can be achieved."
~Mattie Stepanek

Acknowlegments

To my grandchildren:
Ashton James, Madelyn Rose, Michaela Paige
Mima loves you very much.

To Linds and Cindy:
*Thanks for taking this journey with me again, and
again, and again. Your
editing/covers/formatting/graphic design -- make
me who I am. I only write the story!*

To Hideki Naito:
*A very special thank you for letting me use some of
the most beautiful and haunting pictures of
children from South America. As I looked at every
picture in Hideki Naito's portfolio of photographs
from Honduras, Peru, Panama, Nicaragua, El
Salvador, Bolivia, Guatemala, and Mexico of the
young children--the reality of their plight was
etched deeply into my heart. Please check out his
amazing photos on FLCKR: Hideki Naito.*

Sue Ward and Philomena Callan, my dear UK ladies:
It amazes me that you stop everything to beta each new novel of mine. You started with Bishop Street and it has never stopped. I truly feel blessed!

Thank you to all my friends, reviewers, readers, and bloggers (you know who you are):
You are all amazing and I sincerely appreciate all the support. Without you, this journey would be impossible.

CHAPTER 1

MAGGIE STOOD UP AND STRETCHED HER ARMS above her head, trying to relieve the slight ache in her back. She wasn't very tall, but at forty-four, she was still an attractive-looking lady. Her chin-length blonde hair accentuated her beautiful hazel eyes that changed colors depending on her mood. She had been sitting for hours working on her new book. Only, this book was never going to be published or go public. It was a reflection of all the changes in her life over the past four years since she found her childhood family. It was more like a personal tribute to Lucy, Elizabeth, and Randolph. After all, it was their story from the beginning of their time in the orphanage, to now.

And it was going to showcase the incredible differences in their lives after finally getting back together after a misinterpreted separation of twenty years.

Maggie sat down and leaned her head back. She closed her eyes and began to reflect on her life over the past four years. Maggie, Elizabeth, Lucy, and Randolph's tumultuous childhood in the orphanage was finally put to rest. The calculated lies and deceit of Sister Theresa had torn them apart, leaving them all alone after they left the orphanage to find their way in the world. They had all gone through enough in their childhood to last them a lifetime. Sister Theresa had only increased their distrust and securities, tearing them apart from the only family they knew. It wasn't until Maggie had learned of Sister Theresa's death, and her nightmares came back, that she finally decided to search for the real truth of why they had never contacted each other in almost twenty years.

Elizabeth, her husband, and five children were doing well, and enjoying life on the farm. All except for her oldest son, Randall. He had moved from their small farm in North Dakota, and was now living with Maggie in Los Angeles. He was a charming young man, who made the Dean's List at UCLA every year, and his goal was to be a veterinarian.

With the help of Maggie, after twenty years of living on the streets in Los Angeles, Lucy's continued sobriety now allowed for stability in her life. Then finally getting her daughter out of foster care had been the catalyst to push her into helping others. She was now the director and headmistress of Safe House and was concentrating on building another shelter to get runaway children off the streets of Hollywood.

Randolph was still floating between cities and enjoying the solitude of his ranch in Mexico and his billion-dollar Software Company in Silicon Valley. His wealth had imprisoned him into a life of constant bodyguards. The anonymity on a ranch located in a small town in Mexico was his only secret reprieve from tabloids and prying eyes.

Maggie's constant friend and outspoken secretary, Denise, was still enjoying marital bliss, along with her two daughters, Briana and Maddie. She was still in the office pushing Maggie to her limits, and after nearly twenty years together, nothing had changed.

Damon, the investigator who Maggie hired to find her friends, was another story in itself....

Maggie opened her eyes and sighed. Three months ago, her new novel had come out and the media blitz had nearly sucked the life out of her. After taking a few years off to solidify her relationships and reorganize her life, she had finally gone back to writing. Fortunately, her time off had only strengthened her creativity and introduced a new dimension into her storytelling—romance. Her new book had gone to the top of the New York Bestselling List in less than two months. It was a little different, and the genre spread out a little more than the stories she had previously written, but the reviewers embraced it with open arms. The novel was about a strong-willed detective that walked on the edge, and at the end, he finally finds romance. A smile crossed her face and she leaned forward in her seat. How silly she had been to bring a part of her private life into the limelight of her newest novel. Although most authors tended to do that, it was always something Maggie shied away from. For years she did everything possible to stay as private as she could. She never fed into the publicity or opened herself up to the tabloids. She had led a very sheltered existence, filled with an almost nonexistent social life. She had closed herself off from the media that was bent on destroying her reputation. Except for the past year—she didn't care anymore. So many things had changed, and the tabloids had had a heyday printing trashy rumors about her. She was constantly hounded like an animal; and everything she cherished privately was now scrutinized by the stories of the supermarket gutter press.

Maggie put down her cellphone, leaned over and pushed the button on her intercom. "Hey, you...."

Denise laughed. "You mean, you're not texting me on my cell? Make up your mind, Maggie—one or the other! Lately, you are driving me totally crazy! You either need to get out of the office more or take up a new hobby like knitting! This text-buzz, text-buzz has got to stop!"

Maggie smiled and said into the box, "Sorry! I'm so confused with all this new technology. Randall keeps pushing me more and more into using my new iPhone; and I keep fighting it tooth and nail! Texting someone across the room is the big thing nowadays with those young kids, but the intercom is easier, only one button to push!"

Denise opened Maggie's office door and walked in. She strolled over to her desk and sat down in the chair in front of her. She picked up her hand and waved directly at Maggie. "How about in person? This is even easier than texting or the intercom!"

Maggie gave Denise a big smile and nodded her head. "Much better! How are you feeling?"

Denise shrugged her shoulders. Then, she took the Kleenex out of her pocket and blew her nose. "I was up all night with the girls. Briana brought home a cold from school and proudly gave it to the whole family. Schools are a breeding ground for nasty germs that can't wait to infect a whole damn family!"

Maggie scrunched her face into a pained expression when she asked, "Did David get it too?"

"Oh...yeah! He's not a happy camper!" Denise's angry face suddenly burst into laughter and Maggie joined in.

"The lovely perks of having children! And something I don't wish to experience." Maggie continued, "I think Mary Jane is sick, also. Winter is that time of year...."

Denise sighed. "When Christmas break comes maybe we will all be able to stay healthy for a while!"

Maggie's face lit up like a light bulb. "Maybe you should go with David to Hawaii for the winter break? Beautiful sunny skies, hot humid breezes, and leave the children with Emma."

Denise shook her head. "I gave Emma the holiday off. She's been such a help with the sick kids and making sure they are well taken care of. David and I love the fact that she comes early in the morning and leaves when one of us gets home. Great idea, Maggie, except David is going crazy at work and can't take off much during the holiday."

Maggie blushed and said, "I'd give you my beach house in Malibu, but I have plans."

Denise smiled and lifted her brows. "Humm...with Damon?"

Maggie reddened again and said, "Yes, Miss Nosy! Actually, the whole family is coming for Christmas like every year. Plus, we have the 'grand opening' of the new shelter for the children. I'm going to give Elizabeth and her family my penthouse and I'll take the beach house."

Denise sat straight up in her chair, threw her arms across the desk and leaned forward. "For cripes sake, how am I being nosy! For two years I watched him drop by the office just to hang around and be your friend. Then last year, I can remember the exact day and exact time he opened the door, paraded by my desk, pushed open your door, and marched right up to you! I think that was one of the most romantic scenes I had ever witnessed in my whole entire life. It even beat Scarlet O'Hara and Rhett Butler, when he carried her up the stairs in "Gone with the Wind." And I watch that scene over and over all the time!"

Maggie's face was deep red. "Really...?"

Denise sighed. "Geeez, Maggie, you are one of the most naïve people I've ever met!" She continued, "Yes, it was very romantic the way he pulled you out of the chair and planted the biggest, longest kiss any person could ever imagine! And...wasn't it romantic or a deal breaker for you?" Denise laughed.

Maggie started drawing circles on her blotter with the pen she was holding. "It was something I had secretly dreamed about for years. I was just too shy to initiate any kind of relationship, and too afraid of rejection to pursue it."

Denise sucked in a deep breath and let it out slowly. "Well, thank God he finally grew a set of cajones! I was tired of seeing him hang around here waiting for you to give him a sign that you were interested. And I was getting damn tired of watching you moping around like a 'lovesick' teenager!"

Maggie's eyes opened wide in surprise. "Was it that bad?"

"Worse!" They both started to laugh.

Denise stood up. She shook her head and clicked her tongue in bewilderment. "I hope you have a very romantic time at the beach house! Was there something you needed when you called me in here?"

Maggie cleared her throat. "Yes! Lucy is looking for volunteers for the open house at Safe House next week. I thought I would go over tomorrow and wanted to know if you wanted to join me. She's going tonight to straighten things up, but I'm just too tired."

"I'm going to pass. I have two sick little babies and one cranky husband at home who need some TLC; and I'm leaving right now to go home to them! Give Lucy a hug for me."

"I will. And in case I haven't said it enough, I will say it once more.... 'Thank you for all your help with the new book. We hit the top of the charts yesterday'!" Maggie and Denise did a fist bump.

An hour later, Maggie was pulling up into the underground parking of her building. She was exhausted and hungry. Damon had left a text on her phone earlier saying, 'I'm still out of town. I will try to catch the red-eye back tonight, hugs.' Maggie's face lit up with a smile at just the thought of him coming back into town. She missed him and couldn't wait to touch his handsome face or kiss his seductive lips. They had been lovers for the past year and spent most of their time together when he wasn't busy with his heavy schedule of clientele, or she wasn't on her publicity tour for her newest book. Maggie was in love with him, but had never said those three words out loud. Neither had he. Nevertheless, there was a bond that kept them moving forward with their solid relationship.

Herbie watched as Maggie got out of the car and walked toward him. He hit the elevator button as she approached and stopped next to him. "Evening, Miz Maggie." His big toothy smile and eagerness to please was always so endearing to Maggie.

"How's my favorite doorman?" Maggie smiled.

His dark eyes gleamed and his spotlessly clean, dark blue jacket flaunted four rows of shiny brass buttons. The trousers in the same color bore the crease of an iron and the elevator light reflected off his patent leather shoes. "You's be lookin' jus' as tired as me, Miz Maggie. I'z be retirin' real soon, hows 'bouts you?"

Maggie touched his wrinkled face and said, "You're such a sweet man. Don't you think now that you are going to be ninety years old, that you deserve to retire next month?"

Maggie wrapped her arms around Herbie and hugged him. He shuffled his thin legs and smiled. "I will miz you, Miz Maggie."

"I shall miss you, too!"

The elevator doors opened and wearily Maggie walked inside and waited for the doors to shut. It ascended to the penthouse and the doors opened again. She slowly stepped out of the elevator and walked to her front door. She typed in the passkey number and pushed the door open. Sitting on the foyer table was a large, beautiful arrangement of Maggie's favorite flowers. Immediately, she could smell something delicious coming from the kitchen. Without as much time as it took for her heart to beat again, she swiftly walked into the kitchen and threw her arms around the tall, handsome man standing in front of the stove.

She nearly knocked him over from behind. He laughed and said, "Whoa...babe!" He turned around and lifted Maggie up off her feet as they celebrated his homecoming with a long, passionate kiss.

Maggie adoringly whispered in his ear, "Welcome home."

Damon pulled her tightly against his body and let his need be known. "Now, this is the way a homecoming should be!"

Maggie laughed and said, "Only in the romance novels...." Then she leaned over to see what was on the stove. "I'm so hungry I could eat a cow! I didn't have lunch today. And I surely didn't expect you to be back early, so it looks like I got two welcome surprises, without another night of eggs and toast!"

Damon shook his head, released her, and started to laugh. "I guess we should eat dinner first and then you can show me how really welcome I am!"

Maggie stood on her toes and kissed his cheek. "You're on..." she barely whispered. Then she looked around and asked, "Where's Randall? I haven't seen him most of the week."

"He left a note on the foyer table. Looks like him and his buddies are hitting the fraternity parties tonight and he'll be home in the morning." He made a deep growling sound and pulled her tight against his muscular body again.

Maggie cuddled up to him and looked up with her shining hazel eyes. "Well then, it looks like it's just you and me tonight, big guy!" Unexpectedly, her stomach started to growl.

Damon unwrapped his arms and laughed. He walked over to the stove to plate up what he had prepared. Maggie followed, holding onto the belt loop of his jeans. For some reason tonight, she felt this need to stay connected.

They talked about his trip to Denver over a delicious dinner of rib-eye steaks, sautéed mushrooms, and roasted asparagus. Maggie always loved listening to his client stories and the aggressive way in which he dealt with them. He had been a private investigator for years and was now considered the best in his field throughout the country. He was always being sought after by the rich and famous, or anyone who could afford his substantial fees. Maggie remembered the day she hired him to locate her three best friends. He had assertively walked into her office looking like a pirate with his tall, muscular body and long, rakish black hair. She thought he was a movie star hoping to audition for the movie of her newest book. Not only was she rude and abrasive, she was also sadly mistaken. However, she did wind up hiring him to find her missing friends. For the next two years, Damon had remained close to Maggie's new family and they continued to be friends...until that day he stormed into her office, declared his intentions, and planted a slow, passionate kiss on her lips. Maggie was shocked, but when her tumultuous emotional state had finally settled down, their friendship had blossomed into a comfortable relationship. Denise, Elizabeth, and Lucy couldn't be happier. It was Randolph who kept an open eye on Damon to make sure he didn't hurt Maggie.

This was a whole new level for Maggie and Damon. Maggie had never been in a relationship before. Her life had been very reclusive and sterile and consisted of only a few dates. The orphanage had left her with a lack of trust in people; and the thought of getting hurt left her frozen in fear. So, with her antisocial lifestyle, only an occasional date had crossed her path. On the other side, Damon had sowed his wild oats during his youth, but as life began to move forward and become more hectic, his time was then consumed with his fast-paced business. That day he had responded to Denise's request for investigative services and walked into Maggie's office, his life was turned upside down. He didn't expect to meet an aloof author with a chip on her shoulder and a viperous tongue that could cut like a sword. This had immediately sparked his interest and continued to surprise him. He was a handsome man who always had women clambering to get his attention. He could have had the pick of anyone, including some of the movie industry's famous starlets. He was picky, and over the years had become withdrawn from the social scene. Nobody had caught his attention the past few years, and he was okay with that. He had a thriving business that kept him traveling all over the world.

That first meeting with Maggie left him guessing about her. Once she hired him, his curiosity began to hit a high note. Although she was reclusive and isolated, he could also see this raw passion she had never even realized she had. Whenever he got too close, she would close down and flee, like a naïve little girl. Then one day, after he obsessed over her passive-aggressive behavior of stubbornness, sarcasm, and emotional shutdowns, he marched into her office with every intention to confront her. Only, when he grabbed ahold of her shoulders and looked into her surprised eyes, he knew that very second, his life as a wandering loner was over.

After dinner, they settled down on the couch in the family room to watch the news. This was their favorite time together. When everything had slowed down for the day and they could finally just relax. Damon was reclining on the couch and Maggie was curled up next to him. Suddenly, Damon startled Maggie and sat straight up. He immediately grabbed the remote and turned the television sound up louder. Maggie sat up, clutched Damon's hand, and gasped.

A special newsbreak had appeared and a reporter had just announced a shooting. "There is a shooter in the main lobby of the Safe House, a well-known rehabilitation center in the heart of Los Angeles. The police have surrounded the area, but we still don't have any word as to what is going on. Shots were fired, but we don't know how many have been wounded, or how many are dead. Stay tuned for updates."

Maggie gasped and her body began to shake as their eyes intently watched the television.

Maggie began to panic. "I need to get down there. Lucy is there tonight preparing for the open house next week!"

Damon demanded, "Are you sure?" He stood up and pulled Maggie with him. "Let's go!"

Tears began to slide down her cheeks, as the reality of the moment took both of them by surprise. Maggie and Damon were slipping into their coats and walking toward the door. "Please God, watch over and protect my little Lucy!" Maggie pleaded.

The front door slammed shut....

CHAPTER 2

Damon was driving wildly through the streets of Los Angeles, maneuvering through the congested traffic. Maggie picked up her phone to call Lucy's number.

Damon gripped Maggie's hand and said, "Don't dial her cell number. If she is hiding or holding her phone, it will just draw the attention of the shooter. Call her home and see if she answers there...not her cell!" Damon was very perceptive when it came to emergency situations that required a lot of concentration to details. It was his job to make sure of the safety of his clients and himself in extreme cases of emergencies. Maggie never stopped to think about the ringing of the cellphone, or the attention it would bring.

Maggie nodded and dialed her home, but no one answered. She sucked in her breath and the fear caused her to hold it in. Damon nudged her and said, "Calm down, Maggie. Don't panic, we'll be there in a few blocks." In the dead silence, Maggie's phone began to ring. She closed her eyes and let out a big breath before she answered.

She thought for sure it was Lucy. "Hello, Lucy?"

"No, this is Randolph, Maggie! I'm watching this shooter on television. What the hell is going on out there and where the hell is Lucy? Please tell me she is home and safe!" Randolph pleaded.

"Damon and I are on our way to Safe House. She's working there tonight. We're only a few blocks away. I'll call you when I find out anything."

"Do I need to fly home immediately? What is that little fucker doing shooting innocent people?" Randolph screamed into the phone.

Maggie started to cry and couldn't answer. Damon took the phone and said, "Hey, pal, I'll give you a call as soon as we find out what is going on. Hang tight, Rand." Damon hung up the phone.

They pulled up three blocks away from the crime scene. The entire area was roped off and the police command center was set up. The media was sitting around like a pack of wolves just waiting for the feeding frenzy to begin. Red lights from the police cars were flashing everywhere, and the police were shouting orders in every direction. Damon parked his truck and grabbed Maggie's hand as she slid across the seat and out of the open door. Maggie held his hand tightly as he pulled her along towards the command center. He was determined to find out what was going on and where Lucy was. With reporters, photographers, and people running in all directions, Maggie became confused. The chaos was everywhere. Once they stopped in front of a group of men, Damon stepped forward and aggressively began to ask questions.

"Home many people have been shot?" he asked.

One of the policemen answered. "Two, we think, but it could be more. That's all we can see at the moment. We have no reports of how many shots were fired. We're not sure. We can't get in there until we're sure the shooter has stopped. We're trying to contact him now!"

Damon shot back, "Do you know how many are still in there? Have any come out?"

The policeman pointed to a curb, where there were a few people sitting down, garnished with the protection of law enforcement. They were crying and distraught, as the pandemonium was surrounding them. Maggie noticed one of Lucy's young assistants sitting on the curb. There was a photographer shoving a camera in her face. Then she saw a reporter come over and shove the photographer away. It looked like he was yelling at the man and threatening him with his fist, but she really couldn't see that well.

She tugged at Damon's hand and said, "Breezy is sitting over on the curb...let's ask her if she's seen Lucy or if she needs any help!"

Immediately, they ran over to the curb and Maggie squatted down and touched Breezy's face. "Are you okay, darling?" Maggie wiped the tears off of her face.

Breezy was still a child, barely twenty, and here she was going through the craziness of this country. She was crying and hugging her knees. Her body was shaking, and she was probably in shock.

Maggie, like many others, was having a difficult time accepting the insanity of America;

people were walking into schools, offices, anywhere, pulling out guns and killing innocent human beings. The disintegration of society and the spread of violence had grown to astronomical proportions. Intercity violence was out of control and social problems were forcing people to take alternative action to feed their pain and delusionary needs.

Here she was standing in the middle of a violent criminal act, that just took the life of at least two people that deserved better protection, and all she wanted to know, at this moment, was if Lucy was one of them.

Maggie inhaled a deep breath and asked, "Do you know where Lucy is?" She pushed the hair out of Breezy's face and leaned in to kiss her forehead.

Breezy nodded her head and started to cry. Maggie softly gripped her shoulders and knew this innocent child was in shock. "Is she still in there? Did she go home? Or has she been shot?" Maggie and Damon waited patiently as Breezy tried to explain.

"I don't know. She left her office to help others and then I heard the bullets fly by." Then she began to get hysterical and Maggie held her tight against her chest.

Softly, Maggie said, "It's okay, sweet girl. I'm glad that you are out of the mess safe and sound." At that moment, Breezy's girlfriend showed up and sat down next to her. Breezy laid her head in her friend's lap and began to cry again. Her friend rubbed her back and crooned soft words for only her ears.

Maggie and Damon stood there for a moment and then she noticed the photographer who had been pushed earlier.

Maggie walked over, pulling Damon with her. The photographer was talking to someone and when he stopped, Maggie tapped his shoulder. "Excuse me...." she politely said.

The reporter turned around and looked directly at Maggie, as though she was bothering him. "Yes?"

Maggie asked, "Could you let me know what is going on and anything you might know."

He looked at her with questioning eyes. "Who are you? Why do you want this information?" He pulled up his camera as if he was going to snap a picture of her.

Maggie's back went stiff and she placed her hand over the lens. "I'm Margaret Gray, and I think my family is in there! And if you dare take a picture of me, I will sue the crap out of you! And let me tell you Mister Fuckhead—you can't afford my anger! Don't you dare push me!"

He gave her a cocky look and said, "Who are you looking for...?"

Damon's face turned bright red and his fist grabbed the man's shirt. "Look, you asshole, have some respect!"

Suddenly, another man came running over and carefully extracted Damon's hand from the shirt. "I'm Bradley Lane, I'm sorry if this jerk has irritated you." Then he turned to the photographer and said, "I told you once. If I see your face again, I'm going to beat you to a pulp! Now get the fuck out of here; or I will report you!"

The guy smiled and walked away. Bradley held his hand out to Damon and said, "I'm Bradley Lane, from Channel Four news. I'm sorry about him. It's very chaotic here, who are you looking for?"

Maggie spoke up. "Is the director, Lucy Ann Smith, still in there?"

He pursed his lips together in thought. "I believe she is in a closet with five others. When the shooting started, she grabbed all those she could find and put them in her office closet. Then she went back to find more. We don't know if she was shot doing that or what. But I will tell you, this lady, she is a 'hero' in my eyes!"

Maggie leaned back against Damon as tears ran down her cheeks.

Damon looked at Bradley and started to say, "Will you keep—"

All of a sudden, there was yelling from all directions. "Get down—everyone down—get down—get behind cover!"

Damon threw Maggie to the ground and covered her body with his. There was a rapid succession of gunfire everywhere. Maggie covered her ears and Damon flattened himself on her to keep her safe. Maggie could hear the bullets hitting cement, metal, everything. When the gunfire finally ceased, there was a deathly silence. Then, jarring voices were screaming all kinds of orders. Damon heard the 'all clear,' and slowly lifted Maggie off the ground. He cradled her in his arms and held her tight against his body as she tried to make sense of what had just happened. He brought her over to the curb and sat her down. She was in shock and could only do as he said.

He crouched down and looked at her face, "Maggie, it's all over. They got the gunman, but we don't know who else he shot. Stay here and do not move. I'm going to see about Lucy. Do you hear me, Maggie?"

Maggie nodded.

Maggie hugged her knees as tight as she could. She had never experienced this kind of violence before and could not even conceive of how people lived around this constantly in the inner-cities. It was beyond her comprehension and more than she could absorb. She sat there as people sped around her like racecars.

Ambulances were driving up and idling, waiting to transport victims to the nearest hospitals. Reporters and photographers were everywhere with their cameras and microphones anchored in their hands. Maggie wanted it all to stop, but it wouldn't. After what seemed like a lifetime, things started to calm down and a semblance of peace began to prevail over the scene.

Maggie was still hugging her knees, rocking back and forth, when a body slid next to her and a familiar voice whispered, "I'm okay, Maggie."

Ear splitting wails slipped from Maggie's lips. Lucy's arms slid around Maggie's shaking body and they both began to rock back and forth. It was the same rocking that had taken place five years earlier when Maggie had finally found Lucy in a sleazebag motel and had felt powerless as she watched Lucy's emotional breakdown. That night, Lucy's screams of agony tore at Maggie's conscience while she quietly stood there and let Lucy purge twenty years of homelessness. She could only imagine that she was weeping for all those pitiable lost years that had led her to what she had become: a pathetic drug and alcohol-addicted transient, whose less than perfect life ended up in a dilapidated, roach infested hotel—just like her mother. And now, Lucy was rocking Maggie, waiting for the trauma of the day to subside.

At the sound of Lucy's soft voice, Maggie finally released her knees and looked up. Lucy smiled and brushed the hair from Maggie's wet face. "Are you okay?"

Again, as he did years ago, Damon watched from a few feet away and waited for the emotional rollercoaster to wind down. He let the two women take care of each other. They needed to be strong for each other, as the sights and sounds of the crime scene increased around them.

When Maggie finally calmed down, her nerves and her voice came back. "I'm supposed to be asking you that. Not the opposite...." Maggie grinned slightly as she touched Lucy's face. "I was so scared I had lost you."

"Never...." Lucy sighed. "I've lived through years of violence on the streets, but this was perpetrated against people who didn't deserve it. He was a young kid, barely seventeen. His parents had thrown him out of the house at thirteen, and he had nowhere to go. He'd lived on the streets for years; and he finally couldn't take it any longer. He thought his only way out was in a blaze of gunfire." Lucy's heavy heart was breaking in two. Lucy began to cry. "I couldn't stop him. I couldn't save him. I couldn't...."

Maggie touched Lucy's face. "This isn't your fault. You couldn't change a thing if you wanted. He needed more...."

"Randolph and you will never know how much it means to me, for all you have donated to the new shelter that we are building. A place for young children, like that young boy, to have and call home. A real bed to sleep in, instead of the cold, unforgiving streets. A hot meal to fill their empty stomachs. The soft words of someone who has been through it and really cares...." Lucy began to sob again.

Maggie quietly said, "Of all the people we know, Randolph knows what it means to you. He was that little boy who slept on the streets, cried from an empty stomach, and longed for those soft words from someone who cared. He has never forgotten his roots, the same as Elizabeth, you, and me. He's anonymously donated the money for your dream shelter, knowing how it would help those young children."

Lucy looked up at Maggie as an epiphany hit her. "That is what we are going to call it...Dream 'Scape. I want it to be a dream 'escape' for those lost children. Most of them have never had dreams. The only thing they've had in life is a cold, hard world that has forced them to survive on the streets. They need a sense of value and a place to belong."

"Yes, we know what it is like to dream." Maggie hugged Lucy.

Damon squatted down and tapped Maggie. "I found out some information. Two people were shot and they are going to make it. The only one who died was the young boy. Thanks to you, Lucy.

You saved it from becoming any worse by shoving everyone into that tiny closet. They're calling you a 'hero.'" Damon smiled. He leaned over and ruffled her hair.

Unexpectedly, that nasty photographer came over and pushed his camera in Lucy's face. As Damon stood up, the reporter they had just met ran over and punched the photographer in the jaw, deftly grabbing the camera. Then the reporter, Bradley Lane, yelled for a policeman, "Hey, someone come get this guy and charge him with assault!"

A policeman came over and grabbed the photographer by the arm. "Listen, buddy, you've been given enough chances to get the hell out of here. I really don't give a damn what tabloid you're working for, we're going to take you down to the station and book you on disorderly conduct, disturbing the peace, harassment, and public endangerment. Any one of those will work just fine. Take your pick!"

Damon smiled. He liked this reporter's style of handling that jerk.

The reporter bent down and looked at Lucy, smiled and said, "So, this is what a hero looks like!"

CHAPTER 3

Lucy was tucked under Maggie's arm. Her body was shaking and she just wanted to go home. Bradley Lane, the reporter, had left, and then came back. With him was a paramedic holding a big black bag.

"This is the young lady that saved everyone. Do you think we can clean up her bloody legs and check to make sure everything else is okay?" he asked.

"Of course," the paramedic said, as he crouched down next to her.

Maggie and Damon didn't notice the blood that was dripping out of the large gash on Lucy's leg until Bradley brought the paramedic over. Everyone had been so busy concentrating on just comforting her rattled nerves and bringing some stability to the situation, that everything else went unnoticed, including Lucy's leg wounds. All excepting one person—Bradley. He had almost been like a guardian angel watching over Lucy.

The paramedic smiled at Lucy and asked, "Hello, my name is Lou. Would you mind lifting your skirt up so I can take a look at what is causing the bleeding." He pointed to the small pool of blood.

Lucy lifted her skirt and a few large gashes appeared on her shin. Lou opened his black bag and took everything out that he needed to clean and sterilize her cuts. After several minutes, everything was cleaned and bandaged and he carefully pulled her skirt down over her legs.

Lou asked again, "Are you sure you don't want to go to the hospital and get those looked at? Your blood pressure is a little high, but it's safe to say that might be because of the stress of the evening. You should contact your personal physician tomorrow. Okay?"

Lucy shook her head.

The commander had come over during the dressing of her wounds and asked her questions. He took lots of notes and also asked her if she wanted to go to the hospital or come down to the station. They needed to talk some more, but Damon and Maggie insisted she be permitted to go home. Damon told him where she could be reached and gave his own personal number in case he needed to talk to him.

They wanted her to go home where she belonged, with her daughter, Mary Jane. The drama and intensity of what had happened was more than Lucy could take for one night. Going to the station was bound to push her over the edge. She knew that and she also knew, she needed some space so her mind could slowly process everything that had happened—including the death of that young boy.

Lucy looked at the commander and said, "It should have never happened. I lived on the streets for years. There should have been a safe place for him to release all this anger without choosing to shoot others and take his own life. You have no idea how many times I thought about closing that door on myself when I'd had more than I could possibly handle. Life isn't fair. Dr. Jan, Berty, and I have lost this young man who couldn't hold on any longer."

He looked down with sadness. "I'm so sorry. We don't know what to do and where to put all these lost kids."

She looked at the commander and said, "I promise I will come down. You and I need to talk of how we can change things for these misfits. Just let me go home and get some sleep and rest my nerves."

Maggie called Elizabeth and explained what happened before she could turn on the television and see the newscast. Damon was more comfortable with calling Randolph and talking man-to-man, and letting him know exactly how everything went down. They kept the conversations short and promised to call once they were settled in. Randolph wanted to fly home, but Damon insisted that he would handle everything.

Bradley Lane sat there patiently until everyone was getting ready to leave. He had protected Lucy from the frenzy of photographers and media whores that wanted to get to her. He wedged himself between and made them keep their distance, giving them no space to pursue or harass her. Then he stepped in on her behalf, and made an announcement that they would get their story once the police had thoroughly investigated the whole incident. He also made it a point to keep his distance, not wanting to trespass on Lucy's fragile instability.

As Lucy stood up and got ready to leave, Bradley came over and respectfully asked, "Would you mind if I came over in the morning to get the whole story of what happened from you, rather than to speculate or embellish on what might have happened? I promised the media I would contact them instead of them harassing you."

Maggie and Damon were standing there when Bradley walked up. Maggie was sure she had seen him on television as an investigative reporter. She made a note to call Becca, her dear friend who was also an investigative reporter. Maybe she knew him—Becca knew everyone— and everyone knew her. Maggie wanted to really know what his intent was and if it was honorable.

Bradley was a tall, muscular man that looked to be in his forties. His dark hair was too long and hung over his eyes and his hand was constantly sweeping it back. His crooked nose brought character to his face, but it was his smile that could charm anyone. Casual clothes, jeans and a leather coat, along with sockless loafers, added to his charisma. Damon had seen his kind before. Investigative reporters were hard, calloused media whores most of the time—only looking for their next big story. And Lucy was not experienced enough to protect herself against an aggressive opponent.

Damon had begun to put up a barrier. He was very protective when it came to Maggie's family. After all, he knew them intimately after his search to find them. He wasn't sure he wanted this reporter anywhere near Lucy or her daughter. He didn't want this guy snooping around and finding out about Lucy's past. She had struggled enough in her life, the thought that someone could play her for a fool and plaster her rancid past across the newspapers and tabloids for everyone to see was reprehensible. She was a very private person and there was no telling what he would do with all her information.

Lucy looked up and answered Bradley, "Tomorrow would be fine. I'm afraid there isn't much I can tell you that I haven't already said the commander."

"I guess I would just like to make sure you are okay," he said in a heartfelt voice.

Damon stepped forward. "We'll make sure...."

Lucy touched Damon's arm and grinned. "I can handle this, Damon." Then she continued, "Sure, you can come over tomorrow. Say, about ten."

Damon and Maggie tried to persuade Lucy to pick up Mary Jane, and come home with them, but she refused. She wanted to keep things normal and she didn't want to make this bigger than what it was. Lucy had learned to assert herself and had grown prodigious strength from her journey. Before Maggie had found her on the streets, she had let herself dwell in a world of misery and dejection. Dr. Jan Johnson, the former director of Safe House; Berty, her longtime companion and assistant; and Judge Joe, who had put Lucy into AA meetings, were important participants in her continuous recovery. Each person shared a large part of who she was now—a strong woman. Most of all, she knew that she owed Maggie her life. Without Maggie, and her determination and stubbornness, she would still be back on the streets, trying to survive—or possibly dead. Each one of the orphans owed Maggie a fistful of gratitude and they all let her know it. It was Maggie who always felt indebted for their years of devoted friendship in Bishop Street that was filled with pain and emptiness.

Maggie and Damon headed home feeling relieved; and they were beyond thankful that Lucy had been spared her life and had managed to save others. On the other hand, they were emotionally drained, thinking about Lucy and all that she had gone through, and for that young boy who felt the need to end his life, filled with agony at the young age of seventeen.

Lucy heard the knock on the door and immediately looked at Mary Jane, who was engrossed in watching a movie. She got up from her couch and calmly walked toward the door. She could barely remember the night before. It all seemed like such a blur because it happened so fast, and it seemed so surreal. She was going to try and answer his questions the best she could but she knew she had to be careful. She had gotten herself into a mess before when she spoke to an investigative reporter. He had twisted everything she said, and embellished what she didn't. It had been another one of those learning lessons in life where you made a mistake and you swore you'd never let it happen again.

Lucy opened the door and steadily said, "Hello, come on in."

Bradley reached out his hand and she grasped it in a handshake. He smiled and said, "It's nice to see you again, Lucy. I'm really sorry you had to go through that horrible experience last night."

Lucy looked at him with honesty in her eyes. "That was hardly anything compared to other situations I have experienced through my lifetime. Come on in. I only have a few minutes."

He followed her and took a seat on the couch. For the next twenty minutes, they talked about how she knew the young man and why he was there. She explained the circumstances and the anger he carried. She also let him know that she had been raised in an orphanage and could feel his pain, along with the loneliness and abandonment he had experienced. His parents were both drug addicts without any responsibility to him or their other four children. He had no idea where his siblings were or if they had even survived. With all that pain, he could not cope, and it festered into a burning anger.

"How can we make this better? Why are these children on the streets?" He wanted to know.

Lucy folded her hands in her lap. "Because we have a society that doesn't give a damn. The rich don't care and the poor languish in self-pity. Only a few really understand this problem. Kids twelve, thirteen, and up live on the streets in all the big cities. More so in Los Angeles. Unless you've been there to see it and hear their stories—most don't have a clue."

He looked at her with questioning eyes. "How do we stop this?"

"We can't stop parents from throwing their children out of the home because they can't afford to feed them, or they are addicts, or their parenting skills suck! What we can do is find the funds to open homes where these lost children have a place to sleep, food in their tummies, and a kind hand to help them. We are opening a new shelter just for children of the streets, in a few weeks. It's called Dream 'Scape."

"Is there anything I can do to help?" he asked.

"Do a big article in the paper and online, and cover the grand opening. Help get the word out to the street kids, that they finally have a place to sleep. Get law enforcement involved with bringing them to us, instead of letting them get raped in jail. That would be a great start!" Lucy smiled.

"How is this being funded?"

Lucy looked up and exhaled. "By some great people who know what it's like to be alone with nowhere to go."

He looked confused. "Somehow, I think I underestimated you. You're a very strong and persuasive lady!"

Lucy stood up, and silently walked him to the door. She reached out her hand and said, "Thanks for watching over me the other night, I appreciate it. Enjoy your day! And please consider my request."

The sun was out and shining on this beautiful day in the middle of December. Lucy was standing in the front yard of a large building with tears in her eyes. The rest of the group was going to meet her here in an hour. Her eyes shined with pride as they scanned the large piece of property located in the middle of Los Angeles. It was the most beautiful new building Lucy had ever seen, and after months of heavy construction, it was exactly how she had imagined it for years. In the backyard, there were rows and rows of chairs that had been brought in for the 'grand opening.' Festive banners and balloons were everywhere. Tables draped with tablecloths lined the area, and were waiting for the caterers to arrive with the food. Also, in the back was a full-size basketball court, a pool, and another small building that housed a school, complete with a staff of teachers. Lucy could not have been prouder—today was her day to shine. Thanks to Maggie and Randolph, this dream of Lucy's had come true. This house for children had been built mostly on their donations from start to finish. Now, she had to keep it going and prayed that other contributions would start to flow in.

Everyone Lucy knew was going to be there today, including Elizabeth, William, and their children. It was another milestone and celebration of their family. The last few years had been happy ones, with new celebrations—and new beginnings. Lucy could not be happier, in spite of the shooting the week before. Bradley had kept his word and had jumped onto the media blitz, publicizing the hell out of the grand opening. His articles and columns in newspapers and on the Internet had created not only a big hoopla regarding the building; they had also collected enough charitable contributions to completely furnish the house.

He had also kept in contact with Lucy, on occasion stopping by her office and taking her out to lunch. He never overstepped his bounds, and always referred to their meetings as 'strictly professional.' Everyone kept a wary eye on this blossoming friendship. Maggie constantly inquired and Damon shook his head in question at Bradley's motives. Only Dr. Jan approved of what was starting to ignite. She liked Bradley, and the way he was gently handling the situation. She also thought it was good for Lucy to engage in a slow-moving, personal relationship. Lucy had never been in one; and if she by chance 'burned her fingers,' the experience would be good for her. Dr. Jan had been Lucy and Maggie's therapist for years, watching them grow emotionally stronger and stronger. Maggie had finally let go of her trust issues, and now it was time for Lucy.

Mary Jane ran up to Lucy with all the excitement of a twelve-year-old girl. She grabbed her mother's hand, and started pulling her in another direction. "Come on, Mom! Auntie Elizabeth and Uncle William are here. I just saw the car. Hurry, I can't wait to see Sarah and Katie!"

Lucy smiled as her daughter pulled her down the cement walkway. Excitement was in the air, not only for the grand opening, but for all of the family getting together for the Christmas holiday. Elizabeth and William had had a tough year with the crops, but managed to squeak by without defaulting on any of their loans. Randall was living with Maggie, going to UCLA, and working in a pet store in Westwood. Elizabeth and William still held on to their stubborn pride and refused to take any monetary handouts, except for room and board for Randall. They struggled with the student loans for Randall and Meg, but never said a word. Maggie and Randolph constantly wanted to share their wealth—William refused adamantly. He made it a point that he wanted to provide for his family, as his parents had done for him. It was his mid-western pride that was continually challenged, and yet, he still never gave in. Meg had a hard time with her father's decisions because she wanted to go to school in California—like her brother. But her parents couldn't afford it until the following year. Meg's anger sometimes leaked out, and Maggie had to constantly defend her parent's decision. This didn't sit well with Meg, and sometimes it strained their relationship. Maggie knew that something had to be done soon or Meg would take off. Maggie had promised her that she would talk to her parents during this trip, but it wasn't going to be an easy task.

Nothing had changed. James still chased his dog, Blue, through the sprinkler on occasion, and dragged him across the clean kitchen floors. He was a senior in high school and was being scouted for baseball scholarships to some major Universities—he hadn't made a choice yet. William wanted him to stay close to home, so he could go to some of his games. However, the choice was given to James.

Mary Jane was jumping up and down and pointing across the large parking lot. "Look, Mom, there they are!" She was waving her hand high in the air at the limousine. "I can't wait to see them."

Lucy smiled and said, "Yes, I can see that!"

As always, the group had pulled up in a limousine. That's how it had been for years. They all wanted to come and go together, and Maggie wouldn't have it any other way, when 'The Martins' came into town. That was something that Elizabeth and William gave into—they had no choice. When the family came to visit, Randolph and Maggie were in control. They had all sat down years ago, and tried to work it out—somewhat. It was just enough for Elizabeth and William to feel comfortable—as long as Maggie didn't over step their boundaries with the children. After all, William and Elizabeth came from a small town in North Dakota, and their needs and wants were far from those who lived in a lifestyle of indulgence. They didn't know what it was like to have a savings account, or extra money to buy frivolous things. They were just hardworking 'farm folks' who valued the earth they plowed, appreciated the vegetables they grew, and enjoyed the town's people they so dearly loved.

When they first got back together, there was always chaos, noise, and children everywhere. Now that all the children were older, things had calmed down a little, with the exception of Mary Jane, Sarah, and Katie. Those three were inseparable. 'Best friends until the end,' they would tell their parents. And whenever they visited, it was days filled with fun and happiness.

Mary Jane was tugging her mother's hand. "Gosh, Mom, can't you run?"

Lucy laughed. "No! I'm too old!"

Walking as fast as she could, Lucy and Mary Jane finally made it to the limousine. Suddenly the door opened, and two screaming young girls jumped out, and ran over to Mary Jane. They all began to jump up and down, screaming and yelping in excitement. Lucy rolled her eyes at Elizabeth, who was still sitting in the car. William stepped out and Randolph followed. Finally, William held his hand out and Elizabeth emerged, and so did James. Maggie and Damon were last. The younger girls took off in the direction of the yard, where the ceremony was going to take place. More casually, the adults gathered amongst hugs and smiles, as they slowly walked toward the same direction as the children.

Elizabeth hugged Lucy, and didn't want to let her go. "I thanked God so many times that Sunday at church that you were spared that night. If Maggie hadn't called, I would have bitten off all my fingernails! I just want to hold you right now."

Lucy let Elizabeth hold her a little longer than normal. "It feels good to have your arms around me. That night, I felt God's arms around me. I just had a hard time thinking about that poor young boy...."

Elizabeth let her go, looked at her, and then scanned the building in front of her. "Be proud of this and how much this is going to help the others like him!"

Lucy slowly nodded her head. "Thank you, Elizabeth."

Elizabeth's eyes opened wide. "I hear you have a suitor?"

Lucy groaned, and looked at Maggie with suspicious eyes. "I won't ask who is spreading this rumor. I *will* tell you that he's just a friend!"

Maggie walked over, and left the men to talk amongst themselves. Maggie slipped her arm around Lucy's waist.

Lucy backed away, and said, "Traitor!"

Maggie began to laugh. "So be it!"

Lucy looked around, and then back at Elizabeth. Then she asked. "Where's Meg and Randall?"

Elizabeth looked down at the ground. "I'm afraid Meg is not happy with William and I. She wants to go to school out here with Randall, but right now we can't afford it. She decided to wait at the house until Randall got off of work, and then they will both meet us here. Meg is a stubborn—"

Maggie interrupted Elizabeth. "—let her come out here. She can stay with me, or I'll let her stay at the beach house. I don't know what the problem is. Why won't you let her come?"

Elizabeth's voice dropped to a low whisper, "I've told you many times now, Maggie, the out-of-state tuition is just too expensive for our budget right now. In six months, we will take a look at the possibility again. If we have a good summer crop, we can probably consider it."

Maggie closed her eyes and shook her head. "Sometimes I just want to throttle your little neck! My new book is a bestseller, and I'll never be able to spend what I have now! Geeeez, let *me* pay her tuition!"

Lucy clasped Maggie's hand, and softly said, "I don't think that is the point, Mag. Let's not go there right now and ruin Lucy's day! Okay?"

Maggie turned and gave Elizabeth a big hug. "Sorry."

Elizabeth looked at Maggie and said, "We've got a whole week to talk this over. Let's enjoy this lovely day that God has given us, and enjoy this beautiful sunshine! After all, it is our little girl's finest hour. This dedication is all because of her!"

Lucy looked puzzled. "Little girl's...just because I'm a few months younger than you guys, doesn't mean I'm the baby!"

Maggie and Elizabeth nodded their heads in unison. "You were always the baby!"

The three women hooked their elbows and walked toward the chairs. The men followed, but at a slower pace. They were just happy being out of the chaos and noise.

The ceremony was over and it had brought plenty of tears to everyone's eyes who had listened to Lucy's story. There was standing room only with city and state politicians, the rich and famous, and supporters who had been working with Lucy since the conception. Maggie, Randolph, and Elizabeth sat in the fourth row listening to their childhood story. The Dream 'Scape had been built in their honor, and carried a lifetime plaque on the front door. Four scrappy little kids, who grew up at Bishop Street Orphanage without knowing what life was really about. Years of shared secrets and dreams were all they had. They created a nurturing environment for one another that encompassed the only world they knew. Together, they had developed their family and set up the roles. They forged a closeness to cover the absence of a mother's touch, or a father's strong arms to encircle and protect them from all their fears. The love of a parent never entered their sterile world of isolation. It ceased to exist. Yet, they had survived to become role models for others who needed them. And today, they were here to open the doors of a loving home for those young orphans that were living on the streets of Los Angeles, and lost in a world that just didn't care.

In the first row, with tears in their eyes, was Dr. Jan Johnson and Berty. They could not be prouder of Lucy, who had barely survived the treacherous streets of Los Angeles and had come back to save others from the same fate. They had been there unconditionally to wean her off of addiction, to build her self-esteem, and then watched her succeed.

Randolph was one of the richest men in the world. He had contributed millions to build these dreams for the children, and refused any form of recognition. He just wanted to see the Hollywood unwanted waifs and runaways off the streets and given a second chance to begin being productive with their lives. Then he had startled the audience, and his family, with a large fund for scholarships to those who wanted to further their educations.

This had been a large milestone in his life, but the biggest was yet to come. Only Maggie, Lucy, and Elizabeth didn't know it yet. He had a secretive surprise, and they would find out soon enough. He had been spending a lot of his time in Mexico at his ranch and hacienda, and they all knew that. He loved that small town in Mexico, and the town's people that had given him anonymity, and saved his life from the loneliness of being the hunted billionaire—he owed them. He looked happier today, and there was a deep smile that never left his face. Maggie could see subtle changes, and wondered what it was all from.

Lucy was standing next to Randolph, and everyone was coming up to congratulate her for all her hard work. She was laughing when Bradley quietly came over and tapped her on the shoulder.

She turned around, and her eyes opened wide and a big smile crossed her face. "Thanks for coming, Bradley. I can't thank you enough for all your help with the advertising, and pushing for more contributions."

He beamed and said, "I wouldn't have missed it for anything. Congratulations, Lucy, I had no idea you had such a rough beginning to life. Listening to your story actually broke my heart."

Suddenly, Randolph turned around at the sound of Bradley's name. He held out his hand and said, "I've heard a lot about you, lately. My name is—"

Bradley interrupted Randolph, clasped his hand, and grinned. "—I know exactly who you are. Randolph Parker, right?"

Randolph nodded with a very arrogant smile on his face.

"I did many articles on you, and Compsoft. Of all the press releases I read, not one of them mentioned Bishop Street, or your friends. In fact, it mentioned nothing about your childhood." He looked confused. Then he looked at Lucy, and nothing registered on her face.

Randolph began to laugh and kissed Lucy on the cheek. He pulled her tighter into his arms and began to rub her back. "Humm...do I know you, babe?"

Bradley looked stunned when he called her 'babe.' Speechless, he just stood there with a look of bewilderment, wondering what the relationship was now. Were they friends, family, or lovers?

When Randolph had fucked with Bradley's head enough, he finally said, "She's my family. And...I've heard lots of rumors about you two. I just wanted to check you out for myself."

He looked dazed and confused. "Family...but you just called her 'babe'?"

Randolph laughed. "Yes, she was the youngest of the girls. Lucy, Maggie, Elizabeth and I were raised in Bishop Street Orphanage, together. We are family and she was the baby! It's nice to meet you."

Bradley looked at Lucy with pleading eyes as he stuttered. "What...did he hear about...'us'? Anything I should know?"

Lucy decided to go along with Randolph's head game. "They found out I was pregnant!"

Bradley's eyes opened wildly, and he began to stutter, "I...don't know what she's...a...talking about! I have had only...honorable intentions!"

Randolph and Lucy started laughing. Lucy said, "He's just 'fucking' with your head...he loves to play games." She pushed Randolph's chest and continued, "Who put you up to messing with Bradley's head.... Damon? You guys are a bunch of bullies!"

Bradley took his napkin and wiped his brow. He was so stunned, he was wordless.

Humbled by Bradley's silence, Randolph held out his hand again and said, "I'm sorry, I was just playing with you, and I had no idea that Lucy would play along, too!"

Bradley grasped his hand and said, "Wow...you had me going. I had no idea about any of this. I think Lucy is a very sweet lady and I do have good intents...."

Lucy blushed.

Randolph said, "Well, now you know who you're up against...if you do anything to hurt her...."

"Never," he rapidly shook his head.

"Great, why don't you join us for dinner, Saturday night? The family is getting together for a big celebration, and they all want to check you out and get to know you better." Randolph clapped him on his back.

Lucy spoke up, "Hello...I'm standing right here, Randolph. Don't I have a say in anything?"

Randolph asked, "Sure...where do you want to go for dinner?"

The men started to laugh.

Bradley got serious and looked directly at Lucy. "Dinner Saturday night is entirely up to you, Lucy!"

CHAPTER 4

CHRISTMAS WAS EVERYWHERE. THE STREETS OF LOS Angeles were decorated with colorful lights, and the windows in the shopping centers were dressed with the holiday spirit. The younger children were filled with uncontrollable excitement as they got dressed. Lucy, Maggie, Elizabeth were taking all of the kids to Disneyland for the holiday festivities and especially the Christmas parade down Main Street. It had become another new tradition they had started since the first Christmas in Los Angeles when Mary Jane had been introduced to her mother, Lucy, and her new extended family. Only, after their first visit to Disneyland with the full family, the women decided not to make the men suffer through a full day filled with the unlimited energy of the children. So many normal family traditions were starting to develop year by year.

As the family was walking down Main Street, Maggie was holding Meg's hand. "Don't you love watching the crowds filled with excited children, as they feast their eyes with enthusiastic wonder on this amazing land of fantasy?" Maggie asked Meg.

"It's okay...." she said, pouting.

Maggie stopped and looked at Meg. She felt this aloof attitude was beginning to annoy her. "What is this anger I'm detecting? I surely hope it is not directed at me. I can see you really need an attitude adjustment, young lady!"

Meg pulled her hand away and kept walking. "I'm really angry with Mom and Dad, Auntie Maggie. I just don't know why they won't let me come to California to go to college. There are some of the best art and design institutes out here. Instead, I'm stuck at that dumb junior college, wasting my life away."

Maggie stopped again and looked openly at Meg. "Patience is a great virtue. You need to get your lower general education classes finished; and then we can decide the next step. Right now, your parents are struggling financially. Hold tight and let me see if I can gradually do something," Maggie pleaded.

Meg looked angry. "They are always struggling. I told them I would find a full-time job to help with the expenses. You even said you would help me get a job. I can pay my own way. I'm not asking them for anything other than their blessings!" she hissed.

"They have your brother almost finished with his degree and then he'll be in graduate school. Be patient." Maggie squeezed her hand.

Meg pulled her hand back. Then she crossed her arms over her chest and frowned. "It's always about my brother. He gets everything, and I get nothing! That is so unfair. Can't you and Rand talk to them?"

Maggie shook her head and narrowed her eyes. "We will not step over your parent's decision. No matter how much Rand and I love you...your parents make the rules!"

Meg stomped her foot and raised her voice. "That's not fair. I'm twenty now and I can do what I want. I don't have to listen to them, if I choose!"

Maggie saw the rebellion that was boiling deep inside Meg. She knew Meg was a stubborn young woman who wanted to break away from her parent's strong hold. She was also a naïve young woman who was raised with a small town mentality. "Please know they will come around. Right now, give them the respect they deserve, as they are working very hard to get you there."

"I don't know if I can wait, Auntie Maggie!"

Maggie turned, grabbed her shoulders, and said, "Don't do anything stupid. Look at the mess your Auntie Lucy was in for years. Please be patient." Maggie could see she was preaching to deaf ears. She felt this restless need in Meg. It was apparent that changes were going to take place, she just didn't know what or when.

The day was warm and sunny and everyone enjoyed the world of make-believe. Unfortunately, the conversation between Meg and Maggie was weighing heavy on Maggie's heart.

On the way home, Elizabeth sat next to Maggie. They were holding hands when she said, "What a beautiful day. Thank you, Maggie."

Maggie touched her lined cheek. "For what? The kids had a blast and so did I."

Elizabeth looked sad, "All except Meg."

Maggie frowned. "It will work out." Maggie thought about it and realized it was not going to work out. Something was going to happen and she hoped it wasn't soon. She didn't want her and Randolph being blamed for their influence.

Elizabeth took a big breath and exhaled slowly. "It's going to be hard to go back to our unforgiving cold winter. I hear they had a big blizzard today. Reba thinks we are in for an awful winter. I remember years ago when we nearly lost half the town with the record-breaking snowfall and horrible winter storm that brought tornados and flooding. We barely survived that storm."

"Anytime you need a break, give me a call. I'll fly you out with the kids."

Elizabeth smiled. "You always make everything sound so easy."

"It doesn't always have to be so hard."

Elizabeth and her family were staying at the penthouse and Maggie and Damon were at the beach house. The children floated back and forth, depending on the day, and what exciting activities were planned. If it was a nice, sunny day, they would gather at the beach house and play at the beach. Walking along the shoreline was something Elizabeth, Maggie, and Lucy loved to do. It was a great way to catch up without other probing ears. On one of their beach days, Katie lost her ring while building castles in the sand. Everyone panicked as they began to wildly sift through the sand with their hands. Katie was hysterical, because the ring was given to her by her best friend before she left for the holiday. Suddenly, Lucy stood up and ran into the house. When she came back, she had taken a screen off one of the windows. Awkwardly, she was carrying it down to the beach.

Everyone sat with their mouths wide open. It was an excellent idea; they used the screen to sift through the sand, and finally found the ring. After the immediate crisis was over, and they were sitting quietly again, Maggie leaned over and asked Lucy, "What made you think of that?"

Lucy smiled and shrugged her shoulders. "When I was homeless and really hungry, I used to go down to the beach in the evening where all the teenagers hung out. I brought with me an old screen I had found in the trash one day. Believe it or not, that screen probably saved my life."

Maggie looked at Lucy in amazement. Her survival skills had such long-term effects on her, and yet, they were brilliant in the art of survival.

"Thank you, Lucy. I think you just about made Katie's whole trip by finding her ring. I think we've all developed a fascinating amount of survival skills that we've learned through our lives," Elizabeth added.

Everyone was enjoying the week with the Martins. But their stay was coming to an end and Christmas was the next day. The plan for Christmas morning was going to be a quiet and intimate brunch at Maggie's house, like every year. The women would cook a great meal, the men would sit around watching sports, or sit on the patio with an occasional cigar or pipe. William always brought his pipe Maggie had sent him the first year, along with the cherry tobacco. And each year, without fail, he would hold up that pipe and say to Maggie, "The best damn pipe I ever had!"

The actual holiday celebration was tonight. Randolph had reserved a private room in a quaint little restaurant in Los Angeles. It was a small five-star restaurant known for its delicious Italian cuisine by the well-known chef who owned it. Randolph had learned over the years that 'quaint' was much better and less intimidating than his normal choice of restaurants like The Beverly Hills Hotel or The Bel-Air Hotel that were owned by famous chefs like Wolfgang Puck. Although the elite restaurants were more like what Maggie and he were used to, he now needed to take into consideration what Lucy and Elizabeth's family felt comfortable with. Sometimes it wasn't easy, but he also didn't want to alienate those he loved, either. Compromising was becoming easier by the year.

Tonight's dinner was a chance for everyone to dress up in their Sunday's finest and to open their gifts. Decoratively wrapped presents were stacked in the foyer of the penthouse and made it near impossible for everyone to get to the front door. The children were filled with anticipation, and there was chaos everywhere. Katie, Sarah, and Mary Jane had never left each other's sight. They were connected for life through a series of circumstances—and nobody was ever going to break their bonds. James and Meg went sightseeing with Randall in the new car Maggie had loaned him. He took them all over the city, and showed them places they could not believe. They were from a small town in a state that had little in the way of craziness like the surrounding areas of Los Angeles. Driving around the streets of Hollywood, walking the strand of Venice Beach, and joining the crowded madness of City Walk was enough to open their eyes and minds to the insanity of a big cosmopolitan city. James was a little overwhelmed, but not Meg. Her enthusiasm was pushed to its limits and her eyes wanted to absorb it all. Her new artwork reflected her love of the cultural authenticity she was experiencing—she wanted more.

Finally, they all met back at the house to get ready for the evening. Elizabeth looked beautiful in her new dress she had found in the little dress shop in North Bend. It was very simple, and at the same time, much dressier than the typical outdated dresses she normally wore. It wasn't made of cotton—it was a polyester blend that accented her womanly figure. It had rhinestones around the neck and sleeves that matched her sparkling blue eyes. And although she didn't wear makeup, her natural beauty always managed to stand out in a room. William finished dressing in a dark suit and outdated tie. Elizabeth thought it was a feat in itself to just get him to wear a suit. After all his years of wearing jeans, and overalls, this was a big stretch for him.

As Maggie was walking by their room, she accidently witnessed an intimate exchange between William and Elizabeth as they were getting dressed. Elizabeth had walked up to William, who was trying to tie his tie in the mirror. She touched his leathery tan face and he turned to look at her. She said with the kindest voice, "You look just as handsome tonight as you did on our first date." He reached over and encircled her body with his muscled arms, and bent down and kissed her.

Maggie blushed and walked away from the door, not wanting to be noticed, a tear traveling down her cheek at the heartwarming exchange.

Emotionally moved, a lot of questions started to spin around in her head. *"Was that what it was like to be deeply in love? Is that how you felt after years of raising kids and dealing with setbacks and hardships? Would Damon ever feel the same way? Would she ever be able to tell him those three sacred words? Had she given up on having children of her own?"*

She walked down the hall and made sure the girls were getting dressed and that everyone was running on time. From the front door, she yelled, "I'm going to the beach house to get dressed. Randolph will pick you up. Damon and I will meet you there."

Lucy walked into the foyer, and smiled at Maggie. She looked beautiful in a long, black lace skirt and a matching lace jacket. Her brown hair was long and shiny and her makeup was perfection. Lucy reached over and hugged Maggie. Then she whispered in her ear, "It's going to be a very joyous night."

Maggie laughed, and then she turned to admire the stunning woman in her arms. She tweaked her nose, as she did when they were kids. "Of course it is, silly! When we are all together, I'm always happy. I feel like it is finally complete." But she knew differently, she had been thinking about it recently and questioning it earlier today.

"Is it really complete, or do you feel like you're missing something?" Lucy asked, with a very mysterious hint to those words. "I know, I sometimes feel like I'm missing something. I just don't know what."

"Is there a reason you asked me that?" Maggie questioned, feeling a little antsy.

Lucy looked at her watch, and then she started pushing Maggie towards the front door. "You better get going or you are going to be late for your party! Besides, Bradley will be here in a while to pick me up."

Maggie looked thoughtful, "Do you like Bradley? He seems like a very nice man. I just hope he doesn't have ulterior motives."

A sad look crossed Lucy's face. "It's a chance you take sometimes. He's very nice. I just don't know what he will really think of me when I am honest with him and tell him about my whole sordid past."

Maggie's voice took a serious tone, "He wouldn't be much of a man if he judged you on yesterday instead of today. Remember that. We all have a past."

Lucy pushed Maggie, "Get out of here! You need to get ready! See you later!"

The party was in full swing and the gifts had all been opened. Dinner was fabulous, and everyone was enjoying the good cheer. The children were busy with their gifts. It had been difficult not to spoil the children with everything they had on their wish list with Santa. It was the year for electronics that the kids had requested. Maggie and Rand did their best to keep everything to a minimal. Now sitting amongst the glowering faces of Elizabeth and William, they were sure they had gone over that line. Each of the younger girls got their iPhones and iPads with prepaid service connections, along with other things on their list.

Maggie pleaded with Elizabeth during dinner. "Come on, sweet Elizabeth. The girls love to talk on the phone all the time, so now they won't run up your phone bill. It's just a small phone. Besides, I know it will be safer for them; it has a GPS on it and you can track them."

Elizabeth just shook her head in defeat. She didn't have a chance when Maggie set her mind to something. Although she could see her point, all the gifts were still too extravagant for her children.

"Just think...they can even see each other every day. They can talk about their homework and send pictures as they grow. And I'm really pleased, because now I can talk to them and see their beautiful young faces," Maggie went on.

"Enough, Maggie, I get the picture. I hate when you are condescending. These overgenerous gifts have to stop," Elizabeth pleaded.

Later, Elizabeth cornered Randolph and pointed a finger at his face. "I told you nothing for the adults. This is a kid's holiday. Don't you guys ever listen to me! I just lashed out at Maggie in regards to the kids, and now I'm having to deal with you. Lordy, you people just don't get it. I'm returning the stock options you gave us. I won't accept it."

Randolph's face turned red, and he started to stumble over his words. "Honestly, Elizabeth, my company has to give me so many options a year and I have to find a place for them. I have more than I can deal with. Besides, my accountant suggested I give them to you. I was just listening to him."

"Give them to him. I don't care who you give them too, I don't want them!" She said adamantly.

He dropped his voice, and looked defeated. "It actually is a write off to me. So it was like a double-edged sword."

Elizabeth looked at Randolph's face. "Okay, I will put them away. But you will get them back when your accountant gives the word."

Randolph hugged her, and then turned his face so she couldn't see his smug grin. He was trying, in his own way, to make their lives a little more secure for their later years. He knew they had worked very hard for many years, and he just wanted them to have something to fall back on in case of an emergency. They were down-to-earth, hardworking folks who never took from others, yet they were the first to give to those in need. Their whole town was like that. They all struggled, yet they were there for one another.

The children were having a great time and the chocolate fountain was getting a lot of attention. The dinner had been prime rib with all the trimmings. The dessert trays were filled with all kinds of culinary delights. The men had left the room to catch some fresh air, and the women were enjoying a cup of tea. Maggie looked stunning in her new dress she had purchased from Nordstrom a few days before. Meg and Maggie had an exciting day shopping on Rodeo Drive. Maggie bought Meg a few pricey things she liked, and made her put them away in her suitcase. Then, they spent an hour at a trendy restaurant where they saw a few famous movie stars. Meg was so excited, and her enthusiasm to spend more time with Maggie was hard to curb.

"Pack those jeans and belt in your suitcase, and hide the perfume in your makeup case. And for God sake, don't let your mother see the Juicy bag. Take them out in a while. I don't want your mother angry at me!" Maggie said.

Meg frowned. "When I'm finally on my own, then I won't have to worry about what she says."

"Don't start this again. Be patient, and don't turn this into a big fire that can get out of control!"

When the men walked back into the room, Damon walked over to the waiter, and whispered something to him. Maggie watched him as she was talking to Lucy. A feeling of warmth tingled throughout her body. She remembered hours ago when they were getting ready at the beach house for the evening. She had just stepped out of the shower, and wrapped a towel around her. When she quietly walked into the bedroom, Damon had on his dark suit pants, and had just put something into his pocket.

The look on his face was how he had looked hours before, in the early morning, after they had made love. The look of completion, as the quiet calmness took over. He had pulled her close and placed her hand over his fast-beating heart and said, "You have become my whole world."

Rene D. Schultz

56

Maggie thought at that moment in time, she wanted to say, "I love you." But she didn't. Something inside her made it beyond terrifying to say those beautiful words. Not losing the control over her life that had been predestined since her mother had destroyed her trust in everyone was hard to break. Chipping off the ice that had encompassed her heart was almost impossible. Except with her three dear friends. They had to earn her trust in the orphanage before she ever told them her deep-seeded feelings. And now, she felt this dam was ready to burst, and she feared that rejection deep within.

Staring at him from across the room, she softly cleared her throat. "Hey, you...we have to leave in a few minutes. I don't want to be late."

He looked up and gave her a suggestive smile. He came around the bed and put his arms around her. Still wrapped in her damp towel, she looked up and placed her hand on his bare chest. "What were you thinking about, Mr. Dreamy Eyes?"

He moved his lips within an inch from hers and said, "Wow! That's a loaded question. Do you want me to tell you...or do you want me to take off this towel and show you?" He ran his hand down the towel and along her hip. Then he leaned in and gave her a lingering kiss.

When they barely broke the contact of their lips, in a whisper he could barely hear, she finally said, "I love you...."

He pulled her so tight against him, she could feel his shaking body react. He held her for a few long seconds while he tried to gain composure. Then he groaned, "If we don't get ready to go immediately, then I'm going to throw you down on this bed and have my way with you all night!" He moaned, "I'm afraid that everyone might send out the posse. And I hear Randolph carries a big gun!"

Maggie lifted her hands off his bare chest and moved them to his face. "Save those sexy thoughts and we'll continue this later."

Damon released her and laughed, "You little hussy! I knew that first day I met you in your office—and you acted like a cold-hearted queen— I knew that deep inside, you had the heart of a harlot!"

She lived up to those words. She dropped her towel, gave him a smug, suggestive look, and then walked back around the bed to get dressed.

The waiter took a spoon and tapped it against a glass to get everyone's attention, breaking Maggie's thoughts of the morning. With that done, he announced, "Mr. Depre would like everyone to please take their seats."

Everyone looked up in surprise and did as they were told. Maggie drew her brows together and looked at Damon with questioning eyes. He knew something, and he wasn't going to give it away. Out of the corner of her eye, she watched Randolph give Damon a pat on the back. Lucy had a big grin on her face, and it seemed like everyone knew what his intention for this interruption was for—except her. Fear struck a nerve and Maggie was beginning to feel uncomfortable.

Maggie walked to her seat next to Damon at the head of the table as everyone took their seats.

She leaned next to him and whispered, "What...is going on?"

He looked down and winked. It was the same slow wink that he had used that first day in her office when she was checking him out from the bottom of his cowboy boots, up to the handsome features of his face. That wink had thrown her off guard, just like it was doing now. She sat down like everyone else and waited to see what was next.

When everyone was seated, and the room became silent, the waiters went around and handed all of the adults a glass of champagne. Damon cleared his throat. He lifted the champagne glass in his shaking hand to make a toast:

"To everyone...who I now consider my family."

He cleared his throat again. Everyone watched as his nerves started taking over.

"This has been an amazing journey for me. First, to find Maggie's three friends, and then to bring you back together. The friendships I have experienced are not anything I have ever had in my lifetime. As you know, I've lived a very reclusive life that consisted of just my business. Until that one day, when I walked into Maggie's office. I knew that day, I was in big trouble. Her viperous tongue nearly shred me into pieces. Yet, my mission was to get you all together. Maggie, will you please stand up and join me?"

He held out his hand, and brought her to her feet. A look of confusion was written all over her face. She looked into his face for reassurance, but only found a humbled-looking man. Then within one frantic moment, she spanned the silent crowd that was waiting to see what was going to happen.

"That night in the restaurant when you returned from Elizabeth's house for the first time, you asked me.... 'Am I hiding from the past, and too self-centered, selfish, and blind not to notice life around me?' And I answered it the best I could. I said, 'I don't think you're selfish or blind. What you did was withdraw, and you became too afraid to give anyone a chance to get close. You closed yourself off in a neat little circle, rarely stepping out. If you consider that selfish, I'd disagree. You were protecting yourself from the pain of the past.' Then I followed with, 'I know all the symptoms, Maggie. I have that same disease.' I want you to know...that night, I was talking from my heart. I, too, had been sleepwalking through life."

Damon reached into his pocket and got down on one knee. Maggie silently watched as tears streamed down her face. She knew what was coming, and it seemed like a slow-motion dream. She had waited all her life to be loved. A deep love that finally had a commitment. Not at all like her mother who had left her on the steps of Bishop Street Orphanage.

"Tonight before we got here, for the first time, you whispered in my ear, 'I love you.' I knew that it had taken a lifetime for you to say those three words. But, I didn't say it back, because I was waiting for the perfect moment, in front of all your family, so they could see and hear my words, also, for the first time."

He looked around the room and saw the tears in everyone's eyes. Then he looked directly at Maggie again.

"I love you with all my heart, Margaret Gray. I'm not perfect, nor you. But we are perfect together. You make me laugh, you cause me to think twice, you admit to being human and making mistakes, you have a kind soul that gives more than you get, and a smile that melts any anger I might hold in my heart."

He opened the box and took out the diamond ring. He looked at Maggie and took her shaking hand with his and poised the ring next to her finger.

"I promise not to hurt you or break your heart. I don't want to change you or expect more than you can give. I will smile when you make me happy, I will let you know when I'm mad, and I will miss you when I have to go away. But today, I want all of you and forever! I will make you a promise to give you back the very best I can. So, with that said, Miss Maggie...will you marry me?"

Damon waited for her answer.

Maggie's whole body was shaking. Small sobs escaped from her lips, and the best she could do was look down into his teary eyes and say, "I'd be very proud to be your wife, your lover, and your best friend. I love you, Damon Depre! Don't you ever forget that!"

Maggie watched as he carefully slipped the ring onto her finger. Then he stood up and they both looked at each other with tears in their eyes. The room was filled with hoots and hollers and lots of emotional people.

Maggie lifted her hand and wiped his eyes. "I don't think that I've ever seen tears in your eyes." She grinned. He took her tearstained hand and kissed it.

HOUSE OF STONE

"You've never given me cause, and I've never said those words before, to anyone." He hugged her again, tight to his chest, when all of a sudden they were besieged by their family and friends.

Randolph lifted his glass and said, "Let's all make a toast to this happy couple. I couldn't have picked a better husband for our Maggie. Welcome to the family, Damon."

"I'll drink to that!" William's voice boomed.

Elizabeth and Lucy came over and surrounded Maggie with hugs. "Let me see that ring!" Lucy cried.

"I haven't even seen it myself!" Maggie joked. She looked at the beautiful four-carat ring and her mouth opened in surprise. "Oh my God!"

Damon leaned over and whispered in her ear. "Do you like it, babe? If you want to exchange it, we can do that."

Maggie touched the ring and then touched his face. "The ring is beautiful, and I love the man who gave it to me!"

Damon leaned over and gave Maggie a kiss. The crowd started to roar and Randolph yelled, "Hey, you guys, go get a room!" The crowd went wild with laughter.

Meg was jumping with glee and the children were just as excited. Randall heartily patted Damon on the back and shook his hand. "So, I guess you're done with living in sin! When are you making this legal?"

Randolph suggested they get married at the ranch in Mexico. Everyone was giving their opinions as to where the happy couple should get married.

Damon put his hand in the air and said, "Whoa...we just got engaged five minutes ago. I haven't talked to Maggie yet to see what's next!"

Elizabeth said righteously, "Marriage, of course! In front of God and everyone!"

The next evening, after an exciting morning of Christmas celebration, they were all at the airport as the Martins boarded Randolph's private jet to go back to the cold winter of North Bend. Randolph was hitching a ride; and once they dropped off his family, he was traveling back to Mexico. Smiles of happiness were displayed on everyone's faces. The children were busy taking pictures on their new phones, and Randall was hugging his parents with tears in his eyes. Damon, Maggie, Lucy, and Mary Jane looked sad as the door closed and the engines roared to life and the plane started to taxi down the runway.

Rene D. Schultz
64

CHAPTER 5

LUCY HAD HELD ONTO DAMON'S SECRET FOR WEEKS. She knew he was going to ask Maggie to marry him, and so did Randolph. Damon had met with Randolph weeks before to ask permission and for his blessing. That night, Randolph and Damon talked about life and drank until they both passed out on the couch. Two days later, Damon took him to the jewelry store and Randolph helped pick out a ring. Randolph knew the size of the diamond or the cost of the ring would not impress Maggie. She would have been happy with a plastic ring from a Cracker Jack box. It was just who she was.

Elizabeth only found out the day she came in to Los Angeles. And it was hard for her to keep that secret. She didn't dare tell the kids, for fear someone would leak the surprise. They all knew Maggie loved Damon, you could tell by the way she always looked at him. But, like Randolph and Lucy, she held on with a tight grip to her heart. Fear had closed her off for most of her life, and they were not sure if she would ever be ready to let go. That night proved them wrong. They had never seen Maggie happier, nor had they ever seen Damon let go of his tough exterior. It was a good night, a new beginning for two lost souls who had finally let go of their past, and were looking forward to creating a future together.

It was also a new beginning for Lucy. At first, she felt a little awkward bringing Bradley to such an intimate gathering of just her family. It was actually Randolph who invited him while they were at the grand opening of Dream 'Scape. Damon and Maggie were still a little unsure of Bradley's motives, but Randolph wanted to give him the benefit of the doubt. He was going to have a lot of kissing ass to do, and a lot of proving his intentions with this tough group. All the men were adversaries, and you didn't want to mess with them. They were going to keep their eyes on him, especially when it came to Lucy. They had all watched as she fought so hard, bringing normalcy back into her life, and continued her sobriety. They didn't want her to falter. The pain she carried from childhood was almost more than she could handle. Now, being a single parent and raising a child on her own was a tremendous responsibility, and managing her sobriety was a lifetime obligation. *Would Bradley ever be able to share those obligations?*

On the other hand, Lucy was attracted to Bradley from the first night she met him. He was kind and considerate to her, but she also knew, as an investigative reporter, there was a tough exterior that might not be penetrated. She had seen the same personality traits in Damon and Randolph and knew them to have a hard exterior with a soft inside, even though they didn't show it very often.

Bradley had been on time to pick her up and he brought her a beautiful flower arrangement. She had never received flowers from a suitor before. Randolph always sent Maggie, Elizabeth, and her flowers, but that didn't count. Bradley was dressed impeccably and Lucy thought he looked handsome. As the evening progressed, she watched as he blended in with the family and he began to feel comfortable.

Later that night, Bradley drove Lucy home, walked her to the door, and said his goodbyes. "Can I see you again soon? Do you mind if I call during the week?"

Lucy smiled and said, "I would really like that. Thank you for enjoying the evening with me. It was pretty special. Goodnight, Bradley." She closed the door. No kiss, no hug—just a simple goodnight.

Maggie opened the door and started to walk into the office. Denise was standing at her desk, holding two hot lattes.

She put the lattes down and ran toward Maggie. With all the excitement of a best friend, she hugged Maggie and swung her around. Screams of excitement could be heard throughout the office. When the craziness settled down, Maggie told Denise the whole story. Denise's eyes had that dreamy, faraway look to them and she couldn't be happier for her friend. She was part of Maggie's family now, and Brianna and Mary Jane were best friends. She had wanted to be there, but unfortunately the baby had a bad cold, David was still sick, and they couldn't make it.

"I wish I was there. We had to rush Maddie to the hospital. It seems the little one had a raging ear infection!" Denise frowned. "But I want to see some pictures!" Then she grabbed Maggie's hand as her screams bounced around the room. "Oh my God! Oh my God...what a beautiful ring! You lucky little lady! You finally got the 'pirate'!"

Maggie giggled. "He isn't Black Beard, or One Eyed Jack, or Jack Sparrow; he's Damon Depre, who you let into my office one day—and he flipped my world upside down!"

Denise put her hands on her hips and pursed her lips. "Your world needed that pirate, and lots of excitement—we both knew that!"

Maggie nodded. "Thank you, my dear friend. I'm sorry you weren't there, but I'm so thankful the baby is okay. I know what a responsibility it is, with children, after watching and helping Lucy with Mary Jane."

"Forget the sick kids. I'm just so happy I don't have a lovesick puppy hanging around anymore!" Denise laughed.

Maggie looked puzzled. "How come I never saw that?"

Denise handed Maggie the latte, and pushed her toward her office, "because you're so damn naïve! Okay, kiddo, it's back to work! I need you to write some 'thank you' letters to the reviewers that pushed your book to number one!"

With that said, Maggie walked into her office, sipping on her latte.

Things settled down and Lucy was absorbed in Dream 'Scape. She was going out in the evenings and looking for lost children—offering them a place to stay. Sometimes Bradley would go with her. They were talking about doing a documentary about a society who washed their hands of these young children and exposing the parents that threw them out into this harsh, cruel world without any remorse. Parents who had discarded them, as though they were the evening trash, either because they were dirt poor or they just had nothing to offer them in the way of stability. Most of the time it was because of their addictions—and how they had consumed all of their parental responsibilities. It brought back a lot of old memories for Lucy. Especially that night the police had found her lying on her dead mother in a fleabag motel room at the age of six. Even though it felt like a dream now, going to the shelters and frequenting the sleazy motels was more difficult than she expected.

Lucy and her family knew how it felt to be abandoned. Maggie's mother had dropped her off on the steps of Bishop Street Orphanage with a note pinned to her coat. Lucy was found lying next to her dead mother in a sleazy motel. Her mother had overdosed on bad heroin. Elizabeth's parents had both died in a car crash and the next of kin never stepped forward.

Randolph was another story. His mother was fifteen and came from a wealthy family. Randolph's father was from the wrong side of the tracks. The grandfather made his granddaughter give up her child, and when Randolph was born, he was immediately placed into the orphanage, along with a sizable charitable contribution.

Nothing changed in life. Each lost child had a story of their own. At least the four orphans had a place to be and food in their tummies. All the street children nowadays—they had nothing, were left with nothing. Most of the orphanages had closed, and government funding for halfway houses and shelters were practically nonexistent. These kids were the scavengers of the streets and the government had nowhere for them to go except into a broken foster care system or prison.

Lately, Randolph had silently taken his money and set his course in another direction. He loved his hacienda and ranch in Mexico and spent a lot of time there. When his success had amassed sudden wealth, his life had begun to spin out of control, and his privacy was stolen—he needed some kind of stability. Robert, his good friend and mentor since Harvard, suggested he find a quiet place outside of the country where he could sneak away. Over ten years ago, he chanced upon a small town in Mexico while he was looking for inner peace. He needed to get away from all the publicity and security threats. The tabloids hounded him around the world and forced him into a life of isolation. It wasn't easy being who he was, with a constant target on his back. Fame and fortune had become his prison. It had also brought betrayal into his life.

Randolph was married once—to a struggling actress who found a means of finding her five seconds of fame. She was a charming and savvy girl who seized the opportunity of a lifetime. Only in her case it was more than five seconds—it was six months of marriage to one of the wealthiest men in the world. Her first mistake, was underestimating Randolph Parker and the prenuptial she signed. The second was the pictures showing her leaving a motel room in the embrace of her ex-boyfriend.

Her duplicity had knocked the wind out of Randolph's pride—leaving him with major trust issues. Lucy, Maggie, and Elizabeth could see a tough, unapproachable exterior that kept him well-protected from relationships. They also could hear that deep ache of betrayal in his voice whenever the word marriage was spoken. Maggie thought it was a pain so deep, he might never trust a woman again.

He hadn't dated in years; and he steered clear from putting himself on the eligibility market. The rumors in the tabloids, at one time, had speculated that he was gay. But, he didn't care. He knew who he was and he had nothing left to prove to anyone. Just because he made a mistake and was lured in by her beauty and deceit, didn't mean he would do it again. Besides, it didn't cost him a lot to get out of it. He had the last laugh. That was what his wealth had given him, along with a great attorney, and an ironclad pre-nup.

Randolph dialed Maggie's cellphone and waited for her to pick up.

"Hello, Rand, what's up?" Maggie was sitting at her desk, sipping a cup of latte.

"I wanted to see if you and Damon wanted to come to Mexico with me this weekend. I have a surprise I've been working on and it's almost done. I wanted it to be a complete surprise to you, but I ran into a few snags and I really need your help. Please come this weekend," he pleaded.

Maggie laughed. "Well, I can't speak for myself anymore. I have to talk with Damon. It sounds great and you know how much I love the hacienda and I'll only go to the ranch if you and Damon promise you won't get me back on a horse again!"

Randolph laughed. "Okay, I promise. But, is it okay if Damon rides?"

There was a second of silence. "Only if you don't put him on Beast! We've only been engaged a few weeks and I don't want to be a widow this young!" Maggie laughed. "Besides, I'm fascinated to see what this surprise is. You've been working on it for a long time. Can you give me a hint?"

Randolph cleared his throat, and said in his deep baritone voice, "Now it wouldn't be a surprise if I told you what it was. Looks like you're going to have to talk your 'old man' into coming!"

Maggie sighed. "You're so transparent, my friend! I'll bet you built a new wing onto the ranch for the family? Or did you add a kiddie pool for the little ones?" Maggie chuckled.

"Come find out. Let me know later today. My plane leaves Friday, early evening, and I'll have you back late Sunday!"

"Sounds good to me...but—"

Randolph cut her off, "Later, Maggie!"

~~~

Damon and Maggie drove up to the plane just as the engines roared to life.

Randolph was just finishing a phone call when they walked up the stairs and stood in the doorway. A big smile lit up his face and he clapped Damon on the back. "How's life treating you now that you're actually a 'couple'?" Randolph hooted.

"Like a hen-pecked rooster who lost all his feathers!" Damon smiled.

Maggie slapped his shoulder as her eyes opened wide. "You don't know what hen-pecked is yet! Once we are married, you won't have a damn say about anything." Maggie giggled.

"Oh, I must be mistaken; I thought that was how it was—now!" He pushed Randolph the rest of the way into the jet and the pilot closed the door.

Randolph pointed to the couch and the seats. "Come on in and have a seat. Put your belts on. It will only be a short two-hour flight. I've got food and drinks, so make yourself at home," he announced.

The bathroom door opened and a pretty, dark skinned woman stepped out. She looked to be either part Hispanic, or part Filipino, Asian, or a mix. Slowly, she walked down the aisle and stood next to Randolph. Maggie's eyes opened wide in disbelief. She looked her over and guessed her age to be in her thirties. She was small and petite, with a light complexion, and shiny brown hair cut to her shoulder. Her beautiful green eyes were almond shaped and her smile lit up the room.

She held out her hand to Maggie, and in a sweet low voice she said, "Hello, my name is Juliann. You must be Margaret Gray? Randolph told me you and Damon would be on this flight. I've heard so many wonderful things about you. And although I'm too busy to read, I congratulate you on your success as a famed author. It's a pleasure to finally meet you."

Maggie took her hand and looked at Randolph. "Well, this must be my surprise?" Maggie questioned with a wink.

Randolph shuffled his feet. "Not exactly."

"Well, when she says 'finally' I can only assume you've know each other for a while. Am I missing something?" Maggie was very obviously fishing for answers.

"Nope, far from it. This is a dear friend of mine I met a few years ago when she was doing missionary work in China after the earthquake in 2008. I've sponsored some of her charities and we kept in touch. Then we ran into each other again, in Haiti after the earthquake a few years back, when she was working with my buddy, Sean Penn."

Maggie's eyes opened wide after Randolph's introduction. "And what kind of missionary work do you do? This is getting more interesting by the moment." Maggie took her arm and started walking her toward two seats.

Juliann followed with a grin on her face as she looked back at a smiling Randolph. "I'm sure my life is drab compared to yours. I just set up makeshift orphanages for the children who have been separated or orphaned from their parents during disasters. We give them a comfortable place to be when their lives are turned upside down. Then we try to find their family or the next of kin. Unfortunately, it doesn't always have a fairy tale ending." Her soft-spoken voice and kind eyes showed Maggie her tender demeanor.

Damon asked, "Were you ever orphaned?"

She shook her head. "No. I came from accumulated wealth, although that doesn't mean you won't have the same issues of abandonment. With wealth comes great expectations and I did what my parents and society expected of me. I worked hard in school and became a doctor of medicine. I was a practicing pediatric physician at John Hopkins, and I gave that up to do something more meaningful in life. It was kind of like a 'calling,' you might say."

Randolph spoke up, not wanting to ruin Maggie's surprise. "She hitched a ride to visit some friends in the small town outside of my ranch."

Maggie curiosity was showing all over her face. "This is a pleasant surprise. I'm sure you know my connection to Randolph by now. This is my fiancé, Damon Depre. He was the one who managed to bring us orphans together after twenty years."

Damon held his hand out. "Pleasure, ma'am. For some reason, you look very familiar." Damon watched her eyes closely for any recognition.

She didn't shy away. She said, "I worked side by side with Henri Ford, one of the best Haitian-American pediatric surgeons I know, for months after the earthquake. He fixed them, and I gave them a place to stay. Maybe you saw that documentary about him. I also worked closely with Sean. That is probably where you recognized me from."

Damon shook his head, his eyes told a different story. "No it was somewhere else. At my age, memory is not as quick as it used to be, but I'm sure I will figure it out!" Damon hid behind his comment about age.

She smiled. "Don't waste your time."

Randolph heard the engines getting louder and said, "Let's take our seats for takeoff and then we can sit around and chat. It might even give the old man a chance to think about where he knows you from."

Damon watched her closely and he could tell that after years of investigations—she had a secret. Her head turned away when he looked directly at her.

Everyone took a seat and buckled up as the plane taxied down the runway. Once they were in the air the belts came off and they all sat on the couch, engaged in lively conversation. Maggie thought Juliann was a very fascinating woman with lots of interesting experiences and stories. Just knowing that she was once a pediatrician and left the field to become a missionary was thought-provoking. Not only was she well-educated, she was a great conversationalist that never let her discussions lag. Maggie really enjoyed listening to her stories and hearing about all of the places she had traveled.

"Will you be staying with us, at Randolph's?" Maggie asked her.

"I'll have to see. I'm really focused on certain things I need to get done. But I would love to spend more time with you, if I can break away," Juliann said.

"Have you ever been to Randolph's ranch or hacienda?" Maggie was still trying to figure out her relationship to Randolph.

"Oh, yes! His hacienda is magnificent, and the sunsets are amazing on the cliff. But I have a soft spot in my heart for the ranch. I love the old church he rebuilt, brick by brick, for the people in the town."

Maggie nodded. "My favorite place, too. I've done a lot of praying in that sacred little church."

The ranch was Randolph's hobby. It was constructed of historical architecture that was near extinction. The buildings were rebuilt in a multicultural Spanish and Mexican design that was from their heritage. Randolph was very proud of the haunting visions, of the huge, intricately carved cornices of bricks and rocks that were over two hundred years old and restored to perfection by the hardworking hands of the townspeople. Every part of his ranch had been moved from another part of town, brick by brick, and restored to its original appearance. His plan for the ranch was to keep a small part of history alive for the people of the area.

His real pride and joy was the first church built in this region back in the early seventeen-hundreds. The residents constructed it with hand-molded mortar, brick by brick. So, before the building was completely lost to age, he had a team of archaeologists break it down and reconstruct it in a secluded area of the ranch that faced the beautiful mountain peaks that always caught the sunset.

He wanted the people in town to embrace their heritage. That was something he never had. And now, they came every Sunday to enjoy their lovely church, knowing their forefathers had done the same. Many generations of townspeople had been baptized, married, and eulogized in that historic little building. For this, he had gained the respect of the residents and they welcomed him with open arms. Their quiet acceptance had humbled him.

Damon was quietly talking to Randolph in their own private conversation. They both were sipping on small glasses of aged whisky and were completely absorbed in their discussion. Maggie turned to look at Damon; he caught her eye and winked. It was those moments in time when she unexpectedly felt loved. A love deeper than she had ever imagined or ever dreamed she deserved.

Juliann watched this short but heartwarming exchange and smiled. "You are very fortunate."

Maggie blushed. She didn't realize anyone had seen her exchange with Damon. "Yes, I am." Maggie noticed the longing in Juliann's eyes. Maggie didn't need to ask, she knew Juliann had loved once and it was now gone. The mystery of this young lady was beginning to completely intrigue Maggie.

The pilot announced that the plane was ready to land and that they needed to buckle up their seatbelts. It was still light outside as the jet started to descend onto a private airstrip that had a small building attached to it.

"I heard your story about how you and Damon met. Randolph said when he first met your private investigator, he didn't like him. He said he was arrogant and tough around the edges. I don't know what you did, but he seems so gentle and loving. This is quite a surprise to me." Juliann shook her head and smiled.

Maggie held up her finger and waved it side to side in response. "Oh, don't think he's not tough and hard. I've seen that dangerous side when it comes to his clients and dealing with certain situations. You definitely don't want to find yourself on his bad side. Nor do you want to fight with him."

Juliann laughed. "Oh, I bet he is a hard-hitting opponent! You're both very lucky to have each other. It been so nice meeting you, after hearing Randolph proudly talk about his family."

Maggie inquisitively said, "I want to hear more about this mystery woman sitting next to me—and not just about her missionary travels!"

The plane had come to a stop and Randolph walked over and teased. "Don't tell her a thing! And don't let her sweet talk you. I want to keep her guessing!"

Damon was behind him and he said, "That's not smart, Randolph. Have you ever put a red flag in front of a mad bull?"

Maggie stood up, placed her hand on her hips, and gasped. "Are you comparing me to a bull, Mr. Depre?"

Damon took her hand and started walking toward the exit. "I'm the investigator—not you! I already know why she's here. You're going to have to wait to find out! Come on, lady, I'm dying for some authentic Mexican food!" He was pulling her down the steps and laughing at the same time.

Maggie turned around when she got to the ground. "At least give me a hint about Juliann!" she yelled to Randolph above the plane's engines.

He cupped his hands and yelled back, "She's not a 'black widow'!"

CHAPTER 6

MAGGIE COULD STILL REMEMBER THE FIRST TIME she and Randolph pulled into the driveway, surrounded by eight-foot-tall plaster walls of the hacienda. The impressive iron gates opened as a guard waved them in. She had never seen such a masterpiece of architectural and interior design like this, with its rich and vibrant Mexican style. The enormous, sprawling two-story hacienda was swallowed up by a courtyard filled with captivating water fountains. Each one flowed into a large fishpond, as colorful potted flowers encircled the entire courtyard. The well-manicured landscape blended perfectly with the Mexican design. It still took her breath away each time she came back.

They got out of the SUV and began to walk around a brick pathway towards the back of the house. The driver took all of their luggage into the house; and Maggie could hear him telling the staff that the guests had arrived.

Maggie laced her fingers with Damon as they slowly walked the path. Randolph and Juliann followed.

"I thought we would have a traditional dinner and watch the sunset over the horizon. Juliann decided to join us tonight for dinner and then she has to leave." Randolph announced as they were walking.

Maggie turned around and smiled at Juliann. "Thank God, I hate to be outnumbered by all this testosterone! Especially when they are hungry!"

Juliann began to laugh. "Why do I get the feeling that you can handle that—and just about anything else, Maggie!"

Damon and Randolph laughed heartily. Then Damon added, "Because she wants you to think she's weak and submissive."

As they turned the corner, the magnificent Mexican horizon came into sight. The house was perched on a cliff and they had a hundred and eighty degree panoramic view of the ocean around them. The translucent blue sky, the large waves, and mild breeze immediately captured their attention.

Maggie turned and looked at Randolph. "I remember the first time I came here and I asked you if this was heaven," she paused, "you said to me, 'it's about as close as you can get.' I get that answer, now. I, too, have fallen in love with this place."

Randolph took a deep breath of the salty ocean breeze and exhaled. "I feel at peace here, away from the stresses of real life—I was constantly looking over my shoulder." They continued strolling across the flagstone patio, by the free-formed pool that blended in with the landscape. Carefully, they stepped around the large formations of rocks and plants that gave it a natural, exotic setting. The estate reflected the flavor of the country that surrounded it, using nature's resources in their purest forms.

They settled into comfortable chairs in front of a table. Suddenly, two Hispanic women appeared. One with a large tray with two large pitchers filled with margaritas and glasses, the other carried two large platters with sautéed meat, tortillas, beans and condiments. The two ladies placed everything on the table. One of the staff lit the gas lanterns and the large fire pit.

Maggie's face lit up with a big smile. "*Buenas noches*, Lupe!" Maggie stood up, walked over to Lupe, and gave her a big hug.

The petite Hispanic lady blushed and said, "Nice to see you, Miss Maggie. If there is anything you need, please let me know. Your rooms are all ready, and your favorite bath oils are on the sink." Then the two ladies scurried back towards the house.

Randolph passed out Margaritas to everyone. Then he leaned over, picked up a plate, and filled it with the meat and tortillas and the extras. Carefully, he handed it to Juliann. She smiled and whispered, "Thank you."

Damon did the same for Maggie. They ate and enjoyed the perfect balmy weather and slight breeze. As the sun began to set over the ocean, the sky lit up in amazing shades of orange. Maggie could see the stars beginning to twinkle and hear the larger waves crashing against the shore.

"Juliann and I have some business to discuss and then I'm going to drive her into town. Now that we have enjoyed this fabulous dinner, I'm going to leave you to relax the rest of the evening. Why don't you two go to the downtown area, or along the seaside promenade, and have a few drinks in the restaurants with some Mexican hospitality?" Randolph stood up and stretched.

Damon stood up and said, "A nice stroll sounds good. Maybe we'll just stick around here and walk along the beach."

They shook hands. "Great. I'm bouncing you out of bed early so that we can get a head start tomorrow. We're going to have a full day ahead of us, so get plenty of sleep."

Randolph put his hand on the sway of Juliann's back and they walked towards the house.

Maggie smiled up at Damon and held out her hand. "I'm afraid I ate too much. Let's go for that walk down the beach."

When he pulled her up from her chair, he wrapped his arms around her and bent down and gave her a slow, passionate kiss. When they finally came up for air, in a deep, low voice he said, "Maybe we should retire to the room now."

Maggie took his hand and tugged. "I would love a nice walk on the beach. Let's bring a few towels."

They both knew from previous visits to the house that Randolph had a whole staff of bodyguards who silently watched every move of every guest. It was protection from the craziness that had started in Mexico with the kidnapping a few years back. Randolph kept a tight grip on his security, and everyone around him. Mostly because Randolph had to be more vigilant with his privacy and whereabouts, because of who he was.

Maggie and Damon took off their shoes, walked down the stairs to the beach and continued to stroll along the shoreline—letting the warm and damp sand ooze between their toes.

The next morning Maggie rolled over in bed and felt the empty space next to her. Alarmed, she sat up and looked around the room. Damon was already dressed casually in long cargo shorts and a T-shirt, and his hair was still wet from his shower. He was standing on the patio near the railing overlooking the ocean, sipping on a cup of coffee. Maggie thought about the evening and smiled. Every night was more passionate than the next, and it had all been a fulfilling learning experience from her earlier years of innocence. Maggie slid her legs over the side of the bed and slipped on her robe. Quietly, she tiptoed out onto the patio and stood behind Damon and wrapped her arms around him. He turned around, smiled and slid his arm around her. "Sleep well?"

She nestled in his arm and nodded her head. She could feel his body come to life, like the night before.

He cleared his throat, trying to gain his composure. "There's hot coffee in the carafe Lupe brought up to the room a few minutes ago. Want me to get you some?"

"I'll go get some, thanks. You're up early. Couldn't sleep?" She closed her eyes from the bright sun.

"It's not that early. You looked tired last night, I wanted to let you sleep a little longer. So, you better get a move on—if you want that breakfast Lupe is almost finished cooking."

"Oh, hell yes! I love her breakfast menus." She swiftly went into the room, poured herself a cup of coffee, and started to get ready for the day.

Damon smiled. He watched as she opened her robe and let it slide off as she went into the bathroom to take a shower.

After a breakfast of enchiladas, chorizo with potatoes, huevos rancheros, homemade tortillas, and mango and papaya slices, they all got into the Jeep and drove toward the ranch. Only this time, Randolph took a different road toward the outskirts of town in a different direction than the ranch.

"Are we making another stop before we go to the ranch?" Maggie questioned, as she studied the unfamiliar scenery.

Randolph looked in his rearview mirror and smiled at Maggie in the backseat. "How perceptive of you!"

"I'm an author, remember? I have to be two steps ahead of the characters!" she laughed. "Where are we going?"

"I told you that I had a surprise for you! This is something I've been working on for over a year now. It's become my mission in life to start these where they are needed."

They were approaching a large gated complex surrounded by six-foot walls. When they pulled up and stopped at the decorative iron gate, a man came out and opened it. As they drove in, it looked like a small community of different buildings all done in similar architecture to the hacienda. It looked welcoming and cozy. In the front was a gated play yard with swings, slides, tree houses perched above ground, a merry-go-round—everything that would keep the interest of children at play.

Maggie's eyes opened wide with wonder. "Where are we? What is this?" she swung her head around, looking in every direction. Damon and Randolph sat there quietly, letting Maggie absorb her surroundings. "Stop the car. I want to get out!"

Suddenly, a woman walked out the door of one of the buildings with a big smile on her face, waving to the occupants in the Jeep. As she strolled towards them, Maggie smiled when she recognized the woman was Juliann. Maggie watched as Randolph's face lit up with a smile and he opened the door of the car. He stepped out and gave Juliann a hug.

"*Buenos días*, Juliann," he said.

She looked up at Randolph with happiness shining in her eyes, and then she leaned into the car and said, "It's so nice to see you again. Welcome to Casa de Niños."

Randolph lifted his arm and slowly he spun around in a circle and said, "This is the new orphanage we built to house many of the homeless children from this area of Mexico. We've been building it for the past year, and I'm so excited to finally get the opportunity to fill it with a lot of young children, small children who have been living on the streets of our towns and villages, surviving on nothing but what they can find in trashcans or what they can steal from others to allay their hunger."

Maggie and Damon opened the door and stepped out of the car. Maggie slowly turned around, her eyes filling with tears. She walked over and hugged Randolph and then looked into his face. "First you build Dream 'Scape in Los Angeles to keep our homeless children off the streets, and now you build another home for countless others. I'm so proud of you!"

Damon slapped Randolph on his back. "Nice job, Rand. It looks amazing compared to when you started. And you've even kept it a big surprise for our Maggie. That was a feat in itself!"

Maggie turned to Damon with a scowl on her face. "You mean you knew about this? You've been here before and you never told me?"

Damon looked at Maggie and shrugged. "You know I love you Maggie, but I made a promise to Rand and I am a man of my word. I've been here a few times on my way home from some of my investigations abroad. Once at the beginning, a few other times when he ran into some problems we had to take care of."

Maggie was processing his answer. "...you never told me?"

Damon hugged Maggie and whispered, "Let it go, Maggie. You are here now, and he wanted your blessing to continue."

"What about Lucy, does she know?" Maggie asked.

Randolph answered the best he could. "She does. She was a tremendous help to me with the planning while she was working on her project.

We met with the architects and went over all the plans."

"And what about Elizabeth?" Maggie looked dumbfounded.

Randolph smiled and replied. "She knows nothing. But I'm going to fly the family down for a few days when we open it. We still have a lot to do before we bring the children here. And my dear Maggie, I need your help now."

Maggie voice was low, and she looked suspicious, "Okay. But with what? You look like you have everything under control."

He put his arm around Juliann and said, "That's where Juliann comes into the picture. She has been my right hand for the past year helping me with a lot of the details like what it will take to make the children healthy and happy. We have almost everything in place, except hiring the director and staff. I know you have a 'Midas' touch when it comes to people—so will you help us staff the place?"

"Of course. But why look for a director when you have the best suited one standing right here amongst us! Juliann is the best of the best, I would say. Not only does she fit the physiological needs, but she is best suited for the psychological needs of the children!"

Juliann stepped in front of Maggie and hugged her. "What a lovely compliment. And I appreciate the vote of confidence. But, I'm almost done here. I still have this need to work in many countries to help others. I told Randolph from the very beginning that when the day comes that I feel a need to settle down, this would be the place. But for now, I have this burning need to travel on."

Maggie looked sad, and she detected a slight sadness in Randolph's eyes. "Well, I'm sorry to hear that. But I respect you for your choice. All I can do now is celebrate this wonderful Casa de Niños and look to make it a happy home for many children. Places like these are near and dear to my heart."

Randolph gave Maggie and Damon a tour of the orphanage and watched as occasional tears came to Maggie's eyes. It was heartwarming to watch her touch a picture on the wall or stop many times to look at something that brought back both good and ugly memories. Juliann had done a great job at garnishing the different rooms with comfortable and uplifting things that children need to be surrounded with, especially when they don't have family.

There were four beds in every room and each reflected on the gender of the recipients. The boys' rooms were filled with cowboys, spaceships, and cartoon heroes. For the girls, princesses, puppies, and favorite Disney characters were painted on the walls, with bedding to match. Each building housed different age groups and satisfied the needs of those children. There was a library, a school, patios, playgrounds, and nothing was spared when it came to making this place a home. Warm colors and pictures were strategically placed and helped to make everything look cheery and playful. Most importantly, there was nothing that reminded Maggie of Bishop Street and its drab and sterile environment.

After the day at the orphanage, they went to the ranch for dinner. The sun was starting to set when Juliann came over to Maggie and asked,

"Would you like to take a walk to the small church? When the sun is setting, it makes it seem so ethereal. I love that church."

Maggie took her hand and said, "That's a great idea." There was silence for a few minutes then Maggie said softly, "You know, there was a time that I hated God and found it hard, in my heart, to forgive him for my childhood of pain. Then I realized it really wasn't God I hated, it was my mother. Elizabeth taught me that after all those years of holding on to a hatred that really never existed."

Juliann stopped and turned to Maggie. "I truly get that Maggie. I understand that hate and how it eats you up inside. I came from tremendous wealth and my parents were never around. I hated them; I hated God; I hated the power of money and how it took over my parents' lives. Most of all, I hated how it destroyed me, as a child. I didn't know my mother, because I was raised with a staff of nannies. Whenever I saw her, it was only for a few minutes every few days. Then when I was old enough for school, I was shipped away to the best Europe had to offer. So, you see, everyone has a story in life and some of us are even homeless— within our homes. I would have been better off in a place like this. So, some stories are different than others, but they sometimes wind up in that same small place. Mine was a silent illusion for two people whose value consisted of wealth."

"I see that we both carry the pain of a past. It took me a long time to learn to trust again," Maggie whispered.

"At thirty-five, I'm still that wandering nomad looking for 'a reason' to stop. I have this restless part of me that is afraid to stop for fear that I will never be able to trust anyone. My independence is the only thing I have a tight grasp of. I was taught that at an early age."

Maggie smiled, she knew exactly what Juliann was feeling. They started to walk again, still holding hands. "Someday I would love to hear your whole story."

Juliann smiled. "Damon had said earlier that he recognized me. I was not surprised. I was once kidnapped and held for ransom when I was very young. Someday you will hear my story. Not today...today is for celebrating the orphanage."

They got to the little church and walked inside. The church was breathtaking, and there was this feeling that Maggie could or would never be able to explain. It was like coming home, a place where you felt this comfort and a feeling of closeness from deep within. Maggie and Juliann gestured crosses over their hearts with their hand and respectively they walked to a different pew and took a seat. For the next few minutes, they sat as the glorious sunset shined through the windows. Each looking for their own peace.

The plane landed and Maggie, Damon, and Randolph walked down the steps to the tarmac. It had been a great weekend at the hacienda and one of the best Maggie could remember. She started a new close friendship with Juliann, and saying goodbye brought sadness. Juliann was committed to staying on to finish up everything that needed to be done before the orphanage opened. Maggie and Juliann spent the rest of the weekend interviewing many eligible candidates to staff Casa de Niños. They were very specific as to the qualifications of the staff, and their emotional attachments to children. They were not going to let someone like the sinister Sister Theresa come anywhere near their loving home. They wanted a devoted staff that worked well with children and made their lives bright with positive reinforcement.

They were still at loose ends as to the director. Maggie thought maybe they should hire someone from outside of the area. Juliann wasn't sure that would be the best idea, so she was going to stay on and continue to look. Then she announced to Maggie and Randolph that she was eventually going to go to Honduras to open another orphanage. Randolph looked disappointed, but understood that restless part of Juliann and was thankful she had contributed so much to his orphanage.

When Maggie got home, she called Elizabeth. "You would not believe the charming and loving place Rand built for the orphans in his area. I just wanted to cry. And he had a female friend there helping him."

Elizabeth sounded surprised. "Female? Like in a relationship? Or just a companion?" Elizabeth questioned.

"I'm still not sure, Elizabeth. I can't put my finger on it, but I think the both of them are on a collision course, but don't know it. They are both nomads with no solid roots. Except that it looks like his heart is really into this orphanage. Oh Elizabeth, wait until you see it. What are the chances you can come to Mexico and see it soon?"

Elizabeth sighed. "Things are not going too well. Our winter has been extremely cold and wet. They say global warming has a lot to do with it. The flooding is horrendous from the melting snow and we're hoping the rain stops. I'm trying to save what little I can to get Meg to California, but that won't be for a few months. She's angry right now, and I'm worried about her."

"Let Randolph and me help pay for her. You always turn us down," Maggie raised her voice.

Elizabeth sighed again. "For years, we keep telling you over and over that we are humbly proud farmers who don't want your help. You're helping enough with Randall. Even that sometimes hurts William. I don't want him to feel like a failure because he can't provide for his family. Please, Maggie...."

"I try so hard to understand, Elizabeth. But it's hard when Rand and I have enough money that we'll never be able to spend in our lifetime. Neither of us have children to leave it to, so I want to help with yours."

"Let's change the subject." There was a short pause. "Have you set a date? Do you and Damon plan on having children? Maybe you need the little pitter-patter of feet to keep you busy!" Elizabeth reversed the pressure of the conversation back onto Maggie.

"If I wanted the sound of little feet, I'd get another cat. I just don't think I can take the pain of losing another animal. When Sabby passed last year, it broke my heart!"

"I know, sweetheart. We are watching Blue getting old and we will have to think of putting him down one day. No use in letting an animal suffer, you did what you could for Sabby, as we will do for Blue." Sadness echoed in her voice.

"Well, think about taking a short plane trip to Mexico to see Casa de Niños. Maybe Lucy can come too. She's just so busy nowadays with her shelter."

"Love you, Maggie."

"Love you, too!"

Maggie hung up and felt the pain in her heart of not being able to help Elizabeth and her finances. She had to respect Elizabeth and her husband's wishes and appreciated the pride he honorably held on to. But on the other hand, she didn't want Meg to do anything impulsive and reckless.

Rene D. Schultz

Chapter 7

MAGGIE WAS BACK TO WORKING ON HER NEW BOOK, and she was intent on getting it finished. There would be no publicity launch, or reviews, or other people reading this. It was just about her private thoughts and the family within her own circle, where they had been and what they were doing now. It was another one of her cathartic books, like the one she wrote after the death of Patricia, her dear friend and mentor. Patricia was a literary agent who had hired Maggie part-time during her third semester in UCLA, before her writing career had even started. Patricia had believed in Maggie. She knew Maggie had a talent for words and eventually she became the motivational force that pushed Maggie to write her first book. Then, secretly, Patricia sent it to a publisher and it became a bestseller. At times she had pushed Maggie to her limits, but she also had taught her how to hope again—and that was the driving strength that had helped her to rebuild her broken spirit.

Patricia was the closest thing to a real mother Maggie had ever known. When Maggie found out Patricia had cancer, the news was devastating and almost more than she could handle. Her hatred for God back then was beginning to manifest, and hardened her heart once again. With the strength that got her through the orphanage and with loving hands and a broken heart, she nursed Patricia until her death. It was all Maggie could give back to this amazing woman who had taken a small bird with a broken wing and nursed her back to health. After Patricia died, Maggie's world ceased to exist and she went into a deep depression. It wasn't until her fourth book was finished that she emerged from that dark abyss and began to heal once more.

This was a very private part of Maggie that she didn't allow the press or tabloids to exploit. And over the years, Maggie seldom put herself out into the public limelight. She felt uncomfortable amongst her contemporaries and critics. Their deep-seeded jealousy and criticism made Maggie angry and she refused to feed into the tabloid's voracious thirst to destroy her reputation. Maggie didn't want to play *that* game. She had remained low profile, until the tabloids caught her one day with her investigator, Damon Depre. The rumors that circulated were mean and unwarranted, and she tried to ignore their attempts to pull her out of seclusion. It was finally Damon who put an end to the speculation. He started to date an actress to get rid of the rumors. He talked to Maggie over it and they decided that it was the perfect decoy to pull the heat off of her during the time she was reuniting with her family—until Randolph entered the picture. When the picture of Randolph and her appeared in every tabloid, there was no stopping any of that speculation—*the game was on*. For months the press had hounded and followed Maggie, leaving her with little privacy to speak of. Maggie finally hired a publicist to curb the watchful press and it took a while to finally get the media under control.

Maggie never wanted to go through that again; and she didn't want Lucy or Elizabeth to deal with any of that ever again, either. So, when Maggie and Damon finally became engaged, the publicist made a quick and simple statement to the press with a few of the details and eventually the bubble burst and things went back to normal.

Denise opened the office door and popped her head in. "How's it going? I haven't heard a word from you today, I'm getting a little worried," she asked. Maggie was concentrating on something on the computer and didn't hear her. Denise cleared her throat loudly and said, "Are...you...okay...?"

Maggie looked up and smiled. "Oh, I'm sorry! I was reading something. Do I have a call?"

Denise laughed. "No! I said, I thought you were preoccupied all day and I was getting nervous."

Maggie nodded her head. "I have been, sorry! I was on the phone with Juliann and I think we found a director for Casa de Niños. This has taken us longer than we thought. It should have been done weeks ago. I can feel Juliann getting antsy and ready to leave."

Denise grimaced. "That's too bad. I bet Randolph would love to keep her there. She's a very remarkable and intense woman. She reminds me of Randolph."

Maggie frowned also, "I wish she would stay, too. But I get her need to move on. Maybe one day she will come back. I know we will always keep in contact. I adore her!"

"Have you talked to Lucy today? I thought I would give her a call and invite her over for dinner with Mary Jane. I just got off the phone with Briana and she is done with her homework so I thought it would be a great little surprise!"

Maggie glanced back at the computer again and lost her concentration.

Denise's voice hit a high pitch. "Hello…. Earth to Maggie! Are you there?"

Maggie looked up and smiled again. "Gosh, Denise, I'm so sorry. I just got off the phone a while ago with Elizabeth and she said they're having major flooding and she's worried. I've been watching the weather reports online and it looks absolutely dreadful! I'm getting a little nervous, myself. A few years ago she nearly lost the farm when the dams burst and the water crested over forty feet. They built a floodwall a few years ago, but they're afraid it might come down. I can always tell when she is scared or upset. It was something I learned in the orphanage years ago."

Denise walked into the office and looked visibly upset. "I remember that flood a few years back. Elizabeth and her town were filling sandbags day and night to save what they could."

Maggie stood up and stretched her arms above her head. "I'm trying to track the rain and the storms. I think they might be okay. I'm just worried."

Denise asked again, "What's Lucy up to tonight?"

Maggie smiled. "She's going bowling with Bradley, so I'm watching Mary Jane."

Denise's eyes opened wide in surprise. "Wow! She's been seeing him a lot lately. Do you think this might be *serious*?" Denise began to jump up and down, clapping her hands.

Maggie stomped her foot. "Stop that! Don't ever let her see you do that. She's taking it very slowly, and thank God Bradley is a very patient man!"

Denise stopped her dancing around, and looked more serious. "I just want to see her happy. I'd like her to experience a decent relationship for once in her life."

Maggie laughed. "YOU said the same thing about me a year or so ago!"

Denise turned around and walked toward the door and then turned again toward Maggie and stuck out her tongue. "Yes, I did! And look who you got—the pirate!"

Maggie could hear Denise laughing. She shook her head and yelled into the other room. "Go home to your family! I'm done for the day. I want to go home and watch The Weather Channel."

Maggie took a leisurely walk home. She only lived a few blocks from the office in Beverly Hills and always enjoyed window shopping in the stores along the famous boulevard she lived on. She wasn't in a hurry, because Damon was out of town. He was going to be gone for at least the next week on a very big kidnapping case he was working on. So, on her way home, she stopped off in a trendy café and picked up Chinese orange chicken—to go.

When she got to the elevator in her high-rise building, Jamal was standing at the elevator to push the button for her. "Thank you, Jamal."

He smiled and tipped his cap at her. "Evening, Miss Gray. It's a beautiful evening out, isn't it?"

Maggie nodded. "It sure is."

The elevator opened, she walked in, and waited for the doors to close. Then a frown crossed her face. She really missed Herbie and his friendly smile. It was always a comforting thing to come home and have him there to help her with her packages and pour on his charm. Maggie hoped he was enjoying his retirement and his children, grandchildren, and great-grandchildren. After all those years as a doorman, he deserved the time off to finally enjoy his life—or at ninety— what was left of it. This new young man seemed to be very nice, and was always pleasant, but it just wasn't the same. Maggie was a creature of habit. When the chain was broken, it took her a while to rebuild it.

Her penthouse condominium was the only residence on the top floor. When she opened the door, she stepped into the large marble foyer. She glanced down the hall and noticed the sun was just setting through the wall of windows. Soon it would be dark and the stars would appear. She loved this time of day. She put her purse on the entry table and walked into the kitchen and placed the bag of Chinese food on the counter. Then she turned, and walked down the hall to her bedroom. She turned on the hot water for a bath, selected her favorite scent, and trickled drops of oil across the glistening surface and lit a few candles. She slipped out of her clothes, put her cellphone on the counter, and slid into the warmth. With the lights off, and candlelight flickering across the walls, she let the stress of the day ease from her body.

A few minutes later, her cell rang. She slid her oily hand out of the water and tried to pick up the phone. On her second try, she hit the answer button. "*Buenas noches, Señor*," she whispered into the phone.

Damon laughed and replied back with, "*¿Cómo están hoy?*"

Maggie gasped, "Did you just call me a hoe?" She started to giggle and nearly dropped the phone; it was oily and slippery.

Damon whispered, "No...hoy means 'today,' you silly lady! You really do need to brush up on your Spanish! You sound in a good mood. Wish I was there."

"Wish you were, too. How is the case going?"

All of a sudden, there was a loud noise that sounded like an airplane taking off. Maggie could not hear what he was saying. When the plane passed, he continued. "I'm sitting in the damn airport. I was in San Miguel, but a new lead has me busting my ass to Buenos Aires. I used to love all this traveling crap with this job, but I'm beginning to get tired. Oh crap, it's the last call for boarding. Miss ya, babe."

Maggie loved listening to his rough voice. She smiled. "Well, be safe. Miss you, too." And he was gone.

Maggie smiled at her phone, placed it back on the counter, and sat back and thought about her past year with Damon. There had been so many adjustments involved with having another person sharing your life and home. They had their little disagreements, but with his job, they both seemed to get enough space to feel comfortable with the transition of the relationship. Maggie loved turning over in bed and feeling the security of him next to her. She had never had that before, nor did she ever have to answer to anyone since she left the orphanage. Most of all, she had never really known what it was like to be loved, or to love someone with an intensity that could break your heart, at any given moment.

Maggie felt the water getting cold so she slipped out of the tub and wrapped herself in a robe. It was the robe that Becca had given her, with the word 'princess' embroidered across the front. Becca was a dear friend of many years. She was an investigative reporter that Maggie had met early on in her career. They were best friends, but rarely got to see each other because of Becca's globetrotting job that she loved so much. But they always managed to stay in touch, and putting on the robe reminded Maggie to give Becca a call to see how her trip to Israel was going.

Maggie entered her bedroom and leisurely turned toward her four-poster bed that was tucked in the corner and stacked high with an assortment of decorative pillows. The group of surrounding windows showcased the evening sky starting to fill with stars. In her bare feet, she glided across the cold tile floor and down the hall to the kitchen. Her stomach was starting to growl and hunger was setting in. She spooned the different dishes of Chinese food on a plate and popped it into the microwave. When it was done, she grabbed a pair of chopsticks they had given her in the bag, and walked into the family room to watch The Weather Channel. She was still concerned with the rising water in the Red River in North Dakota. She had watched in horror a few years ago what devastation the flooding could do. Lucky for North Bend, it had made it through with minimal amount of damage. With any luck, everything would be the same this time, providing the storm passed over quickly or lost all of its punch.

Maggie watched the news commentator as he explained the growing problem with the pending storm coming within the week. The storm system was currently wreaking havoc in Canada.

Maggie picked up her phone and called Elizabeth's house phone. She became a little concerned on the fourth ring.

"Hello," Meg finally answered.

"Hi, sweetheart, this is Auntie Maggie."

"Hi...." Meg's voice was low and she sounded miserable.

"Are you okay? Where's Mom?" Maggie asked, concerned.

Meg sighed. "They're in the barn securing the animals. The flood waters are rising and they're sandbagging the walls around the barn."

"Why aren't you helping?" Maggie dropped into a deep voice.

"Because I'm still mad at them!"

Maggie inhaled a deep breath. "Don't do that, Meg. Don't get mean-spirited. Please…things will work out, I promise. If you cop an attitude, it's only going to make this harder on everyone and then defeat your purpose—and I won't be able to talk to your mom about it. Just hang in there! And for cripes sake, go help your parents. They need it right now." Maggie said sternly.

In a low whisper, Meg relented. "Okay."

"Have your mom call me and if things get bad, let me know. I know she won't ask for help. So, I'm leaving it up to you—as the oldest child. Okay?"

"I promise…Auntie Maggie."

"Good girl." Maggie praised.

Maggie hung up the phone and sat for a few minutes thinking about how she was going to get Meg out of North Dakota and into the Art Institute of Los Angeles. She was going to have to be careful in how she handled it, but she was going to have to do something soon or there was no telling what kind of action Meg would take on her own.

CHAPTER 8

FIVE DAYS LATER, MAGGIE WAS IN THE OFFICE working when the call from Randolph came in. "Hey, Maggie, what's up?"

"I'm waiting to hear from Elizabeth or William. I've been watching the weather in North Bend and I'm very nervous." Maggie had an apprehensive sound in her voice.

"I'm sure they are okay or they would have called." He tried to reassure her.

Her anger was surfacing. "They never called for help when the big flood hit North Bend, in 2009. That damage almost destroyed everything that they had; and yet, all we could do was watch the television coverage and pray for the best. Then without saying anything, they rebuilt and reinforced their basement because of all the water devastation. But you and I never heard a peep from them until it was over."

Randolph's voice remained calm. "Maggie, get over that! They are private, strong farmers who accept their place in life and everything that goes with it. Just like all their friends, townspeople, and neighbors."

Maggie couldn't understand when they risked their lives and the lives of their children to prove a point. Then Maggie thought, *'were they really trying to prove a point or did they accept the risks that went with their lifestyle? She knew the answer. More than half of the country consisted of hardworking people who didn't have a choice. They left everything in God's hands.'*

Randolph knew more than he was telling her, Maggie could hear it in his calm voice. "Maggie, the storm coming in from Canada won't be there for another few days. I talked to William and he seems to think they are going to be okay. I'm coming home from Mexico tomorrow morning, so if they need me, I'm here."

Maggie sighed in relief. "Okay, I was worried you'd be away and I wouldn't be able to get ahold of you in case of an emergency! I feel better now, knowing you'll be home."

"Maggie, Maggie, Maggie…my little worrywart. I've got it under control. I have an employee glued to the weather, and I've been in contact with Damon. Please calm down and relax a little. I would never let anything happen to Elizabeth and her family!"

Maggie exhaled, and sat back in her chair. "I know you wouldn't. It's just the last time I felt so helpless. And I had wished I was there to help."

"Everything else okay? Just in case you hadn't heard already, Juliann left this morning for Honduras. I'm going to miss her." He paused. "But I like the new director she hired. Great lady with a great insight for children. We are going to start filling those beds; and I can't wait to see the place active with happy faces." He changed the subject to keep Maggie from obsessing.

Maggie could hear sadness in his voice when he mentioned Juliann. "I talked to her a few days ago, and I knew she was leaving soon. I just didn't think it would be this soon! I'm going to give her a call later. Randolph, I think I'll come down to Mexico with you in a few weeks and hang out with the new director. Besides, I want to see some of those precious faces, and get to know some of the counselors."

"That would be helpful to me. You can give me your opinion of her and see if there are any other changes we need. Now stop worrying, I'll stay in touch. And damn it—don't let the news stations scare you about the storms." He hung up.

Maggie felt better knowing that Randolph was coming home. With Damon gone, and Randolph in Mexico, she felt scared in case she got a call from North Bend. Maggie laid her head back against the chair and closed her eyes as she recollected the disastrous flooding a few years back. Elizabeth had called her, horrified with the forecast of potential flooding. The Red River started to overflow along the north end of the river, right near her town of North Bend. It had started with saturated ground and it was exacerbated by a record-breaking snowmelt. Then with additional storms that had passed, dropping so much rain, the already saturated ground had nowhere for the water to go on the virtually flat terrain. Maggie remembered how all those small communities along the Red River prepared for more than a week as the U.S. weather service continuously updated the predictions for the area with an increasingly higher projected river crest. Maggie called Elizabeth every day. Elizabeth was terrified she was going to lose the farm and there was nothing she could do except get the animals to higher ground and start stacking sandbags around the house. Maggie wanted to fly out to help, but Elizabeth adamantly rejected the offer.

The Weather Channel had originally anticipated the crest to reach a level of near forty-three feet, and the only thing that saved the farm was the river had only crested at forty feet. The water started to decline, but then it continued to rise further downstream, just north of Elizabeth's place. But this didn't mean Elizabeth was completely safe quite yet. There was another storm coming in and Maggie wanted to go to North Dakota to be with them. This time, Randolph wouldn't let her go. The town was threatened but it wasn't as bad as the towns further downstream.

William kept on a constant call basis with Randolph. When the governor declared it a statewide disaster, he informed Randolph that the townspeople all pulled together to help each other and they spent days filling thousands and thousands of sandbags. There were volunteers from other communities that had also pitched in to help; and downstream, emergency dikes were being built by the National Guard.

When the river crested at fifty-two feet, the town had already prepared enough that although there was tremendous flooding and a few houses and businesses in town were lost, the townspeople had saved their town from a complete major disaster. Further down the river, two major towns were almost completely destroyed due to the enormous amount of water that broke the dikes. Maggie's mind flashed to all the pictures she recalled seeing on the news as she sat there with tears in her eyes. It was happening again. Only this time, the predictions were worse and closer upstream to Elizabeth's home in North Bend.

Maggie took a deep breath and exhaled, then she pushed the intercom. "Denise, is there any fresh coffee made?" Maggie asked in a low whisper.

Denise heard the anxiety in Maggie's voice. "No, but I can make some. You having a tough day? Did you talk to Elizabeth?"

"No. I think she is with everyone filling sandbags. I know William and James took the animals to higher ground at a friend's farm, a hundred miles away, so that they are out of harm's way. The last time, they lost a horse and all their chickens," she recalled from Elizabeth's conversation yesterday.

In a calming voice, Denise said, "Look, Damon's out of town, why don't you come spend the night at my house with the babies. I don't want you to be home alone worrying all night!"

"No, I'm fine. Randolph is coming home in the morning and he reassured me everything was going to be okay."

Denise asked again, "Can I talk you into at least dinner at my house? Rosa made your favorite—enchiladas and her special refried beans...yummm!"

"No thanks, but bring me leftovers tomorrow or I will hunt you down!" Maggie chuckled.

"Go home, Maggie, and rent a good movie to watch. You can't just sit here obsessing. I know how you are, and you'll drive yourself nuts!"

Two days later Maggie was making herself an omelet when her phone rang. "Hello," she said, pushing the button on her phone without looking at who it was from.

"Hi, babe, how are you doing?" Damon said casually.

Maggie smiled at his voice. "I'm making myself some eggs and toast. How's it going with you?"

"It's going." Damon paused and coolly said, "I just flew in to Mexico and I'm catching a ride home with Randolph."

Maggie looked confused, picked up the plate with the eggs and slowly started to walk out of the kitchen and into the family room. "Randolph said he was coming home yesterday."

Damon exhaled and said, "He's very nervous about the flooding in North Bend. William called him yesterday and he is very worried with the impending storm just a day away. So, Randolph and I decided to pick up some of his ranch hands and head over to North Bend to help."

Maggie dropped the ceramic dish and it broke into pieces when it hit the floor. "I'm packing a bag and catching a flight out!"

Damon's voice boomed into the phone. "To hell you are! You're not getting on a fucking plane in that crappy weather and putting yourself in danger! Rand, William, and I will take care of this. I don't want to have to worry about you, too!"

"That's too damn bad!" she yelled into the phone.

"Hold on a second." Maggie could hear some commotion going on.

Randolph's voice sounded angry. "You are not flying out. I swear I will wring your fucking neck!"

Maggie hissed, "Wring whatever you fucking like. I'm going to go help Elizabeth and make sure she's got someone with her and the kids!"

There were more angry voices in a screaming match. Damon spoke into the phone. "Be ready and at the airport in two hours. We are leaving with a whole crew of men right now. Randolph has a fleet of big semi-trucks and more help headed to North Bend. We're going to try to save the ranch and the downtown area and his neighbors."

Maggie was crying. "I will be there and ready to go when you land."

Damon's voice barely whispered. "If I had my way, you wouldn't be coming. I don't want to risk your life. This two hour delay is going to put us right in the middle of the torrential rains they are getting. Do you think you can handle that?"

"I'm a pretty tough cookie! See you there."

Maggie called her best friend Becca and told her what she was doing. "I have to go."

Becca screamed into the phone. "Let the guys handle it. You don't know what you're getting into, Maggie. I've been reporting on disasters for years and they can handle it. I've been in the middle of a hurricane and we lost a crew member. Please, Maggie...."

Maggie closed her eyes. "Wish me Godspeed." Maggie hung up.

"Maggie...Maggie...Maggie...." Becca's phone was dead.

Maggie dialed one more number as she was finishing her packing. "Hey, Lucy—"

Lucy sounded frantic, and interrupted Maggie. "Elizabeth and the kids are in danger. The storm is stalling and dumping more rain then the area can possibly handle. I'm so frightened!"

Maggie made sure to calm down her voice. She knew that when Lucy got into a frenzy, almost anything could happen. It had happened a few times in the past years and they had to call a doctor to the house to sedate her.

Quietly, Maggie asked, "Lucy, did you take your meds?"

"Yes. I'm just terrified...for...."

"I want you to calm down and take a big breath." Maggie listened to Lucy inhale and then exhale slowly. "Randolph and Damon are on their way here from Mexico to pick me up. They have a lot of Randolph's ranch hands and friends coming also. As soon as they arrive, we are going to take off and head to North Dakota to help North Bend. So, I need you to hold down the fort here. Okay?"

Lucy sounded a little calmer. "Okay, Maggie, but be cautious. I see the pictures of the storm out that way and it is a killer. They said a few tornados were spotted. Please be careful!"

Maggie sighed and said, "I promise. I just want to make sure James, Meg, Katie, and Sarah are out of harm's way."

"Keep in touch!"

"I will be home soon. Love you, Lucy!"

Maggie was packed and called a limousine service to take her immediately to the airport. She had packed an additional suitcase for Damon so he had dry clothes to change into and she packed his warmer attire because of the weather they were heading into. She packed herself lots of warm clothes and figured she'd be able to share with Meg and the girls. Maggie turned on the television in the limousine while they were sitting on the tarmac waiting for the plane. The news reports were tagging the storm as the worst the area had seen in over twenty-five years. Maggie was shaking all over and her adrenaline was nearly coming out of her veins. Her heart was pumping and she was terrified they would not get there in time. She was worried about Reba and Wendell and hoped that because their farm was out of town and on higher ground that they would be okay. Her real hope was that maybe they could make that like a 'home base' for everyone. Only time would tell.

Maggie heard the roar of the jet engines as the plane taxied up the runway and her eyes lit up in awe. Randolph was not in his Lear jet. He was in a much bigger plane that looked more sleek and powerful. When it finally came to a stop, the steps were rolled up to the door. Within a minute, the door opened and Damon and Randolph hurried down.

Maggie got out of the limousine and started to walk toward Damon, instead she took off in a run with tears streaming down her cheeks. He brought her into his arms and held her tight. Then he whispered into her ear, "Hey, babe. You know I don't really want you to go, but if this is what you want, come onboard."

Maggie looked up and touched his cheek. "I want to go with you. They did this on their own a few years ago and I don't want Elizabeth to be alone again."

Randolph laughed. "She is not going to be alone. I have fifteen of my men from the ranch and enough supplies to take care of us for weeks. I have semi-trucks filled with all kinds of supplies for the town, including lots of building materials. That town is not going to be alone!"

Maggie smiled for the first time in days. "Thank you, Rand."

Randolph waved his hand and said, "Okay...let's go. The storm and heavy rain is expected to follow us in. Time is our nemesis right now."

Damon grabbed the luggage that the chauffeur had placed next to them. Maggie grabbed onto Randolph's hand and they walked up the stairs. Once they were in the plane, the stairs were taken away and the roar of the engine filled their ears. The men who came along to help were seated towards the back and most of them were sitting back in their seats and sleeping. Maggie recognized a few, and when they noticed her, they smiled.

Maggie and Damon took a seat next to each other and Randolph across from them. The plane started to move forward and the pilot announced he was just waiting for the tower to give him runway clearance. Within a few minutes the plane moved forward again. It taxied down to the runway, stopped for just a moment, and then it powered up to full throttle and took off. The power of the larger jet was more than Maggie had ever felt before. She tightly gripped Damon's hand until they lifted into the air. Once they were up in the air and they began to level off, Maggie relaxed enough to ask, "This isn't your Lear jet, how come? Where did you get this?"

Randolph grinned. "No, it's not! I pulled in a marker from someone who owed me a favor. My plane was just too small to hold this many people, a few supplies, and luggage. I wanted to keep it at a certain weight going into the storm. We needed something solid and stronger, or we wouldn't have had a chance. But, that doesn't mean we are out of trouble. Depending on the torrents of rain and wind shear factor, this could be a really tough ride. And...if I feel this is putting us in any kind of danger, we will turn around and fly into the nearest and safest airport. Okay?"

Maggie nodded her head. "Does Elizabeth and William know we're coming?"

Randolph's phone hummed and he picked it up. At the same time, he nodded his head.

The flight attendant came around and served drinks, sandwiches, and snacks to all the passengers. When she was done, the lights were turned down and everyone relaxed before they jumped into the chaos.

Maggie leaned back and closed her eyes. Over an hour into the flight, the attendant came out and walked up to Randolph.

"The captain said that everyone needs to belt up and stay put. That also includes me, so if there is anything you want, I can get it now."

Randolph asked Maggie and Damon and they shook their heads. "We're fine, Sue."

"Just to let you know, we are chasing that storm coming from Canada. He especially wanted everyone to know we are going to hit heavy turbulence. I'll let everyone know and I'm going to put everything away and make it safe in here," she said.

"Thanks, Sue, tell him I appreciate the heads-up! Tell him I put my headphones on and to keep me posted."

Fifteen minutes later, the plane started to violently shake. The pilot tried to adjust to the turbulence by dropping down and lifting up with the air pockets. But the shaking was worse than Maggie had ever experienced, and she was terrified. Damon removed the armrest between them and had her lay across his lap and he held her tight. Maggie thought it felt like the plane was ready to explode into pieces—the turbulence was so powerful. The pilot and Randolph talked a few times and he reassured the passengers that the pilot had everything under control and that he would not hesitate to land the plane if their safety was at risk.

Damon and Randolph began to talk about alternative plans. Randolph took out his logbook and some scribbled notes and began to read them.

"If we can't make it into Grand Forks airport, then we have the Grand Forks Air Force Base ten miles away. My pilot has already asked for clearance if we need it," Randolph said as he wrote down more notes.

Damon nodded. "There's also a smaller airport just southwest, and of course, there's Fargo. The problem with Fargo is that it's a hundred miles from North Bend. I'd really think the less driving we do, the better we are with getting to William's. But it's still an option."

At that moment, the plane lurched and Maggie squealed, "Oh my God!"

Damon looked down at her ashen face and said, "We're okay. I've been in a lot worse. This Gulfstream G650 is only two years old and the best there is. We're going to bump around a little, but the pilots know what they are doing. Please calm down, Maggie. I don't want you to scare the other passengers."

Tears were running down her cheeks, "Sorry...."

Randolph got up and slowly started to walk toward the passengers. Once he got to them he held on to a seat to steady himself. In Spanish he explained to the men, "There's nothing to fear. The plane is the best and the pilot too!"

The ranch crew gave him a thumbs up. Then he slowly walked toward the cockpit. He disappeared into the cockpit for the next half hour. The plane continued to pitch and at one point the wings began to sway back and forth a little. Maggie squeezed Damon's hand but refrained from any more noises that might scare the rest of the passengers.

Randolph came back and sat down. "We are trying to get into Grand Forks International Airport. As it looks right now, we beat the storm by a few hours. So we will try to slip into the airport and head out to North Bend. The trucks are there already and some have made it into town and to William's place. So now they have generators and pumps!"

Maggie sat up and happy tears started to flow. "Oh, thank God!"

"Once those trucks are emptied, William and some friends will be loading their valuable equipment into the trucks to protect them from the flooding, including his machinery from the farm. He can't afford to lose that. He also sent some of those trucks into town to Main Street to help the businesses."

Randolph exhaled. "When we get there, we need to really work at strategically getting those sandbags into place to force the water into controlled creeks aimed at the river. Then we need to distribute all the generators I had shipped in to pump the water into those creeks and keep the flooding damage to a minimal, if we can. The town has been through this before so they are all very aware of the other potential hazards of the contaminated water. I'll let my men know."

Damon agreed. "Great idea. With the ranch hands and the trucks, we might have a chance to save most of the town."

"Where are the kids? Did William say?" Maggie wanted to know.

"Reba and Wendel's farm is outside of town, on a ridge. They left the two young ones there with Reba. Wendel, James, and Meg are at the ranch with Elizabeth and William. We are setting up the Library as the evacuation center for the families and children that stayed behind in North Bend. It's the safest building in town right now because the structure was only built a few years ago. Everything else, including the school, is not safe enough. One of my trucks and the Red Cross is already setting everything up," Randolph replied.

Damon stepped forward and showed them some pictures he had on an iPad. "We are going to do a makeshift levee made from sandbags to hold the water out of the residential areas like they did in the Fargo flood in 2011. They corralled the water in certain areas." He held up his iPad. "They literally saved that whole community. Randolph has some men there now doing that. They brought in almost a half million sandbags at the Air Force base. We're going to do that with the small center of town also. Then we will work to save as many farms as we can. We are going to make this happen, hopefully!"

Half an hour before they got to the airport, the turbulence started to calm down and just the torrential rain was pelting the plane. An occasional flash of lightening lit up the darkened sky as everyone sat in silence. Randolph and Damon stood up and went over to the passengers. They explained a minute-to-minute schedule they had planned and were very much in control of the procedures they were going to implement. When they looked out the window, what they saw was devastation that the area had already suffered. There was water everywhere, but the sandbagging had left most of the structures alone to survive. The large areas of overflowing water resembled lakes. Randolph was told that the governor had called a state of emergency and the National Guard and Air Force were called in to evacuate the elderly and the hospital. Residents were evacuated to Grand Forks Air Force Base where the Red Cross was set up. The smaller town of North Bend had secured the new library for its residents; and Randolph had made sure they had plenty of supplies, beds, and help to keep them safe.

Randolph personally shook every hand of the helpers and said, "We may not be able to save everything, but we are going to keep the damage as minimal as possible!" High fives went around the plane and Maggie could only sit there with a gnawing numbness as she watched. She was so thankful and beyond words as to all the hard work that Damon and Randolph had put into their plans to save North Bend. Not to mention the enormous amount of money that was spent to bring in the trucks, supplies, and help. Randolph brushed it off and said, "One life and one farm is worth far more than every dime I have. If I could do this with every disaster, I would. This one just happened to be close to my heart, and close to home, and I watched it coming. Not often does that happen with tornados, earthquakes, and other disasters!"

The plane's landing gear started to come down and the full-throttle of the engine started to roar. Randolph raised his voice across the entire group of passengers inside the plane. "We are going to land in a few minutes. We are not landing in Grand Forks International. We thought it was too risky with the planes that are going in and out and with the wind shear and deep water on the runways right now. We are headed into the Air Force base and we will be welcomed with a lot of help! I want all of you to take care and be safe at everything you do. I don't want any casualties! Buckle up, this is going to be a very tough landing because of the amount of water on the runway!"

With his last words, the plane's landing gear hit the runway and the force of the speed along with the pelting rain—it began to slide. Everyone held on as the plane started to swing to the right and skid as it hit large pockets of water. Damon laid Maggie on the seat and laid on top of her, as the plane groaned and started to spin around— Maggie prayed.

CHAPTER 9

ONCE THE PLANE FINALLY CAME TO A STOP, THERE was nothing but a deafening silence. Everyone came to life and started moving quickly. The pilot came out and talked to Randolph, they shook hands, and the pilot returned to the cockpit. Randolph turned and barked out orders and let everyone know what was going to happen and where they were going. Trucks and vehicles were waiting for them on the tarmac. They loaded the trucks with all of the luggage and the supplies from the plane, and then, immediately, the caravan began driving the thirty miles towards North Bend.

Damon, Maggie, and some of the crew jumped into the back of an open canvas-covered truck with benches on each side for the occupants. They looked like military trucks that Maggie would occasionally see on the freeway back home. The rumble of the wheels and the noise of the rain was thunderous as they traveled along the highway toward their destination. Maggie sat quietly with a gut feeling that the worst was yet to come. When they finally pulled up to Main Street in the middle of town, the trucks stopped. Randolph came around to the back of the truck and started to talk to Damon.

Damon inquired, "How did it look on the highway coming out? Was there a lot of flooding?"

Randolph placed his boot on the bumper, and leaned in toward Damon. "It wasn't too bad, some areas looked worse than others. Large pockets of water were forming their own lagoons. The weather report said we just made it in by an hour before they expect the worst to come. Come on down, and take a look at the town with me. It looks like they worked very hard to get the sandbag walls securely surrounding the downtown area. I think we should look around with the crew and make sure everything is sturdy enough to save these stores in case of more flash flooding. Let's set up some pumps to keep it dry enough inside the perimeters of the bags, so the stores don't flood completely with the final storm. Then let's head toward the farmland to protect those homes, and help protect those farmers' expensive machinery." Randolph sounded and acted like a man who knew what being in control of the helm meant. He had been the driving force of his company for years, and now, for the first time, Maggie began to realize just what a powerful and commanding person he could be. Not only was he powerful, but he was brilliant and resourceful when it came to protecting what was his.

Damon clapped him on the back as he jumped down off the truck. "You, my friend, have done an amazing job. I'm totally impressed with how much, and how quick, you pulled all this together!"

Randolph looked down and when his head came up, Damon saw the tears. "These people are my family. They are the salt of the earth. They never ask for anything, but they'd give you the shirt off their backs if you needed it. How does a person put a price on something like that? I couldn't sit by and do nothing. And if it took every penny I've earned, I'd do it ten times over!"

Damon nodded, and looked at Maggie and winked. "Come on, let's take a look and then head over to the farms. The rain is starting to really come down. The last I heard about the weather, it wasn't going to have the 'kick' they thought it would have. Let's keep our fingers crossed!"

Randolph sighed. "I think our saving grace is the new dikes they constructed after the last big flood in Grand Forks and Fargo. Maybe they finally learned their lesson!"

They finished their inspections and got back in the trucks and headed toward Elizabeth's farm. Some of the flooding was so deep they had to find another way to get there. When they finally did pull up, the rain was causing rivers of water rushing down the roads. It was higher than expected, but the thick and steady walls of sandbags had kept the house and barn safe. William was working with a dozen men, filling and stacking sandbags. Randolph and Damon jumped out of the truck along with the crew and immediately gave the others some relief. The noise of the rain and wind made it almost impossible to speak or be heard. It didn't matter, they all began working hard with one thing on their minds—saving the farm.

Maggie ran up and pulled at William's arm. "Where's Elizabeth?"

"In the house securing the windows and packing anything of value in the big truck Randolph delivered." He turned back to continue what he was doing.

Damon grabbed Maggie's arm before she took off into the house. "Be careful, if you don't feel safe at any time—get into the large truck. You'd be safer there. And no risk taking, okay?" He bent down and kissed her on the lips and turned to help William.

Maggie was soaking wet by the time she reached the eight stairs leading up to the porch. The house was sitting on a raised foundation that kept it pretty safe. She opened the door and walked inside. "Elizabeth!"

"I'm in the kitchen, Maggie," she called out.

Maggie ran into the kitchen and into Elizabeth's arms. They both started to cry. Finally Elizabeth pulled away and said, "I'm so scared, Maggie."

Maggie wiped her tears off her face. "Don't be, everything is going to be okay. Randolph and Damon are out helping and they brought a whole crew from Randolph's ranch in Mexico. We're going to make sure you and your neighbors make it through. Can't promise you everything will be okay, but we can do the best we can. Where are the kids?"

"Meg is around trying to gather up all the chickens. James is outside in the barn loading all the equipment into the large truck. Katie and

Sarah are with Reba at the library. They were going to stay at her place, but she's just too old, if something were to happen, I could never forgive myself. They'll be safe there. Right now I'm making coffee and sandwiches for the men because it's so cold and they haven't eaten for a while."

Maggie took off her wet clothes and Elizabeth gave her a pair of sweatpants and a dry shirt from Meg's closet. She went into the kitchen and immediately started to help prepare the food. When a few platters were done, she put on some rain gear and took the food outside to the men. Parked in the driveway was a large truck that served as a makeshift commissary. One-by-one, the men jumped into the back of the truck and Maggie served sandwiches and hot coffee. Then she would go back in the house and refill the trays and do it again. Soon, crews from the other farms and around the area came to eat out of the rain and relax for a few minutes with hot coffee.

Half the road was blocked off and stacked with sandbags, leaving it barely open for trucks. The other half was raging water from the continuous rain and runoff from all the pumps. It became a manmade fast and treacherous moving stream that had no mercy on anyone or anything it came in contact with. Branches off of trees were traveling at a reckless speed in the current. It was directed, for miles down the road, toward a smaller creek area that eventually flowed into a tributary of the Red River.

Maggie was in the kitchen cutting up vegetables to make hot soup. The generators were permitting them to have dim light and enough electricity to get everything done. Damon and Randolph had set up a Military-size double burner using gas tanks on the outside porch. It was under the overhang so that pots of hot soup could be cooked and protected from the weather. The gas and electric in the area had been shut off to protect everyone from explosions and fires.

Maggie looked up and Meg was walking through the back door carrying two baby kittens. When she saw Maggie, she placed the animals in a box and rushed over to give her a hug. "Oh, Auntie Maggie, I'm so glad you're here. This has been awful! I was so afraid we were going to lose the farm." She began to cry. "I didn't find the mother cat and only the two babies. There are still two more I need to look for."

Maggie rubbed her back. "It's okay, I think the worst is over. We followed the storm and it should be gone in a few hours. At least no one has been injured and we're all safe! Calm down, sweetheart. Damon and Randolph are out front with your father! Don't stray far from home looking for those kitties, the mother cat probably has them safe."

Her sobs continued to crush Maggie's heart. "Thank you for coming to be here with us and help!"

Maggie lifted her chin and looked directly into her eyes. "I love you."

Elizabeth watched from the other side of the room with a heavy heart.

Meg pulled away. "I've got to find the other two kittens. Blue was out there with me looking for them. At least he still has a good 'sniffer' at his age."

Elizabeth yelled across the room. "Be careful out there. The rain is coming down hard and with a vengeance."

Meg sighed. "I will, Mom…"

Ten minutes later, Maggie was on the porch stirring the soup when she noticed a movement along the wall of sandbags. With her vision blurred from the heavy downpour, she watched, mesmerized by the dog.

Blue was slowly walking along the top of the wall with a kitten in his mouth. Meg started running toward him and climbed halfway up the wall, when it suddenly collapsed and Meg, Blue, and the kitten were pulled into the fast-moving current of water. Her hands were flailing in all directions, and Maggie ran down the stairs screaming and yelling, trying to get the men's attention. "Help! Help! Someone help Meg!" Maggie was running down to the group of men working.

Damon turned around and looked at the panic in Maggie's face. He grabbed her shoulders and asked, "What's wrong?"

Maggie was out of control and pointing and screaming. "Meg fell into the water! The sandbag wall collapsed while she was trying to save Blue! Oh my God…!"

Damon started running towards the men but yelled over his shoulder, "Stay here…don't you dare go near there! And don't let Elizabeth leave here either. It's too dangerous…we'll find her!"

James came around from the back of the house after hearing the loud shouting. He came around the corner yelling and screaming something no one could understand, nor did they pay attention. Then he ran around back to the barn again. Immediately, the men started running down the sides of the walls looking into the fast-moving water and trying to find any signs of Meg. James came from the back from the barn dragging his small fishing boat to the front of the house.

Randolph's face lit up. "Nice call, James! This is perfect!" Randolph said as he dragged it over to the wall. Randolph and his men took the small boat with a four-stroke outdoor motor and dropped it over the side of the wall and into the rushing current. Then, Randolph and José jumped in.

"I want to come, too!" James yelled.

William yelled back, "No! I'm not going to lose you too. Wait here with your mother."

James continued to run down the wall, screaming his sister's name. "Meg…. Meg! Blue, where are you, boy? Blue…bark for me!"

Damon got into a pickup truck and stopped for William and some of the men to hop into the bed of the truck. They stood up in the back, holding on to the top of the cab to maintain their balance as Damon drove slowly along the side of the wall. They looked over the wall to get a better view, hoping they could see her.

Maggie watched this, as if in slow motion, and was screaming, "Please, God…. Please, God…. Take me, don't take her! She has a whole life ahead of her…. Don't do this…don't you dare do this!"

Elizabeth came out of the house and saw Maggie crying hysterically and ran as quickly to her side as she could to see what was going on.

"What's wrong? Tell me, Maggie! What happened?"

Maggie grabbed hold of Elizabeth and screamed, a little out of control, "Elizabeth, dear God, Meg fell into the rushing water!"

The fear in Elizabeth's face was more than Maggie could handle, but she knew she had to try to stay strong and hold tight to her friend. "They are all down there looking for her...."

Elizabeth fell to the wet muddy ground and starting crying out in distress, "Not my Meg, God! Not my Meg...you already took Rebekah...not my Meg! I promise...don't do this again to us, God!"

Maggie sat down in the mud and placed Elizabeth's head in her lap as they both rocked and cried. Maggie knew the worst of the storm was over by the feel of the light drizzle. The noise had stopped, and the silence was like an impending doom. In the middle of the large front yard sat two women who had been through enough in life, and yet they were sitting silently waiting to see if death had knocked on Elizabeth's door again...taking another one of her children....

CHAPTER 10

For the next hour Maggie rocked back and forth, in the light drizzle, holding her dear friend. Eventually, some of the searchers came back with grim-looking faces. Maggie sat quietly, as her friend continued to pray to God, asking for forgiveness and begging for the life of her child. When the truck pulled up and William got out, Maggie could see by the look on his face that something was wrong. Her heart began to leap out of her chest, and her body began to shake. Her hatred of a God, who was supposed to be fair, was beginning to build. "Why Meg," she kept repeating. "Why our Meg?"

William bent down when he reached Maggie; he slid his strong arms under Elizabeth's legs and arms, and slowly began to carry her into the house. Mud, tears, and rain were dripping down Elizabeth's face, but the numbness had set in. She didn't move, or say a word, but stared straight ahead. Once they were inside, Maggie could hear the horrible screams and wails of her friend. Maggie sat in the mud listening, helpless and shattered. With nothing she could do, she started to whimper from the pain in her broken heart, as her childhood once again began to flash in front of her eyes.

Maggie never knew what it was like to have a child, let alone lose one—and yet the pain was so deep she could not move. She could not conceivably understand the deep-rooted pain that could tear out a person's insides when they faced this kind of suffering. Why were William and Elizabeth going through it again? Their first child had died four days after her birth, leaving them heartbroken, and yet, they had four more. It was so many years ago, and yet the pain was still like a fresh wound now being opened up again. How unfair could life be? Where was her God?

Damon slowly walked over and sat down in the mud next to Maggie. Gently, he put his arms around her and said, "We couldn't find her. We looked everywhere. The current was too wild and must have washed her downstream. We had everyone looking. Maybe she made it out...somehow."

Maggie looked up in a daze, and Damon's face was filled with deep anguish as tears slid down his cheeks. In a quiet voice, she said, "I don't know what to do or what to say. The storm has passed, and this all seems so surreal. What do you say to them? How do you let them grieve?"

Maggie and Damon sat holding each other as they listened to the screams still coming from the house.

He whispered, "I don't know the answers, Maggie. I've never been in this place, of losing a child." He hugged Maggie tighter. They sat there for a long time listening to their family break into pieces.

Off in the distance, Maggie could hear a slight humming sound, or was it just Damon's heartbeat? As it got closer, the humming began to sound more and more like a small engine. Then, all of a sudden, she heard Randolph yell, "Hey, someone help me! I need some help."

José screamed at the top of his lungs, "Help! Help! Help!"

Damon let go of Maggie, and suddenly everyone was running toward the sandbags. Damon climbed up and reached over. First, Blue was lifted out of the boat. His limp body was pulled up and over and laid down on the ground. Then Meg was hoisted over the wall to Damon, as the men hung tightly to the rope, giving Randolph and José a chance to get out also. Meg threw herself down on the ground and was holding onto Blue. When Maggie saw Meg, she didn't know what to do first. Did she run and tell her mother and father who had already started the grieving process or did she go hug her beloved Meg?

Maggie ran up the stairs and swung open the door. Then she started yelling, "They found her! Randolph found her alive! Come quickly!"

Immediately, William and Elizabeth came running out the door and down the steps towards their daughter. Meg was lying on the ground holding Blue tightly and crying. She began to rock and noticed nothing around her. Elizabeth tried to pull her up but she shook off her mother's hands. She didn't want to let go of Blue. "He saved my life...and died doing it! He saved me, by keeping me afloat. He found a large branch and jumped on top and it gave me a chance to grab it." Meg was crying hysterically while everyone listened to her story and watched.

Randolph wiped his tears, "We found the branch stuck on another one, and Meg was holding on to Blue and the branch. I don't know how it happened, but he saved her life."

James rushed over, and leaned over Blue. His tears were streaming down his cheeks as he slowly and lovingly petted his dear friend who he had chased through the sprinklers on warm summer days. His best buddy who would go fishing with him during summer vacations. He had loved Blue with all his heart and Blue had died a hero—saving his sister.

The group watched as James sat down next to his sister and laid his head on Blue and talked to him about their lifetime together. *"I'm going to miss you, Blue. Why didn't you stay in the house? Why did you have to go looking for the kittens? Why did you leave me, Blue? Who am I going to go hiking with? How am I going to find that sneaky skunk? Who am I going to chase through the sprinklers?"* He kept talking to Blue and asking him questions. Everyone backed away and let James and Meg have that time with their best buddy—their best friend.

The first few hours were tough when everybody had finally stopped to sit down and have the soup Maggie and Elizabeth made. Everyone left James and Meg alone as they wept for their dear friend and companion, Blue. It broke Maggie's heart and she knew it was going to leave a big void in James' life on the farm. Blue had been in his life almost since birth. He was especially close to his dog and considered him—his best friend. Blue was a loyal dog and never once had he ever let the family down, for nearly fourteen years.

They all watched in silence as Meg gently and wearily picked up the dog and placed him by the tree as James dug the hole. The gentle dog had saved Meg's life in exchange for his own, and instead of everyone rejoicing the storm was over, they watched in silence. Both Meg and James dug until the hole was deep and wide. Elizabeth walked over and handed them her most prized family heirloom. It was a large patchwork quilt she had sown the first year she had arrived in North Bend. It was the blanket that she carried each child home from the hospital in. She had been saving it in her cedar chest for her first grandchild. But instead, she silently handed it to Meg, so that she could wrap Blue in a blanket the whole family had loved as much as him.

Meg looked at her mother with sad eyes. "Are you sure?"

Elizabeth smiled as tears ran down her face and said, "Never been more sure in my entire life."

Meg hugged her mom, and together the three of them wrapped Blue, with loving hands, and handed him to William, who placed him in the hole under the big, old Bur Oak tree. It was where James chased Blue through the sprinklers for years and seemed only fitting he would treasure his final resting place. Once Blue was placed in the hole, James left and came back with Blue's favorite ball and tossed it in. Then he tossed in his first homerun baseball. Meg laid a watercolor picture of the family she had won a blue ribbon for in the state fair inside as well.

Sobbing, she said, "He needs a picture to remember us by."

Elizabeth put her arm around Meg's trembling shoulder. "He won't forget us...."

With tears running down his face, James shoveled the first patch of dirt onto Blue. Meg was next, then William, Elizabeth, and Maggie took the shovel. And for the next hour, Randolph, his ranch hands, and everyone else took a turn at putting Blue to rest. It was one of the most touching moments Maggie had ever witnessed, and she would never forget it in her lifetime. The devoted dog had saved his master's life, and everyone was paying their respect—everyone was wiping their eyes.

As it started to get dark, Randolph, Maggie, Damon, and the ranch hands drove to the North Bend Inn, just outside of town. It was the hotel Maggie had stayed in when she first came to see Elizabeth, and the same place that all four of the orphans had stayed up all night talking when they all got back together. She loved this cozy, small hotel. When Damon and Maggie come to visit, they stay there. It had not been severely damaged from the outside during the storm and flood. But when they walked in, the staff was mopping up all the water on the first floor. Randolph reserved a floor of rooms so that everyone could get a good night's sleep.

By the time everyone had settled in, the stars were starting to shine, letting everyone know that the worst was over—tomorrow was a new day and time to rebuild. Randolph and Damon left the hotel to go into town to see what was going on, and if anyone needed a room. The major part of the crisis was over, and from the conversations around town, the townspeople were triumphant. The little town of North Bend, the heartland of America, where generation after generation continued to farm the land, and produce a steady percentage of the agriculture for the states—had survived again. Not without hardship; not without pain; and not without loss. They had survived with their hard work, their perseverance and strength, and their love for their home and the families that had lived there for generations—like William's. With the feeling of renewal, they would come 'together' and rebuild what they had lost—again.

The town had sustained damage, but most was kept to a minimal due to the quick thinking of Randolph and Damon. Without the needed supplies, and the extra manpower that Randolph had delivered, the destruction would have been much worse. There had been no loss of life, unlike the storm a few years back. The farmers in the area were able to protect their expensive machinery and safeguard their homes, as they worked together in teams. Many trucks Randolph had brought carried building supplies to enable the town to start immediate cleanup and repairs. The stores on Main Street were almost without any damage to the centuries old brick buildings.

The town was abuzz when Randolph and Damon showed up to look around. They were greeted by all the local men and business owners, who had come out to look around, also. The continuous chorus of 'thank you,' pats on the back, hugs, and emotional handshakes to Damon and Randolph, from the locals, was overwhelming. The locals were grateful and appreciative to the two men who saved their town. Randolph didn't want the admiration from all his help. He was happy for the respect and acknowledgement that he was now a 'brother' to a town who asked for so little— but always gave a lot in return.

The next morning, their local church, along with some from out of the area, led the way in providing volunteers to help muck out the homes and affected areas. The local Air Force base supplied a lot of manpower to help. They formed assessment teams, Mud-Out, and chainsaw and debris removal teams across the affected area to assist in the cleanup. Within a few days, the Red Cross and numerous charities and relief organizations stepped in to comfort those who needed it and to assist in organizing shipments of food and supplies.

After the fifth day, Randolph and Damon thought the town could manage with the rest of the cleanup. The roads had been cleared, and the water had receded. Most of the reconstruction was started, and the neighbors were helping each other. Reba and Wendell brought Katie and Sarah home, and life started to get back to the typical Martin family routine. With the exception of one. Meg wouldn't leave her room. Depression had set in and she was having a difficult time. It had a little to do with Blue, but most of it had to do with her restless need to go to school in California.

Maggie was sitting on the steps of the porch in front of the house looking out over the storm-ravaged area. Tears were slowly running down her cheeks, when she heard the front door open. Quickly, she wiped her eyes with the apron she was wearing.

Elizabeth sat down next to her and reached for her hand. "Why all the sadness, Maggie? We all worked so hard and look at the amazing results." She swept her other hand in a half circle. "Randolph, Damon, and you were lifesavers. I thought for sure we were going to lose this place, along with my neighbors. They have all stopped by bringing baked goods, pastries, and preserves as a mere appreciation for what you did for them."

Maggie turned and looked at Elizabeth with tearstained cheeks. "What we did was from our hearts, and for the love of your town. Just like the new library we built a few years ago. You had to drive your children forty miles to the nearest library. That should never happen, especially when children need to learn. All those computers we installed gave the ones who didn't have it—the ability to use one now."

"So why are you so sad?"

Maggie kissed Elizabeth's cheek and quietly said, "Please, let me take Meg home with me. It's time for her to get serious and learn from the best at the Art Institute of L.A. I don't want to lose her or watch her do something a normal girl her age would do—rebel and run away. I want to lead her down that yellow brick road and let her see what life has in store for her artistic abilities. Please, Elizabeth, I beg you...."

Elizabeth looked at the sky as though she was thinking. Her eyes filled with tears. "I know she's not happy."

Maggie could only nod her head, she was filled with so much pain. "We almost lost her the other day. If she runs away, you *will* lose her. At least this way we both can watch her grow, and if this is not where she needs to be...like Dorothy, she will come to that realization—*there is no place like home.*"

Elizabeth continued to look at the sky, almost like she was looking for a sign from God. Finally she whispered to Maggie, "Let me think about it, and talk to William."

Maggie nodded again, as a single tear slid down her face. "Fair enough."

That night at dinner, Randolph had announced that they were all leaving in the morning. With everyone gathered around the large makeshift table, the sadness could be felt. The table was filled with the appetizing meal the women had made. Meg was sitting quietly with her hands in her lap. William was ready to say grace. "Will everyone take their neighbor's hand? I want to say a prayer of thanks."

Everyone clasped hands and in a lower baritone voice he said, "First, I want to thank our mighty God for giving us strength through this difficult time. Second, I want to thank my family and friends for all the help you gave. Saving this small town of North Bend that my family has been part of for many generations, for finding my lost child, I can never fully express the depth of my appreciation and deep respect. Randolph, Maggie, and Damon—we owe you a lifetime of gratitude." He looked at each one and gave a nod. "Without you, we couldn't have done it." Then he stopped for a moment as emotions took over and he became choked up. He cleared his throat and wiped his eyes. "And to my dear sweet Meg...your mother and I have decided to take Maggie up on her offer, and though my heart is breaking for my oldest daughter, we know it is the right thing to give you our blessing to go into the world and find your way."

Abruptly, there was a few seconds of silence as everyone absorbed what William had just said. All of a sudden, pandemonium broke out and screams could be heard across the county line. Meg jumped out of her seat, ran over to her father, and kept hugging and kissing his face with an energy that matched the storm they had just been through. "Thank you, daddy!" She kept repeating over and over. Then she did the same with her mother, only her mother didn't want to let her go. When she finally broke away from her mother, she slowly walked over to Maggie, and stood a foot away and stock still. She just stared at Maggie with tears streaming down her cheeks. Their deep emotional connection was seen by everyone who watched. It was a beautiful moment of one generation connecting with another who knew what it was like to chase their dreams. Meg's mother had never pursued her dreams, she had naïvely walked into a lifestyle that dictated what her life would be like—Maggie hadn't. Maggie was independent, and followed her yellow brick road searching until she found what she was looking for. Meg knew that; and Elizabeth was now allowing her daughter that chance to discover her own place in life.

As though in slow motion, Maggie held out her arms and Meg slid into them. Maggie whispered into her ear, "Patience is the key in life."

Randolph and Damon stood up. Randolph said to William, "Looks like this is a 'cigar' kind of moment. I say we head outside and enjoy those stars that finally came out tonight!"

Elizabeth, Maggie, and Meg were filled with excitement. Meg could not contain her energy or her emotional exhilaration. "I don't want to leave you and Daddy. I just want to go to the best art school and see if I can make it. I promise I will work hard, Mom. I won't let you and Daddy down. I'll call every night; and I'll listen to everything Maggie and Damon tell me to do."

Elizabeth hugged her daughter and smiled. "That's a lot of promises. I hope you can keep your word."

Maggie drew her brows together and pursed her lips. "She'd better be good, or I'm going to ship her right back here!" Maggie tapped Meg's nose with her finger. "Sometimes, Meg, you're only given one chance in life. My Lucy got lucky!"

Everyone was down at the Air Force base and the plane's engines were making a deafening noise. Meg had packed and was standing on the tarmac, along with William, Elizabeth, James, Sarah, and Katie. Maggie was hugging the little ones and Damon and Randolph were shaking hands with William.

Elizabeth hugged Maggie. "Thank you for everything. Take care of my baby and keep her safe!"

Maggie hugged her tight and let her go. "She's going to be the best damn artist in Los Angeles!"

Meg laughed. "I don't even know if I can get into that school, Auntie Maggie."

Maggie arrogantly smiled. "All we need to do is take in a few of your etchings."

Hastily, James ran up to Maggie. Very carefully, he pulled a ball of fur from under his T-shirt. It was that little kitty that Blue went diving into the water for. "He needs a home, Auntie Maggie. And I don't have the heart to give him to anyone but you! I know he won't take the place of Sabby, but he sure could use some tender, loving care!"

Maggie shook her head and softly said, "I can't take the kitty, James."

Tears began to form in James' eyes, his spirit had been broken and this was the first time she had seen him show any emotion. "Blue would want you to have him. I named him Storm.'"

Maggie looked down at this little tiny bundle of black and white fur and then back at James. Finally, she let out a big sigh. "Okay. Then you have to promise to visit him!"

James smiled and threw his arms around Maggie. "I love you, Auntie Maggie."

She ruffled his red hair and said, "I hope Damon says the same thing when he sees our new roommate!" Maggie slipped the tiny bundle under her jacket and shook her head in disbelief that she was even considering a cat again.

The pilot stepped out onto the upper platform and waved everyone in. The plane was ready for takeoff. As everyone started to walk up the stairway to the plane, Maggie turned around and blew a kiss. Elizabeth caught it with her fist and put her hand to her heart.

CHAPTER 11

AFTER WEEKS OF CONSTANTLY WATCHING THE storm systems creeping close to North Bend again, things were finally starting to settle down. The tumultuous week they spent in North Bend was beginning to feel like a distant dream. Maggie and everyone arrived home, and Randolph headed back to Mexico. Damon took off to South America to continue on his case. Maggie, Randall, and Meg were in the penthouse only a few days when they made a unanimous decision. Meg and Maggie had found the ideal situation to not only help Meg make extra spending money, it had also been a great solution for Lucy's dilemma.

Meg moved in with Lucy and Mary Jane the week after she arrived in Los Angeles. Lucy only lived a few miles from Maggie and if Meg needed her, it was only a short bus trip away. With Lucy working more hours and going out in the evening to Dream 'Scape, she had a built-in babysitter whom she could trust wholeheartedly. Lucy and Meg got along fabulously and Mary Jane adored her cousin. Elizabeth even said it was the best place for Meg. She was closer to her school and she didn't have to be an extra burden to Maggie with Randall already living there.

One evening on the phone, Elizabeth said, "I didn't want to burden you with both my children at once."

"Oh stop it, Elizabeth! I love both of the kids, they are so helpful and keep me grounded. Besides, they are both adults; and I rarely see them because they go to school and have their own social activities. Actually, this worked out so amazing for Lucy, and she'd have to pay a babysitter, anyway. Meg now has a job and she can defer some of her own costs." Maggie said into the phone, sounding very self-satisfied.

Elizabeth laughed. "You are funny, Maggie. You finally got your way and so did Meg. Now you're describing all the pros with this move."

Maggie's voice grew serious, "I could see it in Meg's eyes that she was on the verge of leaving. I didn't want her to be a statistic or leave in anger."

Elizabeth asked, "Did you ever think about me, and how I would feel watching my oldest daughter move away? It broke my heart to put Randall on a plane. You've never experienced that kind of emptiness. Then when my oldest daughter walked on that same plane...."

"No. I wasn't lucky enough like you to have a whole houseful of children. I've missed out on a lot of things I wished I had done." There was a silent pause, then Maggie continued, "I promise to send her home to visit all the time. She can catch a ride with Randall whenever you need a 'Meg fix.' I know it hurts, but eventually all your little birds are going to leave the nest to get their education.

The younger generations have different philosophies than the older generations. I remember talking to a young woman who was flying home to bury her father. She was from a town close to yours and was going to UCLA like Randall—she didn't want to go back to farming like her parents. I met her on the plane during my initial trip to finally see you again and we had a long conversation. Some of her values are now beginning to make sense."

"Farms are handed down from one generation to another. Who will take on the responsibilities of this farm when William and I are gone?" a slight panic rose in Elizabeth's voice.

"This young woman was so bright, and now, I'm beginning to really understand why these younger generations are not committed to farming. She explained that her parents were proud people and it was hard for them to understand why none of their children wanted to carry on their cultural and traditional inheritance. They were the fourth generation of farmers and the tradition didn't hold the same meaning for these younger ones as it did for their fathers and grandfathers."

Elizabeth sighed. "That's because my generation was not given a choice. We had to take over and do what our parents demanded we do."

"Exactly, Elizabeth." Maggie agreed. "Their values are more self-centered than yours ever were allowed to be. Farming is a difficult life. It's very structured and extremely hard. You're dependent on nature for every successful season. One success doesn't guarantee that next season will be the same, no matter how hard you work.

Meg's generation is not sure they want to accept that kind of challenge. They don't want to predict. They don't want to work hard and lose it to flooding, insect infestation, or tornados. They want to know how they are going to feed our families."

"Why are things changing? Why are these generations so different? Why don't they understand tradition? Why can't their dreams be like ours?" Elizabeth said slowly and curiously, as though trying to understand.

Maggie could hear deep emotions in Elizabeth's voice. "Because they are part of the intellectual, innovative generations that have changed everyone's whole way of thinking and living. Technology has opened their horizons to life, and fed them knowledge that we never knew, or had access to. They think so differently than us. They love their families, but their loyalties are to themselves."

Elizabeth sadly said, "What will William and I do if none of the children want this farm?"

"That is so far off in the future. Why worry about it now? Let your little birds fly and see if they come back. That's all you can do."

Elizabeth inhaled a deep breath and exhaled slowly. "Since when did you become so smart?"

Maggie smiled into the phone. "I didn't! I just learned a lot from you!"

"Give the kids a hug from us!"

"Always…. Love you." Maggie hung up.

The whole time she had been sitting and talking to Elizabeth, the little ball of fur was sleeping on her lap. She thought of James and his smile when she had finally taken the kitten.

Damon didn't have a big smile on his face when she mysteriously pulled him out from under her shirt after takeoff. In fact, he wanted Randolph to stop the plane to give the kitty back. Maggie wouldn't let him. She thought for sure she could find a home for Storm amongst one of her friends, but she hadn't had any luck so far. The little kitten was as cute and mischievous as he could be. Its sharp little teeth had ripped the skin off Maggie's hands plenty of times and it was a good thing Damon had only been home for a day, because Storm was into 'shredding' with his newfound claws.

One morning, she had walked into the bathroom and a roll of toilet paper was torn and strewn all over the bathroom floor. It was such a childish action, and all she could do was laugh when he hid behind the toilet. Maggie loved watching the impish behavior, and sometimes it was impossible to stop giggling. At night he would sluggishly crawl into the box near the bed that she had lined with an old blanket. Maggie worried that he would miss his mother, so each night since she brought him home, Maggie would fill a hot water bottle with warm water and stick it under the blanket. In the morning she would smile when she saw him cuddled up next to it.

She missed Sabby and was heartbroken that he couldn't enjoy the kitten's playful antics. Damon, on the other hand, had never owned an animal. He had never had that tie-down responsibility. He was not happy, but he really didn't have a say, either. Randall enjoyed having the kitten around the house. Half the time Storm would be in his room finding some kind of trouble he could get into. Randall loved animals and that was one thing he had missed, moving to Los Angeles from the farm. That was the main reason why he wanted to be a veterinarian. For years, he had spent most of his spare time nursing the sick animals on the nearby farms back to health. Birthing was always a miracle to him, and calving season was his favorite time of year. On Maggie's first visit, he pulled her out of bed in the middle of the night so she could experience the birth of a calf. It had been the highlight of her trip, and a remarkable contrast to her somewhat mundane city life.

Maggie was trying to make dinner, but the kitten was chasing her slippers as she walked around the kitchen. She was laughing in delight when Randall walked into the room.

"Hey, Maggie, what's going on? Looks like you have an active, little rascal on your heels!" Randall started to laugh and bent down to pick him up. Instantly, his hand snapped back. "Ouch! You little brat!"

Maggie started to giggle. "Did he bite you?"

"Yeah." Randall was holding him by the scruff of his neck so he couldn't bite him again. "Look at him. He's squirming like a little polecat!" The kitten was four feet in the air and didn't care if he fell; he was trying his hardest to get free.

"How's school going?" Maggie asked.

"Great. I have a week off before the next semester begins and I would really like to go home and hang with Mom and Dad. I was hoping I could hitch a ride from Randolph if he is going to the east coast during that time. Think I should ask him. I feel really bad I missed helping Dad with that big flood weeks ago, but I had midterms and if I'm going to stay on the Dean's List, I needed to study. I know my dad must have been terrified about losing the farm. And I know losing Blue must have been real hard on James. I am hoping him and I could have a long talk about that," he said.

Maggie smiled and he still continued to dangle the kitten. "Ask Rand. I don't think he will mind at all. The worst that can happen is that I'll get you a ticket on my credit card points. James is still having a tough time. Your mom says that he sometimes sits next to the tree just staring. Let's hope that with baseball season starting soon, he'll snap out of it."

"Dad said he is really excited about baseball season starting. Him and James go down to the field after church and play catch."

"I'm thinking I might go to Mexico for a few days when you're gone. I want to check out the new orphanage and maybe get some rest. I'm not sure when Damon will be back. That case he is working on is a real bummer. The father kidnapped his son from the mother and is hiding out in Buenos Aires. He is constantly traveling all over Argentina trying to catch him."

Randall dropped the kitten to the floor and Storm took off after Maggie's slipper. Randall and she started laughing. "He has such a cool job. He gets to travel the world and at the same time he's like Sherlock Holmes or Sam Spade. Maybe I should become an investigator!"

Maggie's mouth and eyes opened wide. "I don't think so, buster! Your mom and dad would hunt me down and turn me into kitten food!"

Randall began to laugh. "Eww, yucko!"

"Have you heard from Meg?" Maggie asked.

"She's babysitting for Lucy tonight. I think Bradley got tickets to some concert, or game, and they are going out for dinner, too! What do you think of him, Auntie Maggie?"

Maggie looked puzzled. "Not quite sure, but I guess the jury is out until he blows it."

"Meg thinks he's a nice guy. He gives a lot of attention to Mary Jane and sometimes helps with her homework."

Maggie poured the fettuccini with sun-dried tomatoes into a big bowl and sprinkled fresh parmesan cheese on it. "Did you talk to Meg about going home? You might have a tough time getting her out of California."

Randall picked a piece of pasta up and stuck it in his mouth. After he chewed it, he said, "She loves the Art Institute and the beach house, and I love the new set of wheels you got her!"

Maggie turned around and looked intently at him. "You promised not to say anything to your parents. I'm holding you to your word! You hear me? I only got her that because she has an evening class and I didn't want her taking a bus. Elizabeth would kill me. So make sure you lock it up!"

Randall laughed and walked over to the refrigerator. He took out the bread and some sliced meat and started making a sandwich. "You make the fanciest food, Auntie Maggie. I think I will just have a plain old sandwich!"

Maggie smiled.

A week later, Maggie put Randall and Meg on a plane for their first week of summer break. William and Elizabeth were extremely excited to have the whole family together again, and Maggie didn't want to spoil it by tagging along. Besides, Maggie was going with Randolph to Mexico. She was hoping that Damon could meet her there, but he wasn't sure if he'd be able to make it. She was only going to stay for a few days. She wanted to see the new director and spend some time at the orphanage. She loved spending time with the children. They had a full staff, including teachers, and all the rooms were finally filled with little ones. Maggie was excited and couldn't wait to see some of those smiling faces. She went out during her lunch time and hit up one of the Toys "R" Us stores in the area. When she was done, she had filled four carts with toys of all kinds. All the girls and boys were going to get little surprises and she couldn't wait to see their faces.

The engines were roaring and Maggie was sitting reading a magazine on the couch. Randolph was up with the pilot and within minutes, he was walking down the aisle and taking a seat next to Maggie. She put down her magazine and said, "I can't wait to see the orphanage."

Randolph laughed. "You could have fooled me. What the hell did you do, buy out the Toys "R" Us in Beverly Hills?"

Maggie looked indignant and sat up straight. "No! I just wanted to bring some little things for the kids."

"Calm down, Maggie, I was just teasing you! Sometimes you just take life too seriously." He tweaked her nose like he did when they were kids. "Lay down on the couch and relax. You look tired. It's going to be a quick flight. The tailwinds are perfect and I can't wait for some of Lupe's carnitas and homemade tortillas!"

It was a fast flight like he said and they made it to the hacienda before the sunset. Once they were settled in and had eaten dinner, Randolph decided to take Maggie to Casa de Niños. When they pulled up to the iron gates, Randolph pushed a button and it slowly opened. Walking out of the building was a beautiful Hispanic woman dressed casually in jeans and a T-shirt with the name of the orphanage displayed across her chest.

Maggie and Randolph got out of the Jeep just as she was walking up. "Good evening, Rand. I see you brought Maggie this trip." A warm smile lit up her face.

Maggie stepped forward and held out her hand. Instead, Maria walked forward and encompassed Maggie in a hug. Maggie backed away slightly and smiled. "It's great to see you again, Maria. We never got much time together the last time I was here. You had just arrived and Juliann was showing you around."

Randolph inquired, "How is everything going? I'm afraid to show you the back of the Jeep.

Seems Maggie went on a shopping spree and brought some new toys for the kids!"

Maria's face lit up. "Oh...how wonderful. *Gracias*, Maggie! Kids always like to play with new toys. Why don't you come with me to the younger dorm, we are just about to put the smaller children to bed. I think you might like to see how we do that."

Maggie clapped her hands and jumped up and down. "Oh, I'd love to."

She took Maggie's hand and turned to Randolph. "Once you've unloaded the toys, there is some hot coffee in my office."

He gave her a salute like she was the 'Sergeant-of-Arms.' Maggie followed as she walked into one of the larger buildings. Then they walked into a big delightful room decorated with fairy tale characters on the walls and a large soft area rug that encompassed the whole room. Sitting on the rug were twenty-five young children between the ages of three to six. They were all wearing their pajamas and nightgowns and watching as the enthusiastic young woman sitting on a small chair in front of them was reading a bewitching bedtime story. She had the children mesmerized with her animated voices as she read each character in the book. Maggie watched in awe. When she was done, she had the children stand up and one by one they followed her into their bedrooms. Once they were all in their own beds, she walked from room to room and tucked each child in and blessed them with a kiss on their forehead. As she left each room after this evening ritual, she said, "Sleep, my dear babies—sleep with the angels."

Maggie watched with warm emotions and started to get choked up. Then when she felt herself starting to fall apart, she walked over to a window to look at the stars shining bright in the sky. Maggie's thoughts drifted back to Bishop Street. *This was not how the Sisters put the children to bed. How many empty years had they suffered abusive behavior from Sister Theresa and the others? How many painful beatings? How much humiliation, intimidation, or isolation did they endure?*

Maggie's tears formed as she remembered her childhood. *On those lonely, scary nights, all she ever wanted was to be kissed goodnight. Or to hear some kind loving words that children deserve. Instead Elizabeth, Lucy, Randolph, and she had accepted a childhood of sadness, manipulation, and abuse. Sister Theresa ran the orphanage, and should have never been allowed to be around children. She hated children. Her biggest pleasure was breaking their spirit. She couldn't break Maggie. So, instead she nurtured a hatred toward her that became a constant source of her resentment. Whenever Sister Theresa had a chance, she belittled Maggie and her friends, or shamed them over something small. Maggie was mortified when she hung Randolph's wet sheets for everyone to see. Or she cut off all of Lucy's beautiful hair, just to be cruel.* Maggie touched her cheek, and the scar that had reminded her of those ugly orphanage beatings.

She closed her eyes. Even after all these years, she visualized the children's faces that filled the Bishop Street Orphanage so long ago. Those little ones of all ages yearned for a soft touch, or kind smile, or just a bedtime story. It was so different to watch the children tonight and their enthusiastic faces. They laughed and watched as the storyteller weaved her fairy tale using character voices that kept them wanting more. She kept them spellbound as the atmosphere quivered with excitement. Then when she was done, she tucked each child into their bed and kissed their beautiful faces. Maggie felt a tear slide down her cheek. Why was her childhood so painful, and what did she do to deserve that?

Maggie knew that answer and smiled. Because, in life, even the most hateful and hurtful people unknowingly teach you lessons. They teach you—how not to be. They show what those ugly behaviors can do, so that you don't repeat them. Breaking the cycle is more important than continuing to tightly grip a fistful of agony that you can't release. Lucy was the only one that didn't learn that lesson early enough. Her pain was so deep, and her anger so solid, she couldn't let go. When Maggie finally found her—Mary Jane had been left to the same fate. Until Maggie brought them both home.

Maria tapped Maggie on the back. "Are you okay?"

Maggie turned around and smiled. "I was just thinking how beautiful that was to watch tonight. How lucky those children are to be loved."

"Oh, yes! Katrina is a wonderful storyteller. She is one of the oldest of our children. She loves being here, and she loves all the little ones. She had been on the streets for four years when we found her. She's only fifteen. Her family had been killed by banditos. We think her father was a drug dealer or involved."

Maggie took Maria's hand and started to walk. "She's a lovely child. From what I see, this place is so happy and encouraging to these little ones."

As they slowly began to walk down the hall, Maggie felt a little tug at her blouse. Then she heard a little voice say, "I'm scared."

Maggie turned around and looked at this little angelic face and she stooped down to take a better look. Her long brown hair, big brown eyes, and sad face captivated Maggie. "You are? What is scaring you?"

The little girl's shoulders lifted and she didn't say anything. Maggie's finger swept the hair out of her face and said, "Would you like me to come lay with you for a while?" The little girl nodded. "*¿Cómo te llamas?*"

In the lowest of whispers, "Olivia."

Maggie took her little hand. Then she looked at Maria and said, "I'll meet you back at your office in a few minutes. I'm going to lay down with Olivia for a while." They began to walk down the hall. When they got to her bed, Maggie helped her in and she laid down next to her and wrapped her arms around her. It felt so good to hold the little one in her arms.

Maggie remembered her first night at the orphanage. She was alone and terrified. Her mother had just left her sitting on the steps in the rain with a note pinned to her coat. When Sister Theresa found her, she was mean and left her sitting on a bed. The sister had given her a dry nightgown and just said, "Go to bed and I will see you in the morning." Maggie's world was spinning in fear, then out of nowhere, Elizabeth appeared and helped Maggie out of her wet clothes. Then she laid down with Maggie and held her tight until she fell asleep.

With loving arms, Maggie waited until Olivia was asleep before she got up. Then she bent down, kissed her little forehead, and whispered, "Sleep with angels."

Maria and Randolph were sitting on a couch in her office sipping coffee when Maggie walked into the room. Randolph asked, "How did it go? Is she not the cutest little girl?"

Maggie grinned. "She's adorable. How old is she?"

"Olivia just turned three. She is from a small town over the mountains. She has twelve siblings and her mother died from an infection. Her father had no other family and couldn't take care of the youngest two children, so he dropped them off here. She has a four-year-old brother, Pablo."

Maggie sat there and listened to the little girl's story. Every child in the orphanage had a story in how they ended up here.

Randolph sat forward and asked Maggie, "So what do you think of Casa de Niños?"

Maggie smiled and he could see she was emotional. "I think this is a great place for children. All I saw were smiles tonight. You did an amazing job, Randolph!"

He stood up and pointed to Maria. "Juliann gave Maria lots of tips to comfort the children and Maria is doing a fabulous job!"

Maggie inhaled and exhaled slowly. "I wish we had been here, instead of Bishop Street."

"Me, too! Come on, Maggie, let's go back to the house. Tomorrow is another day. Wait until you meet all the children and see what a great place this is. Night, Maria!" Hand in hand, they walked out of the building into the night air. When Maggie saw the stars, she stopped and looked up. "Star light...star bright...first star I see tonight...."

Randolph added, "I wish I may...."

CHAPTER 12

IT HAD BEEN A WONDERFUL FIVE DAYS IN MEXICO. THE orphanage was housing and lovingly taking care of those misplaced children of the streets. This had turned into a very cathartic and healthy experience for Maggie. Life was filled with changes, and learning to accept those changes had become easier as she watched all the little ones so trustingly adapting to their new environment. The school staffed teachers for all the age groups; and some of the children for the first time in their lives had the opportunity to go to school. Others, it was actually the first time they slept in a real bed.

Mexico had a much higher poverty level than the United States, and it left a lot more families impoverished. Necessities such as nutrition, clean water, shelter, education, health care, and basic services didn't exist for most and they lived in extreme poverty. Sometimes to the point that they couldn't afford to feed their families, or they were forced to live in a tent with no running water. Traveling with Maria and Randolph through some of the small villages opened Maggie's eyes to a lot of things she had never experienced, or even acknowledged in life. Most of these children lived a lifetime without getting out of the squalor.

Going back to Casa de Niños only made Maggie want to do more for those children who never knew what it was like to have three meals in a day or clean running water. Maggie's eyes absorbed all she could, and her heart broke every time she thought about leaving. She always made it a point during the day to find little Olivia, and spend some time with her. Eventually, she got to know her brother, Pablo. He was a quiet little boy who seemed to hold a lot more in than Olivia. His bashful, yet distrustful, demeanor always intrigued Maggie. Olivia and he were such opposites. Olivia reminded Maggie of Lucy with her carefree, risk-taking attitude. Pablo was more rebellious and hidden.

The last day Maggie was there, Damon flew in to surprise her. Maggie was in the courtyard of Casa de Niños playing with the children. As usual, Olivia was following her around and always trying to hold her hand. Maggie tried hard not to let Olivia become too attached, so she tried to keep some distance between them. Maggie was at the swing set pushing the children on the swings. It was one of her favorite things she loved to do at Bishop Street when she was seven. Bishop Street had an old rusted swing set with a shiny metal slide that the children loved. It was Maggie's favorite time of the day when the young children were allowed to go out into the yard area and be energized and carefree. She loved to fly high in the sky, kicking her legs up in the air.

At Bishop Street, they all stood in line waiting for the three swings, or a chance to slide down the hot metal slide. Watching the children brought happier memories and a smile to Maggie's face as she pushed Olivia and the other children high in the air. There were lots of swings and four different size slides. Olivia would only go down the small slide. She was too afraid of the three larger ones. Her brother, Pablo, didn't have a fear of anything. He was a brave little soul, who always seemed to test the limits—not only of himself—but of others.

Maggie watched Pablo climb to the top of the largest slide. When he got to the top, he stood and stared down at the kids laughing, waving and pointing his fingers. Maggie ran over and said, "Pablo, sit down. You're going to fall. Please be careful."

His inbred boldness reminded Maggie slightly of some of the bullies in Bishop Street. Billy the Bully, Joseph, and Charlie Grimes were the worst. They used to constantly intimidate the children and do awful things to them. Maggie hated their cruel behavior aimed at some of the weaker kids, like Randolph. They never got in trouble and no matter what mean things they did, Sister Theresa ignored them. Until Maggie decided to give them back what they deserved. She came up with ways to secretly turn the tables on them and found ways to hold them accountable without bringing in the Sisters. Randolph and Maggie, one summer night glued the window shut in Billy's room with their morning oatmeal. For days the four of them laughed at all the trouble Billy got into when the Sisters found the empty oatmeal dish tucked away in his closet. He was angry and wanted to retaliate, only he couldn't figure out who had done it. He had been so mean to so many kids. Maggie and Randolph were relentless in their pursuit to teach him a lesson, and a few weeks later, they hid his only pair of shoes. After years of putting up with those bullies, they were beginning to learn a big lesson. Trying to the stop the bully's behavior was impossible, but giving them some of their own medicine kept the four laughing.

Yes, Pablo was a typical bold, defiant little boy who was going to learn through his mistakes. He wasn't mean-spirited or vicious to the other kids; he was just one of those risk takers who challenged his circumstances. Maggie looked again and yelled, "If you don't sit down, Pablo, I'm afraid I'm going to come get you!"

Pablo began to dance around and laugh. Maggie was not one of those people who idly threatened; she was a firm believer in following through. She marched over to the slide with a scowl on her face and her hands on her hips. Damon had been secretly watching from a distance with a big smile on his face. He was waiting to see who was going to win at this game—Pablo or Maggie. Just as she was about to step on the first rung, a set of strong arms grasped her around the waist, as his baritone voice boomed, "Whoa...young lady!"

Maggie swung around in utter surprise and threw her arms around Damon's neck. She wanted to kiss him, but she didn't think it was a good idea in front of the children.

He asked, "Are we having a problem?"

Maggie pulled herself out of his arms and said, "Little Pablo has a mind of his own and has listening issues."

Damon laughed. "Seems to me, Pablo is just having fun pushing your buttons, like most little boys!" Taking two rungs at a time, within seconds Damon was at the top of the slide. Pablo's eyes opened wide in shock. Damon picked him up and lifted him high in the sky. Pablo began to panic and grabbed onto Damon for dear life. "Don't like it this high, Pablo?" he teased.

Pablo shook his head, while he tightly held onto Damon. Finally Damon sat down on the slide and together they slid down. By the time they got to the bottom, Pablo had a big smile on his face. Maggie and Olivia were at the bottom of the slide laughing. The children continued to play in the sandbox as Maggie and Damon walked over to sit under the tree.

Maggie sat down and Damon sat next to her. "Hey, baby, I see you're having a fun-filled day! What would you say if I asked you out for dinner and took you into town to that romantic little restaurant near the ocean you like?"

Maggie grinned. "I'll have to think about it!"

"What...?" His jaw dropped down and he looked stunned.

Maggie stood up and tugged at his hand until he got up. "I'm just teasing you—for surprising me!"

He laughed. "Let's enjoy this beautiful evening, seeing as we catch the plane home tomorrow. I brought you back a gift from South America."

Maggie's eyes opened wide, "What?"

He smacked her ass and laughed heartily. "Me!"

Juliann flew in from Honduras to see Randolph and decided to surprise Maggie at the office. They had been communicating back and forth for months since she left Mexico. Juliann was building a small orphanage in a smaller, impoverished area of Puerto Cortés on the coast of Honduras. She had been there three months and this was her first time back in the States. Some of their main contributors, of the organization of Honduran refugees, were located in Los Angeles. She was meeting with them to try to procure more contributions.

Maggie was sitting in her office concentrating on her computer screen. Denise opened Maggie's door and peeked her head inside. "You've got a visitor."

Maggie didn't hear her because she was fixated on what she was doing.

At the top of her lungs Denise yelled, "Is anybody here?"

Startled, Maggie looked and started to laugh. "I guess I was in my own world! Sorry!"

"Having your own world is a good thing, but I think it has more to do with old age!" she teased.

Maggie stood up and looked indignant. She knew that Denise was pushing her buttons and yet she was still going to feed into it. "I am not OLD!"

Denise put her finger to her cheek—thinking. "I think you're as old as Roxie, and she's already lost her hearing, too. So no wonder you didn't hear me!"

Maggie stomped her foot. "I'm not as bad or old as her. Your dog is fifteen years old. When you multiply that by seven for dog years, which is like saying I'm one hundred and five!"

Denise nodded her head. "Most of the time, you act it!"

Maggie picked up a book sitting on her desk and threw it at Denise. Just in time, Denise slammed the door. The crash against the door was very loud and Juliann began to laugh. When Denise reopened the door and poked her head in, Maggie and her burst into laughter.

Suddenly, Denise flung the door wide open and Juliann walked through. "You certainly have an interesting relationship with your secretary! After listening to that, I want to join in on the fun!"

Maggie's mouth dropped open and she gasped. She leaped out of her chair and rushed toward her friend. "Oh my God! When did you get here?"

Juliann kind of shook her head and said, "Fifteen minutes ago. And just long enough to hear the book hit the door!"

Denise started to laugh. "Maggie, I tried to get your attention to tell you that you had company, but you got caught up on my dog's age!" They all started to laugh now.

Maggie hugged Juliann and looked at Denise. "Denise, I'd like you to meet a sweet friend of Randolph's and mine. I told you about her when I got back from Mexico. This is Juliann the 'child whisperer.'"

Denise walked in the room and hugged Juliann, also. "Pleasure to officially meet you."

"*De nada*," she answered.

Maggie released Juliann and turned toward Denise, "This is a very dear friend since college and my best friend for life. Well, except for those days she compares me to her old dog."

The girls all laughed again. Denise closed the door, and Maggie took Juliann's hand and led her to the couch in the corner of the room. That was Maggie's favorite place in the office. It was her comfort zone over the years. Whenever things got really tough, you could find her 'vegging' on the couch with a hot cup of coffee and tabloid magazines, or taking a nap when sleepless nights overwhelmed her with exhaustion.

Once they were seated, Maggie looked excited as she said, "What brings you out this way? I'm so honored you stopped by."

"I had some business in town, and I thought maybe Randolph, you, and I could go to dinner tonight," she answered.

"Oh, that works for me. Have you talked with Randolph?" Maggie asked.

Juliann shook her head. "Not really. I haven't talked to him for a week or so. I get so busy at times, I barely am able to catch a few hours of sleep."

Maggie picked up her cellphone and dialed. "Hey, you. Are you in L.A.?" she asked.

"Yes, I am, but I'm in a big meeting right now. Anything important?" he barely whispered into his phone.

"I think so! Juliann is sitting in my office and we were wondering if you wanted to join us for dinner tonight?"

"What...she's in town? Really? Hell yes, I'll meet you for dinner! I'll cut my meetings short and meet you somewhere. Or should I send my driver to pick you up?"

"I'm going to take her home and I'll make dinner at my house. I don't feel like fighting the paparazzi tonight. Damon is home, but he leaves in a few days for Buenos Aires, again. We'll cook some steak on the barbeque and sit outside at the beach house. Does seven work?"

"Perfect. See you then!"

Maggie and Juliann slowly strolled along Rodeo Drive in Beverly Hills, enjoying a great conversation and catching up on their lives. Then they stopped at the grocery store, picked up steaks and other groceries. Maggie called Damon and let him know that Juliann was in and they were all meeting for dinner at the beach house. Juliann loved the beach house with its modern simplicity. It sat on a small cliff off Malibu Beach and had a large deck that gave them a panoramic view of the ocean. Maggie started the barbeque while sipping a glass of wine with Juliann, enjoying the sun setting over the ocean and a cool California breeze. They had thrown together a quick salad and were planning on cooking asparagus, in tin foil, with lemon juice and olive oil on the grill.

By eight, everyone had finished dinner and they were relaxing on the patio. Juliann had told them all about her past months in Honduras. She loved the people, but sometimes she felt the unstable political climate was interfering with her ability to get things done. It was going slower than normal, and there were just a few major repairs she needed done. The orphanage had more than enough children, and it broke her heart that she couldn't take them all. It wasn't in the best part of town, but it was a solid place for them to eat, sleep, and go to school.

"I'm just in awe of all that you do for those countries and their children who need a place to belong," Maggie said.

Juliann smiled. "I don't do it for them. I do it for me! I think I get the best deal from it all. Each one of us, sitting at this table, has firsthand experience of how a child feels when they are abandoned with nowhere to go. They feel helpless and hopeless. The smaller ones on the streets have little chance at all, because it's a 'fend for yourself' attitude."

Maggie nodded.

"The smaller they are, the more they trust, as they get older, they turn to their survival mode. Sometimes we are lucky to find them when they are not so damaged. Today, I heard from Maria that Olivia and Pablo are doing much better," Juliann stated.

Maggie's eyes lit up. "She has really become the social butterfly with each passing day. I was just there and she followed me like a little puppy dog, she wanted acceptance so bad. On the other hand, Pablo is trying harder to deal with his trust issues. He is more independent and doesn't want to listen."

"It's just amazing to watch how most of them learn to adjust, mainly the 'under-fives.'

Occasionally, a few just have the hardest time dealing with being trapped in the orphanage. They become so used to living on the streets, and being scavengers, that they become bored and feel tied down. Especially the older ones. That's why it is so important to catch them at a younger age."

Randolph looked concerned. "I hope you're careful. I've seen them turn on you with a click of your fingers."

Juliann patted his hand that was on the table. "I try to think that I exercise reasonable caution when it comes to these kids. I have only been in a few small altercations."

"I love what you did with Casa, and I'm curious as to the others you build," Maggie inquired.

"The one in Honduras is interesting. It's not quite as extravagant as Casa, but I've been to see it a few times and there's going to be some really happy and appreciative children," Randolph stated.

Maggie's face lit up. "You've seen it, Rand?"

He nodded. "That's so unfair. I'd love to go see it and give a contribution."

Juliann sat up and said, "Come back with me. I leave in a few days. Come with me!"

"That sounds great. I just finished up a book, but it's not being published. And just a few days sounds perfect," Maggie answered.

Damon's eyes opened wide. Then he suggested, "I don't think it's the safest of places right now, with their civil unrest and major drug lords. Why don't you wait a few months?"

Maggie raised her voice a little and slightly frowned. "If she can go and feel safe enough, why can't I go for a few days?"

Damon leaned forward. "I'm not saying you *can't* go, I'm just not sure you have the street smarts that Juliann has to see danger or how to deal with it."

Those were the wrong words, and the conflict was beginning to fester. "Are you calling me stupid? Do you think you can tell me what I can and can't do?" Maggie was getting madder by the second and she stood up.

In a gentle voice, Damon said, "Sit down, Maggie, we will discuss this later. We have guests right now." He paused. "For the record, 'stupid' never came out of my mouth. There is a difference between being stupid and being street smart! Enough said until later."

Juliann and Randolph looked at each. Then she said, "Talk about it with Damon and let me know. I'll be around for a few days."

They finished off their after-dinner liqueur and decided a nice walk along the beach would calm some of their ruffled nerves.

"Are you sure you ladies don't want to take my jet into Honduras?" Randolph asked.

Maggie was standing with her arm around Damon's waist, but his face showed his apprehension of her going with Juliann. Maggie smiled and said, "No, but thanks. I think we are fine going commercial." She looked up at Damon. He looked down at her and looked away. Then she whispered, "Please don't let me leave with you being mad. It's only going to be four days, and besides, this is great research for my next book. I think I'm going to model it around our little Juliann."

He looked down and said, "I am just feeling a little uneasy. Four days, right?"

Maggie was concerned about the conversation that Damon and she had that night when the company left. He was very angry and didn't want her to go. He had heard a lot of disturbing stories while he was in Brazil. Not only was Brazil having very violent outbreaks of cartel murders, but the mayhem was bleeding into Honduras, Nicaragua, and El Salvador. San Pedro Sula was considered one of the top twenty-five most violent cities in South America and that was exactly where she was flying into. Maggie was not a street-smart person. Her knowledge on survival skills ceased to exist. Now, if you were talking about someone like Lucy, she had lived on the streets for years and was savvy enough to recognize dangerous situations—but not Maggie. He knew that Juliann was also another very sharp lady who knew how to get around and what to watch for. There was no talking to Maggie and she would not listen to his concerns. She was determined to go with Juliann, and nothing he said fazed her in the least. That is what scared him the most.

Juliann walked over and laid her arm on Damon's. "I promise I will have her on a flight in four days. We won't do anything risky or 'stupid.' I promise." She looked directly at him.

Damon's face showed his concern. He bent down and gave Maggie a hug and a kiss on the forehead. "Be safe and be careful. I love you."

Randolph gave Maggie a hug and then walked over and gave Juliann a hug. "I guess if I can't convince you to settle down in Mexico with Casa de Niños, then Honduras it is! Be safe, my friend, and keep this one out of mischief!"

Damon flinched at the word 'mischief.' Maggie picked up her carry on, and so did Juliann. They waved goodbye to the guys and walked down the passenger hallway.

The airport was calling for their final boarding, so they started to run, while laughing. When they finally got to their plane, they were just getting ready to close its doors. They gave each other a fist bump and boarded the plane.

After a long twelve hour flight, with one transfer in Houston, they finally made it into the tiny airport with just four landing strips. The block-style, cement-walled buildings looked very old and primitive. As the plane taxied on the runway, Maggie could see the impoverished condition of this country, from the potholes in their runways, to the deterioration of its buildings. When the plane had stopped, one metal set of stairs was rolled over to allow the passengers to leave the plane.

Once they were in the terminal, it was just as simple and modest as the outside. Inside, it was filled with people all standing in different lines waiting to fly out. The lines for customs were wrapped around and out the door. Maggie followed Juliann as she slowly and nondescriptly managed to get to an office door just inside of the customs area. There she talked to a younger gentleman in fluent Spanish at the desk. They laughed and the conversation seemed very animated. Then he left the room and came back with an older man dressed in a military or law enforcement uniform. Within minutes, he was stamping their passports and escorting them to another door to leave.

Once outside, Maggie asked. "What was that about?"

Juliann took Maggie's hand and began to walk toward a rotating carousel that had their luggage spinning in a circle. "I hate to stand in lines. It would have taken us three hours to get out of here and this place is pretty quiet today. Usually it's packed wall-to-wall with people coming and going on the inside and outside. Thank God I know people. Their names and my pretty face get me out of a lot of bullshit!" She pulled their luggage off and handed Maggie hers. "Come on, let's get out of here. The orphanage is thirty-six miles out of town, near the coastal town of Puerto Cortés."

Maggie looked at Juliann and said, "This country is extremely poor. Flying in, I could see the shacks, tents, and dilapidated houses. Why did I think this was going to be more like Mexico?"

Juliann shook her head and stopped. A look of exasperation was all over her face "Because the U.S. is the gold standard, Mexico the silver, and this country is the 'rocks.' You haven't seen anything yet. As we drive through the towns, I will show you what the real faces of poverty look like and how survival doesn't work for most.

Starvation, disease, and death is their way of life. Unless you live right on the coast of Puerto Cortés. It's one of the largest seaports for shipping in all of South America. It's also one of the nicest resort towns to visit along the coast. It has very tropical and lush forests filled with wild avocado and mango trees, along with wild orchids. Unfortunately, we are located about four miles from the coast in a small town that is poor."

Maggie had no idea what she was walking into and had never seen such haunting looks on the faces of the people waiting patiently to get out of the country. She didn't expect this trip to be easy, or an extravagant vacation, but she was almost afraid of what she was going to experience. Maybe Damon had been right. Maybe she was naïve and completely unaccustomed to a world filled with homelessness, starvation, and disease.

Damon knew Maggie only too well. She was naïve, trusting, extremely impulsive, and vulnerable. He had initiated her into the world of homeless street people when she went with him to look for Lucy. She had never been on the streets to witness what vagrants went through just to find food and shelter. She didn't know what it was like to be stripped of your dignity and beg for money to feed yourself. Her life after the orphanage had continuously moved in a positive direction with accumulated wealth. The few days they had gone to search for Lucy was just a small exposure to what she was going to experience in Honduras. He knew all about this country, he had been here a few times and could not wait to leave. He tried to tell her that, but she was stubborn, and thought she could handle those four days.

Maggie was surprised by how uncharacteristic the country was compared to certain parts of Mexico. Most places inland in northern Mexico like Juárez and Chihuahua were hot deserts and dry. Other areas along the Pacific Ocean, just south of the California border, were cooler and the people used the ocean for most of their food source. The southern tip of Mexico was situated between the Gulf of Mexico and the Caribbean Sea. With world-famous archaeological sites, enchanting colonial cities, romantic haciendas and resorts, beautiful beaches and distinct cuisine—it was like another world. Maggie had been to Cancun many times, but any form of poverty was always hidden away when that part of the country made most of its income on tourism. It was the same from the coastal cities, following the coast of the Pacific Ocean. She knew that the Mexican people were proud and hard workers whose culture and way of living sometimes didn't even include running water or electricity. Randolph had built a purified water plant specifically for the town he lived in. That also generated most of the electricity. Most areas were not that fortunate.

They were standing by the curb when Juliann raised her hand to flag down a car. The vehicle pulled up to the curb and a young man got out. He came around to give Juliann a hug. She introduced him to Maggie. "I'd like you to meet my *amigo* Ricardo. He works with me at the orphanage. He is the best of the best, and I adore him, dearly."

Maggie held out her hand. "*Hola*, Ricardo. *Me llamo* Maggie."

Juliann started to laugh. "It's okay, Maggie, everyone that works with me speaks better English than I do!"

Maggie blushed. "Oh...."

Juliann patted her on the back and opened the back door of the car. "Come on, I want to get to the orphanage before it gets dark." She climbed in amongst the boxes of food and stacks of bottled drinking water.

Just that sentence began to make Maggie second guess her reasons for coming, reminding her of what Damon had said.... '...*before it gets dark*.' Maggie wondered what happened '*after it was dark*.'

CHAPTER 13

THE OLD CAR WAS BUMPING ALONG THE PITTED DIRT road at a very slow pace. Maggie could hear the shocks rattling as the car jarred up and down. As they traveled through the small villages and towns, Maggie was having a hard time holding the bile down that was creeping up her throat. The disintegration of the towns was conspicuous and depressing.

As they were driving through a large city, Juliann turned to Maggie and pointed out the window. "Over there is the square, or some call it the plaza of San Pedro Sula. See the man in front of McDonald's? He sells nothing but glue! He sets up his card table and fills it with these little tubes of solvent-based glue. That glue is for street children to buy and inhale. It is made in and exported from the United States or made by U.S. companies in Central America. Unlike glues of a similar kind sold in the US, this glue does not contain nausea-inducing mustard seed. These greedy pigs can be seen selling glue to Honduran street children in every major Honduran city. It's sickening, disgusting, and breaks my heart."

Maggie gasped. "Oh my God! Really?"

"I don't joke around when it comes to children. I spit on those men." Juliann made a spitting sound. "Most of those street children don't live past ten or twelve."

"The government allows this?" Maggie's angry voice hissed.

Juliann gave a wretched laugh. "The government doesn't care. Street children purchase the glue because inhaling it reduces their hunger and numbs them to the emotional and physical pain they endure every day—plus physical and sexual abuse, in addition to the sense of hopelessness and abandonment. And you want to know why I can't stay in one place too long? There are too many children who need someone who cares, because these fucking governments don't!"

Maggie felt tears welling up in her eyes and she could barely breathe.

"I go to the parts of the city where tourists do not go. I check under the underpasses; visit the city dump; or go to rural areas to look for them and bring them to the orphanage. Some stay, and some are so used to surviving on the streets, they go back." Juliann sat back in her seat.

"What can you do? You can't save all of them. The streets are swarming with them," Maggie said, her eyes now trained on the window, looking for the homeless children.

Juliann sighed. "I save what I can and that's all I can do."

They continued to drive at a slow pace, skirting in and out of different areas on their way to a small village outside of Puerto Cortés. The shacks, and makeshift living conditions, in most of the small villages were beyond poverty. The filth and squalor was overwhelming to Maggie. The homeless on the streets of Los Angeles were nothing compared to what Maggie's eyes were absorbing. She was having a hard time keeping from vomiting, and watching Juliann's unemotional face was a dichotomy to the kindhearted woman she had first met in Mexico.

The silence was broken by Juliann. "Are you okay, Maggie? I didn't think this would upset you that much. I wanted you to spend a few days with me so you could really see why it's hard for me to stay in one place."

"I truly get it. But you will never be able to stop it. And you live such a perilous life," Maggie stated.

"Whatever you do in life is dangerous. Walking across a street in Los Angeles is dangerous. So, why not do something meaningful in life. My parents had a zillion times more money than they could ever spend. And yet, a Gucci bag meant more to my mother than feeding a thousand children. I need more meaning than that in my life." She exhaled slowly.

"So, Randolph has been here?" Maggie questioned.

Juliann turned and smiled. "Yes. I think his heart broke in two. That meeting he was at the other day was a group of people that help support my children's home. Their charitable donations run this home; and I was hoping to get a little more money so we could build another wing for twenty more children."

"Only twenty?" Maggie sounded surprised.

"One child is a lot more than none. When I can save twenty more, I'm beyond thankful!"

Maggie nodded her head and thought, one was better than none.

Juliann announced. "Where we are going is three miles outside of Puerto Cortés —that's on the North Atlantic coast of Honduras. It's on the rim of the Bay of Omoa. We're almost there. We didn't take the highway because they've had some trouble along it a few days ago and Ricardo didn't think it would be safe today."

Maggie looked up in surprise, but didn't say anything. What had she gotten herself into and would she ever get out? That was all she could keep asking herself.

A few minutes later, they were driving through a town with a main street filled with decaying and dilapidated brick and sandstone buildings, houses, and three-story apartments. The cobblestone streets were bumpy and the town had aged and was showing its rundown remnants of what a beautiful place it must have been—years earlier. The ruinous conditions were reminiscent of a war-ravaged Europe after World War II. Maggie was horrified on one end of the spectrum, and on the other, her heart broke for all the people who managed to survive in this environment that had little to offer.

In the middle of the block there was a large seven-foot plaster wall that went across from one apartment building to the next, in between was a single story set of buildings nestled behind the heavy wall. Ricardo pulled into the short driveway and got out of the car. He shoved a key into the lock and opened the gate. Then he came back to the car, got in, and drove it through the gates. Once in, he shut off the engine, got out of the car again, and went to lock the gate. Everyone got out of the car and Juliann took Maggie's hand.

"Welcome to My House."

Maggie looked confused. "Your house?"

Juliann grinned, "No, it's called My House. We have thirty-two children here and every day we bus twenty-seven of them into another city to go to a private school. Our bus should be here any minute. That is why I was in a hurry to get back."

"Oh, I thought you were in a hurry because it is dangerous after it gets dark!" Maggie laughed.

Juliann shook her head. "Doesn't matter if it's dark or light, it's always dangerous in this country. You have to keep your eyes open and constantly be alert. Never—and I mean never—mistake a nice person as a friend. That doesn't exist. Everyone in this country always has an ulterior motive."

Maggie frowned. "It's such a broken down town. It really was hard to see the deterioration of these buildings. And most of the people looked depressed, also."

"Most of it was from a large earthquake a few years ago. They never could recover and you know how hard it is to get the government to repair or fix anything. This country is so dirt poor, they can't afford to feed their own children. It's another Haiti." Juliann's face looked sad. "Come on in. All the little ones are here now."

"How little?" Maggie asked.

"Between three and six years old. We have five little ones that stay behind because they are too young to go to school. I have two wonderful young women, Sofia and Chica that stay with them. They were both homeless when we found them, so this is now their home and they help us take care of all the children. They are sweethearts and really bright young girls." Juliann started walking across the large driveway toward the main house. Maggie followed and they walked up the three stairs to the porch that went from one side of the house to the other. The massive wood entry doors to the house swung open and a bunch of little children came running out, laughing and giggling.

In the background, Maggie could see one young woman walking toward Juliann. "*Hola*, Sofia. How did the day go?"

Sofia's face lit up with a big smile. "These little ones always keep me busy. Today it was all about the chalk." She pointed her finger at all the funny drawings all over the cement driveway.

Maggie never noticed the chalk etchings as she walked across the area. Now, all she could do was look down at the imaginative artwork and laugh. Nothing made any sense, it all looked like a lot of scribbling in different colors. "Well, they must love their chalk, because it is one beautiful picture. Not sure what it is—but it is very colorful!"

Juliann started to laugh. "You mean you can't see the houses, animals, or the people these little ones say they draw? Shame on you. We just might have a Van Gogh or Picasso in this group!"

Maggie pulled her brows together in concentration and said, "You're right! I see it all." Everyone laughed.

The little ones stood in front of Juliann and started to jump up and down. The excitement on their faces was priceless, and Maggie could see that they loved their 'head mistress.' One of the little boys tugged at Juliann's hand over and over, until she bent down and said, "What do you want to tell me, Marco?"

He looked slightly shy when he finally got her full attention and announced, "I went to the bathroom by myself."

Juliann ruffled his short black hair and kissed his cheek. "I'm so proud of you, *hijo*!" The little boy threw his arms around Juliann and gave her the biggest hug. "You are getting to be a big boy now!"

Maggie watched and felt this wonderful tug at her heart. To be loved with such innocence and to have it be unconditional was sometimes beyond her comprehension. Juliann stood up and touched the heads of each child to let them know—she not only could see them, but they needed her touch.

"Okay, let's get the trunk unpacked."

They walked down the stairs and went to the car. Ricardo had taken all the boxes of food and bottled water out and everything was stacked neatly next to the car. Juliann grabbed two cases of water and everyone started picking up the rest of the boxes. Even Maggie lent her hands carrying a twenty-five pound bag of rice. "Follow me, Maggie."

They slowly walked along a cement path between the tall wall and large building until they got to the back. Maggie noticed there were two smaller buildings and a much smaller storage structure made of cinderblocks. On the front of the storage structure there was a steel door that was double padlocked. They all stopped and Juliann took a key out of her pocket and unlocked the padlocks. Sofia kept the children outside, playing with a stray cat that had wandered into the yard area. Juliann opened the door and turned on a light bulb that was hanging from the ceiling on a wire that looked like an ordinary extension cord. It barely lit the room enough for them to be able to bring the packages inside. Maggie looked around and spotted an old refrigerator tucked in the corner, along with a white oblong freezer. There were strong steel shelving units that were used to store the boxed foods. Everything was stacked neatly, and it all basically consisted of just staples like rice, beans, flour, corn meal, canned vegetables, and canned fruit. There wasn't anything that Maggie could actually call child-type snacks that filled her favorite markets as she walked down the aisles. There was nothing that was wasteful in that shed, either. Juliann began to put away the groceries. When Juliann opened the refrigerator, it was filled with milk, stacks of egg cartons, and perishable vegetables. The freezer had an icemaker in it and bags filled with ice. In the corner was frozen meat and chicken.

When everything was neatly put away and they walked out, Juliann replaced the padlocks.

Maggie inquired, "Is this where you store all the food? How come not the house?"

"We had a problem a few times with staff and some of the children stealing it, so we thought this was a great solution. I have the keys and I have a set hidden away. We keep some supplies in the house, but this is our main storage area."

"Okay, now I get it." Maggie nodded her head with the reasoning behind the outside storage.

Juliann smiled. "I don't even know if I get it! I don't know what it feels like deep in the pit of your stomach when hunger eats away at you. I just know that I have to help these children. They didn't ask to come into this world."

Maggie frowned. "I know that nauseous feeling of hunger. I remember when I was living with my mother. Most of the time, we didn't have food. My mother used to steal it from stores. She used me, hiding it under my heavy coat."

"That sounds like a tough beginning in life, Maggie."

"Hunger for a child is difficult. Stealing is part of the need."

"The staff that we found stealing was just giving it to their street friends. It was a tough call, but with limited funds, we have to hold on to what we have for the children here. The children within the house, on the other hand, were hording it out of fear that if anything happened, they would at least have food! Sometimes it's a vicious circle. Come on, let's go inside and I'll show you around and to our room—you'll be sharing with me."

The children followed. She opened the screen door, and then unlocked the thick wood door at the back of the house. When Maggie walked in, she was standing in the middle of the kitchen. It was clean and organized, but without any kind of style. It was not pretentious like the kitchens Maggie was used to, nor would it make it into her favorite, *Interior Digest Magazine.* There were used and chipped Formica countertops instead of granite or tile. The cabinets were old and looked like they had been painted many times over. The stove and refrigerator were old and looked well-used. There were two thick plywood tabletops attached to four-by-four wooden legs. The chairs nestled around the table looked to be from a banquet hall. Maggie slowly turned in a circle. Then she realized that all-in-all it was clean and bright with four big windows. It was a decent kitchen that was probably better than most of the houses Maggie had seen as they drove down the streets. And better than on the streets where these children used to live.

They left the kitchen and entered a large room that looked like a study hall with four couches. None of them matched each other, then again, life was not a fashion statement in this part of the world. Furniture was simple, useful, and suited a purpose.

Maggie noticed there were a few overstuffed chairs and a few desks that were placed along the walls. Maggie asked, "Is this where the kids do their schoolwork?"

"Yes and we have a smaller room for the little ones with toys and a VHS player where they get one movie a night. The children love Disney movies—and because everything is now DVD, I can find hundreds of VHS movies really cheap!" Juliann laughed. "The kids don't care about technology and how good the clarity of the movie is, all they want is a captivating movie that keeps their undivided attention." She took Maggie's hand and left the children with Sofia.

They walked through a hall that had four rooms. In three of the rooms, there were three sets of bunk beds. One set on each wall. Under the bottom bunk bed there were three large drawers. That's where they stored their clothes and personal items. At the end of the hall was a bathroom. It was very simple, with a shower, one sink, a toilet, and done all in white tile. Past the bathroom was a large door. When Juliann opened the door, it was another large room with three single beds, a few dressers, and some boxes stacked along the wall.

"Welcome to my room. That messy bed in the corner is mine. The other two belong to my helpers Sofia and Chica." She sat down on her bed and Maggie joined her. "We have the smallest room in the house because the younger ones need more care. The two smaller buildings in the back have one large room and a bathroom. Each of those house eight older children and Ricardo sleeps on the floor in one of those rooms. I have seventeen children outside the house and twenty inside. So, we are running at full capacity. I would love to build up and put another floor upstairs for another twenty children. That would be in a perfect world, of course!"

"In a not-so-perfect world, at least you have saved the ones you have!" Maggie stated.

"Well, my friend, the best I can offer you is Sofia's bed. She'll sleep with one of the little ones."

"Don't be silly. I can sleep on the couch in the big room."

"We know this isn't the Ritz-Carlton. But it's pretty damn close to these children, who work hard at studying because they were given one chance and they don't want to blow it!"

Suddenly, the front door opened and the entire house was bursting with noise. Voices, laughter, singing, and typical childish noises filled the house. Maggie smiled and got up to look. She slowly walked down the hall and back into the big room. All the older ones were home from school. Lots and lots of kids were everywhere. A young girl walked up to Maggie and held out her hand. "Hola, I'm Chica."

Maggie smiled and extended her hand. "Hello, Chica, nice to meet you, I'm Maggie."

"Juliann said you would be visiting with us for a few days. I've heard a lot about you. You are so lucky. I wish I could live in the United States. Maybe someday if I work hard enough, my dream will come true!"

"I hear you are a tremendous help to Juliann and how wonderful you are with the little ones."

Chica blushed. "Gracias." She looked around at all the restless children, and said, "I need to go start dinner. We can talk later."

Maggie turned around to go look for Juliann, but when she turned around, she bumped right into her. She had been standing behind Maggie the whole time. "Come, let's go help Chica. Feeding a lot of hungry children takes a village." Juliann laughed.

Dinner consisted of rice, a creamy sauce with vegetables and some kind of meat it in. Maggie didn't dare ask what kind of meat it was, rumors online had listed a few domestic animals that were considered pets in the U.S. and consumed in third-world countries. Then of course, there were homemade tortillas. You scooped up some rice, added the saucy mixture and ate it like a small burrito. It actually wasn't that bad, Maggie thought. But she definitely didn't want it as a staple in her culinary world unless she knew it was chicken or beef.

When dinner was over, each child washed their own cup and plate and placed them in a neat stack on the counter. They did the same with their utensils, and placed them in a drawer. It was an interesting concept that worked perfectly in this group house. All except for the little ones. Sofia did their dishes. Each young child stood in line next to her and, one-by-one, they handed her their plates, and looked so proud when they did. Maggie's heart did a flip-flop as she observed them. They were all little helpers who only wanted to please and tried so hard at doing so.

That evening, some of the children retired to their bedrooms, others hung in the large room and studied. The little ones got to pick out a bedtime movie and they sat in one of the bedrooms, watching with their eyes wide open, and completely transfixed with each word. Part of the evening, Maggie snuggled on the bed with little Elena. Juan and Marco lay on a bed giggling, and playing with pretend swords. Gitana fell asleep early, and Luz's eyes were glued to the movie. Luz was the shy one that distanced herself from the others.

Juliann sat in the kitchen with Ricardo, Sofia, and Chica, going over the next day's menu, chores, and other things that needed discussion. When they were done, the little ones were put to sleep by Chica and Sofia. Juliann found Maggie talking to one of the older children on the couch. Maggie saw Juliann come out of the kitchen. With two cups of coffee in her hands, Maggie followed Juliann out to the porch. They sat down on one of the steps. The moon was shining high in the sky and the stars were brighter than Maggie had ever seen.

Maggie looked up in the sky. "What a beautiful evening. Look at those stars."

Juliann smiled. "They do have beautiful stars here, but not as nice as Mexico. I really enjoyed my time there. It was a lot more peaceful and comfortable than I had imagined."

"Then why didn't you stay? Why did you come here? Don't you ever want to settle down in one place? Or have a relationship?"

Juliann inhaled and exhaled slowly. "At one time I had those dreams, but my fiancé was kidnapped and killed by the rebels. It was horrible and I swore I would never invest my heart into something that would hurt so much again."

Maggie patted her hand. "I said the same thing, and lived reclusively for years. When I first met Damon, I thought he was a jerk. I had never met someone so arrogant." Maggie smirked. "I don't know why I hired him to find my friends that day he barged into my office. He did a great job and he just decided to hang around for a few years. I think he was waiting to see how long it would take for the 'ice maiden' to melt."

"Well, patience is a virtue, and I see the pirate got his maiden," she chuckled.

"It was terrifying, and we did this 'passive-aggressive' dance. He moved forward, and I moved back. Then he moved back, and I stepped forward. Until one day he took the bull by the horns, and just walked into my office and laid his heart on my desk. I couldn't breathe. I was so scared. But he promised we would go slowly and we did." Maggie turned, and Juliann noticed the tears in her eyes.

"I was there once, Maggie, and lost it. Now, I'm just a wanderer," she said sadly.

"You sound like Randolph. He's never in one place for too long. Although he loves his ranch and hacienda, he is constantly on the move. I'm hoping the 'Casa' will get him to settle down."

Juliann smiled, "Yes, Randolph and I are a lot alike. He's a wonderful friend. And I like that he is loyal to those he loves, and he never flaunts what he has. What he has, he puts to valuable use of others in need." Juliann looked up at the sky. Her face had a wistful look on it. "Yes, he is an interesting man."

Maggie noticed the look but did not say anything. "What's on the agenda tomorrow?"

"Well, we have the large school bus." She pointed. "And the small VW bus, and that small car we used from the airport. I'm taking the children to school in the big bus. Chica is going into town for our mail and some supplies. And I thought you might want to stick around, for the morning, with Sofia and the little ones. Is that okay?" Juliann asked. Then she added, "You will get to see how wonderful Sofia is with the little ones."

"That's fine with me."

"I thought, later, we might take the little ones to the beach. It's only a few miles from here, and the older ones will be in school until we pick them up at five." She stood up and took Maggie's hand and pulled her up. Leisurely, they walked back into the house and down the hall to their room. Maggie put on a pair of sweatpants and a T-shirt.

They both were sitting on the bed when, unexpectedly, it began to shake slightly.

Maggie looked surprised. "What was that?"

Juliann smiled. "Oh, just a little earthquake or tremor. We have those occasionally. It's a way of life around here."

Maggie nodded, but suddenly her mind went off into a thousand different directions. *She had lived through the large earthquakes in California and this made her nervous!*

CHAPTER 14

Maggie woke up when she heard the alarm go off at 5:30 a.m. Chica and Juliann quietly got up and went into the bathroom before the kids took it over. Maggie put on her robe and started to walk down the hall to the kitchen. On the way, she noticed the little ones doors were shut so that they could sleep in. When she got to the kitchen, Chica had already put on a large pot of coffee. Sofia was beginning to make eggs in three large frying pans on the stove. She added chilies and tomatoes into the scramble. Chica was heating up the leftover tortillas, and for those who didn't want scrambled eggs, she was stirring a pot of oatmeal.

Maggie poured a cup of coffee and sat down at the table. "You girls are amazing. Do you pack their lunches also?"

They both smiled. Chica said, "No, they get a lunch at school."

Juliann walked into the kitchen, poured herself a cup of coffee, and sat down next to Maggie as Chica placed a tablecloth on each table. "We don't want to sit here when the kids roll in.

Trust me! They are a noisy bunch. We will be gone soon and you will have a few hours with peace and quiet. Grab a plate of food, and your coffee, and we'll sit on the front porch."

Maggie got up and followed Juliann to the stove and then out the door. They sat down and began to watch the sunrise. "It's a lovely day out," Maggie said, sipping her coffee. She pulled her cellphone out of her pocket and looked at the bars. "I don't get reception out this way but just a few minutes a day. I've been texting Damon and I don't know if he even gets those."

"Yeah, this part of the world doesn't have a lot of towers. When I go into town to drop the children off, you want me to call him or text him anything?" Juliann asked.

"Just let him know I'm really enjoying myself and that I'm bringing some little ones home with me!" Maggie began to giggle.

Maggie sat on the porch, sipping her second cup of coffee, and watched Juliann pack the large, yellow school bus with all the children. Ricardo sat in the driver's seat, and Juliann came over to where Maggie was sitting. "See you soon, I'll be back before noon and we'll take the kids to the beach. Ricardo will stay in town with the bus. He makes extra money for our orphanage by becoming a bus system and transporting people around the town. Chica will pick me up in the car. If for any reason you need the VW bus, Sofia knows where the keys are."

Maggie got up and hugged Juliann. "See you soon!"

Juliann bounced down the stairs and waved goodbye.

Sofia and Maggie cleaned the rest of the kitchen. The little ones were waiting patiently, in their rooms, for Sofia to come and get them for breakfast. The routine was always to wait for the older ones to leave for school. This made it less chaotic and a lot easier for the older ones without the little ones following them around. The children sat down to the table and ate their oatmeal. Then they each received a buttered tortilla and a glass of milk. Once they were done, they stood in line with their plates for Sofia. When the kitchen was completely cleaned, Sofia took them into their rooms and picked out the clothes they were going to wear for the day. Each child slowly and meticulously put on their own clothes, except for Marco. He was having a tough time so Maggie stepped in to help. With a shyness that made him so adorable, Maggie bent over and gave him a big hug when they were done.

Maggie walked down the hall to her room and got dressed in some jeans and a lightweight sweater. The sun was out, but it was still brisk enough in the morning that a heavier garment would keep her warm. She combed her hair, brushed her teeth, and then went in search of Sofia. She found Sofia and the children outside playing in the back courtyard. They were all neatly sitting on the ground, in a big circle, rolling a ball to each other. Maggie was smiling at the children as she came down the stairs. Without warning, the ground began to rumble and the earth began to shake, and then it was over. Alarmed, she immediately looked over at Sofia; and nothing was registered on her face that acknowledged the earthquake.

Maggie recalled the big one in California. How could she forget? She was in her early twenties and had never been through any major disasters before. California really didn't have tornados, heavy flooding, whiteout blizzards, or hurricanes. She soon learned that it had major earthquakes. On Monday morning, January 17, 1994, at 4:31 a.m.; she had just moved into her new apartment, in Santa Monica the year before, after she graduated college. Her writing career had just taken off, and her first book was a huge success. She had spent the evening before with dear friends, Patricia Cohen and her husband Thomas. He had been her English teacher, at UCLA, and his wife was a literary agent. Patricia had taken Maggie under her wing and was very instrumental in starting Maggie's successful writing career. Maggie had taken a part-time job with Patricia at her literary agency. Within that year, Patricia had not only realized what a talented writer Maggie was, she also was influential in soliciting her book to a well-known publishing house to pick her up as a client.

Maggie drove home from Patricia's that night and was extremely tired. When that earthquake hit the next morning, Maggie was unprepared and had no clue as to what was going on. Her building shook so fiercely that her walls began to crack, and her dishes all fell out of the cabinets. Her television fell off the dresser, and she barely made it out of the apartment when the second aftershock hit again. Crying and hysterical, Maggie stood in the middle of her street with all her neighbors. Everyone was shocked and confused as to what was really going on, and if they were going to survive it. Maggie, at one point, thought it was the end of the earth and that the ground was going to open up and swallow her, along with everyone else. Finally, after huddling with her neighbors for an hour, she ran back into her apartment, packed some needed clothes, and went to Patricia's house. She was thankful that her car was parked on the street and not in the underground parking. Her neighbors were angry and scared and could not get their cars out of the underground parking area for fear of the apartment building collapsing. Those gates had sustained damage and would not open in spite of everyone who tried.

The earthquake had a 'strong' moment magnitude of 6.7, but the ground acceleration was of the highest ever instrumentally recorded in an urban area in North America. The strong ground motion was felt as far away as Las Vegas, Nevada—about two hundred and twenty miles from the epicenter. The epicenter of the earthquake struck in the San Fernando Valley, about twenty miles northwest of downtown Los Angeles. Santa Monica was just another few miles away. As Maggie drove through those areas on her way to Patricia's house, the damage she witnessed almost reminded her of the town she was in now. That morning, Maggie couldn't believe her eyes as the ground began to spout water from broken mains, and small fires exploded in some of the houses from broken gas lines. Devastation and destruction was everywhere and there was no way out. The Santa Monica freeway had collapsed and they would not let anyone near it. The surface streets were filled with panicked people as everyone tried to get out for fear of more fires and more earthquakes. Maggie had never been so scared in her entire life. And yet, Sofia did not flinch with the shake of the earth a few minutes ago.

Maggie stood there watching the children roll the ball. Then, all of a sudden it happened again—only this time it was shaking so hard the walls surrounding the building began to crack and tumble. This time Sofia got up and they gathered the children in the middle of the courtyard away from the shaking buildings. The shaking began to get violent and the buildings surrounding them began to tumble. Sofia screamed and held on to the children, who were crying now.

Maggie grabbed ahold of Sofia and screamed, "Where are the keys to the VW and the food shed? We need to get these children out of here NOW! And we need to pack some stuff in case we can't get back in. I'm deathly afraid that since we are only three miles from the ocean, there could be a tsunami on its way. We need to get to higher ground!" Maggie's panic was surreal. But her mind knew exactly what needed to be done.

When the shaking stopped, Sofia ran up the stairs that had nearly separated completely from the house. She jumped over the twelve inch separation and into the house and disappeared for what felt like a lifetime to Maggie. She came out carrying some things and the keys. The shaking began again...and again, it was just as violent. Back and forth, back and forth, with an increasing rumble; it sounded like gods under the earth were angry. Sofia went to the shed and opened the padlocked door. Maggie went in and started grabbing cases of bottled water, boxes of cereal, oatmeal, rice, macaroni, and anything easy they could make to keep the children from starving. Bags of ice were placed in two large coolers that were stacked in the corner. Sofia had calmed the children down, and now they were just sitting on the cement and waiting. Parts of the walls from the two smaller buildings had tumbled down. Maggie sidestepped the walls and climbed into one of the rooms. As she was doing that, Sofia padlocked the shed again so that nobody else could come and steal their remaining food and water.

She handed some pillows and blankets to Sofia and said, "Let's get the hell out of here. One more tumbler like the last one and it will bring all this down. You watch the kids, and I'll start carrying the stuff to the front and only hope we can pack it and get the hell out of here!"

"Let me help, too. The children will listen to me and they will stay in a little circle; we can move this more quickly with the two of us. I'm afraid of a tsunami, also. I know of this great secluded area above in the mountains that we can go, just in case."

Sofia smiled at the children to let them know she was okay and to make them feel like everything was going to be fine. "I want you to hold hands and stay in a little circle. Maggie and I are now going to pack the car for a little trip to the mountains. We are going to have fun today, but I need you to sit here and hold hands. Okay?" The children nodded and Sofia tapped each of their heads.

Maggie and Sofia took three trips, back and forth, to the little VW van until it was packed. They took out the two bench seats and made a place for all the little ones to sit on the floor. There was no need to buckle them in and Maggie didn't think it was a good idea for their little eyes to see all the destruction as they drove to their destination. Sofia came back and got the children and they followed her quietly and got into the van.

Maggie and Sofia were standing outside of the van when Maggie asked, "Do you know how to drive this van? I don't know how to drive stick, but if I have to learn today, I don't have a problem with that."

The ground started to shake again and it seemed to Maggie like it was harder than the last one a few minutes before. The van started to sway and Sofia and Maggie silently held on to the open sliding door on the side to keep from falling on the ground. When it finally stopped they both heaved a heavy sigh of relief.

Sofia looked directly at Maggie with slight panic in her face. "I drive it all the time and I know my way around all over. So, let me drive and I promise we will get there safely. But first I have to run back again and get a can of gas. I'll be right back." Sofia took off in a run and disappeared. When she came back around the corner, she was carrying a five-gallon, bright red gas can.

Sofia tied it in the back of the van and made sure it was securely in place. Maggie could tell she had done that before. It was a wise decision to take that and she appreciated Sofia's knowledge of everything to help them survive.

Maggie looked at Sofia. "Is there anything else you think we might need for a few nights if we have to stay in the mountains?"

Sofia thought again and said, "Give me another minute." She left again, and came back within a few minutes. In her arms she was carrying a large box. She placed it in the van and ran toward the gate and took out the key and unlocked it. "Get in, Maggie."

Maggie got in the passenger's side and waited for Sofia to come back. Sofia opened the door and jumped into the van. She turned to the children and said, "I'm so proud of you, *hijos*, you're being so good for Maggie and me. We are going to have fun. It will only take us a little while to get there."

A little voice squeaked out, "Where are we going?" Juan asked.

Elena spoke up, "Juan, didn't you hear Miss Sofia? She told us to be quiet."

Juan whispered, "Okay...."

Sofia started to back out and down the short driveway. The devastation they both witnessed was overwhelming and terrifying at the same time. Most of the buildings looked like they had been bombed. Some of them were flattened, others were precariously leaning and the next big shake would topple the rest. Others were still intact. The street was lined with debris and people were sitting, standing, and walking everywhere. Everyone looked to be in shock and those who weren't were sobbing and screaming. Those painful sounds could be heard passing through the van. Maggie gripped her waist as a powerful agony ripped through her for the loss she was witnessing.

People were hysterical as they dug into the rubble looking for whatever they could find. Maggie could only assume they were looking for family or friends, buried alive. Nothing looked good and everything was beyond comprehensible. Sofia got out of the car and locked the gate. She didn't want anyone trespassing or invading their home. Scavengers were the biggest fear after watching what was going on in this small town. Despite the initial earthquake and the aftershocks, their buildings did not look as bad as the ones on the streets. Maggie was thankful and prayed that Juliann and the others had made it through and that eventually they would all be together again. Right now, her only concern was getting the children to a safe place and higher ground. She had read a lot and watched on television the tsunami that hit Japan and the damage it caused in a matter of minutes. There was no fighting the ravaging water and the power it possessed. She watched it completely flatten an area in seconds. These little ones would not have a chance at all, and neither would she and Sofia.

Sofia hopped back into the van and very slowly started to drive down the rubble-filled streets. The dust from the collapse of the buildings was like looking into a dense fog. It was thick and filled with all kinds of particles that could destroy the lungs if breathed for a lengthy period of time. It was beginning to build on the windshield and after a few blocks, Sofia had to get out of the car and wipe it off. At that moment, another aftershock hit. Sofia and Maggie sat in the van as it swayed back and forth, nearly tipping over twice. The little ones started to cry and Maggie jumped into the back to calm them down.

"Hey, guys, let's pretend we're on a merry-go-round ride." They looked at her with confusion in their eyes. Maggie had to think of something else. These children had probably never seen a merry-go-round or carnival ride, and almost certainly had never even heard of Disneyland.

Sofia smiled at Maggie. "They don't know what a merry-go-round is." She turned toward the kids and said, "Let's pretend that someone is shaking us in an empty box. Remember when we used to do that? I would have you close your eyes and I would shake the box? It was so much fun, we laughed."

The little ones began to cheer and laugh. "That was fun, Miss Sofia," Luz said.

"Yeah...." Marco whispered.

Sofia started to drive down the street when the shaking had stopped. One or two houses were on fire from broken gas lines and black smoke streamed from them. Twice, Sofia had to stop and they got out of the car to move some larger pieces of wood and debris, to make a path for the van to get through. There were only a few cars that were moving on the street and at times the pathway was only big enough for one. Turns were taken as people tried to leave the town. Many cars littered the street, incapable of moving because of the damage on and around them.

Along with all the other loss, parts of the street had buckled and other parts had cracks a foot wide. Sofia did a great job in finding her way slowly out of town and once they were on the main highway, they were not sure if it was the safest place to be. The highway was buckled and the road broken with jutting pavement sticking up from the earth. Other cars were having a horrible time getting around the wreckage.

"Is there another way we can go?" Maggie asked.

"We can try some of the winding roads leading up to the mountains, but I don't know if there were any landslides. I've seen those before during real rainy weather. Let's go see, okay?"

"Sure, what have we got to lose? I'm just afraid that this highway might have some sink holes and then we're in trouble! Besides, people are really reckless and driving like maniacs."

The van started to shake again, and Maggie was sure this road was going to open up and swallow them whole....

CHAPTER 15

"**W**HAT DO YOU FUCKING MEAN THERE WAS AN 8.2 earthquake in Honduras a few miles from the orphanage?" Damon yelled into his phone. He was sitting in a restaurant and, immediately, he signaled the waiter and pointed, signaling that he needed to leave. As quickly as he could, he ran outside.

"Calm down, Damon. There's nothing we can do to change things. We have to gather our senses and pull it together and find a way to contact them!" Randolph yelled back.

"Where are you, Randolph, Los Angeles or Mexico?"

"I'm in New York. I'm on my way home as soon as they refuel the plane. Where are you?" he asked.

"I'm in fucking Argentina. Let me see if there are any flights going in or out of Honduras. I'll call you back."

Randolph hung up the phone. He was terrified something had happened to Maggie. He tried every number he could and he couldn't get a hold of anyone. The lines were all dead and it was a constant busy signal. He tried Juliann again. Nothing! He began to pace back and forth. What if something happened to Maggie? What was he going to say to Elizabeth and Lucy? Why the hell did he let her go? He knew that they had been having tremors for the past year, but nobody thought anything about it. It had become the way of life in that area. He sat down and turned on CNN news; and right there in front of his eyes was an emergency station break, "Mass Destruction in Honduras, Guatemala, and Belize!"

The reporter was standing in front of the camera, with pictures flashing as he announced, "The earthquake decimated Puerto Cortés and all the way along the coast to Le Ceiba. Guatemala, Belize, northern Nicaragua, and Honduras took the blunt of the earthquake and there were a few tidal waves along the coast that had wiped out part of the city of Puerto Cortés. What they were watching for now was a large tsunami building up and heading for the Isle of Roatán, directly across the bay from Honduras."

Randolph clinched his hands together and was taking deep breaths. He had to find a way to get in touch with Maggie and Juliann. He needed to get into Honduras to look for them and make sure they had survived. The death toll was up to ninety-two people, so far, and he feared the worst was to come. He called a friend at the White House and asked for some help. He wanted to talk to the embassy there and see if they would let him fly in or just cross over one of the borders. Sometimes they closed off the borders. If he could fly into Belize and drive over the border, it would only take a few hours to get to the orphanage, providing the roads weren't too damaged to use or the pandemonium wasn't too extreme. Most of the time when a disaster hit in a country, the first thing they did was close off the airports and the borders. The only planes allowed to fly in were for disaster relief and the military.

A small, poor country like Honduras didn't have a huge military; and something like this happening could create uncontrollable chaos. Randolph heard the engines roar to life and he was unsure as to where he was going to fly. He was waiting for Damon to call. Damon was in Argentina, which was just as far from Honduras as New York. They were both about four thousand miles away, which was an eight-hour flight nonstop.

"Eight fucking hours!" Randolph screamed out loud as he kicked a small trashcan across the plane.

His phone rang. "Hello!" he barked into the phone.

"They aren't letting anyone fucking fly into Honduras right now. The government is run by a bunch of lunatics, and they stopped domestic flights until the aftershocks calm down. Seems they had the big one, and now the aftershocks are almost as bad." Damon said. He took a sip of the bottle of water he had in his car.

"I can't stay in New York knowing Maggie and Juliann are over there with thirty children. God only knows what that damn old house looks like or if it is still standing. Or if it came down with the kids in it. They said that the earthquake was at 9:42 a.m. That means Juliann had just dropped the kids off at school and she must be in the bus in the next city. That leaves Maggie either with her, or she stayed home with the little ones. There's no cell reception now and I don't know if the towers were damaged or they just cut it off. Have you heard anything? Now what the hell do we do?" Randolph took a sip of his glass of whisky.

"I wish we could fly into Ramón Villeda Morales International Airport. It's a little over fifty miles if we have to drive to their city. I'm not sure if that airport is closed down, but it's fairly close to the epicenter. We could give it a shot. If we can both get into that airport, I'd like to go into the country in search of them, together." Damon's stress showed deep in his voice.

"Okay, call me back in five minutes. Let me see what I can do about getting into Guatemala. Hang tight, Damon, we will find a way into Honduras. I think they are both very resourceful ladies."

"Juliann is, I'm not so sure about Maggie." He sighed.

Damon sat in his car and stared at his phone. He had never felt so vulnerable in his life. He had never let anyone get this close to him and now he knew why. He was terrified, for the first time in his life, over losing a woman who had crawled under his skin and into his heart. He was willing to give up just about anything to make sure she got home safely. He didn't care what it took; he was determined to bring her home. *If she is dead, how am I going to make it through, knowing I had let her get on that flight to Honduras? I should have put my foot down and stopped her, knowing how dangerous it was from the beginning.* Damon was fighting with himself and he was losing that battle.

Damon's phone rang. "Okay...I got you on a flight leaving Argentina in forty minutes. I'm fueled up and taking off to fly into Mundo Maya International. Once we get there, I'm picking you up, along with some supplies, so that we can justifiably fly into Ramón Villeda Morales International Airport in San Pedro Sula. They are closed to commercial, but are open for planes coming in with supplies. I had to pull a lot of strings to get this done. It's the closest to Puerto Cortés—Thank God! Get it together, and get as much sleep as you can, because the next forty-eight hours are going to be hell on wheels!"

"Thanks, Randolph. How did you do that?"

Randolph was silent for a few seconds and then he said, "It doesn't matter—I just did it."

"I owe you...."

CHAPTER 16

JULIANN AND RICARDO HAD JUST DROPPED OFF THE students at the school. With smiling faces, and the excitement to actually go to school and learn, they couldn't wait to get off the bus and go to their classes. They were all dressed in their required uniforms and carrying their books as they stepped off the bus and onto the curb. With five minutes left before the bell rang, they waved goodbye and disappeared into the century-old Catholic school. Juliann had always loved this old part of town that reminded her of old Europe and the Catholic cathedrals.

The unique mixture of buildings in this old city was reminiscent of old Spanish colonial architecture features, strong Native American influences combined with Moorish, Gothic, and Baroque designs. Some of the buildings were three hundred and fifty years old (repaired over the years) and displayed the history of Honduran culture with Mayan and other pre-Columbian architecture. The problem was that during the last large earthquakes and minor aftershocks, most had sustained substantial damage and their foundations were not stable or solid. Most had come down already, and the ones that were left needed extensive renovations to make them completely safe.

The school was housed in an old church that was renovated for the children in the area. It was very imposing to look at, with the three wide steps leading up to the doors. The columns in the front and the massive wooden doors were hundreds of years old. The two stained-glass windows next to the door were beautifully crafted by locals in the area over a hundred years before. The floors were polished stone that kept the building cooler than most. It had a main lobby with a high ceiling. A door opened to the larger room where the congregation would spend most of their time praying. It was cleared of all the pews and was now a study hall with tables and chairs. On each side of the large room, there were three doors that belonged to smaller rooms that had been refurbished into classrooms. The six rooms were filled with children whose parents could afford a small pittance to get their children educated. The children from 'My House' were lucky to get contributors from the United States to enable them to go to school.

It had government subsidized teachers and very little in way of being educationally updated. They used outdated books, had little in the way of supplies, and only two working computers. The teachers were incredible and Juliann loved each and every one. They loved the children and did everything they could to keep their education going. Two of them were young missionaries, who fell in love with the town, and the children, so much that they had decided to stay in Honduras. Juliann spent many days in that old church with the children and the teachers. Their education was very important to her. She wanted them to be the first in their families to succeed. For those off the streets, she wanted them to see there was always hope.

Ricardo sat there for a few minutes while Juliann went over her day's schedule. When she finally looked up, she told him to go to the plaza in town and she'd meet Chica there.

He started the bus and headed down towards the center of town. He parked along the curb and they both waited for Chica. As always, Chica was late. They continued to wait another twenty minutes, until Juliann looked at her watch and said, "I'm not waiting much longer…damn it!"

Juliann tapped Ricardo on the shoulder. He was sitting back in the seat with his eyes closed. "If she's not here in five minutes, we'll take off and you can take me home. This really annoys me when she's—" Her words were cut off when the bus began to sway back and forth and a deep rumble filled the air. "What the hell!"

Everything was shaking with a violent strength that began to scare Juliann and made Ricardo sit straight up in his seat. The violence got much stronger, and they both ran outside of the bus and stood in the middle of the park where nothing could harm them, unless the ground opened and swallowed them up. The buildings around them began to break apart and tumble as if someone was knocking them down with a wrecking ball. Pieces of cement and debris were flying everywhere. People were coming out of their homes and businesses screaming and yelling, in horror, as they watched around them. Others, riveted in shock, were just standing there dazed and confused. Juliann watched, in shock, as part of a building fell on an older woman, probably crushing her to death instantly. Ricardo stood there mesmerized by the whole scene as the shaking continued to ravage such destruction in the small, old town. Within the space of only one minute, they watched as this once beautiful town was reduced to rubble.

He turned toward Juliann and she could see tremendous pain displayed on his face. Tears were rolling down his cheeks when he sadly said, "I'm not sure what to do or how bad it's going to get?"

Juliann was forced to make a split decision. "Get in the bus. This will protect us from the tumbling buildings. Let's see if we can drive down the street to the school. I'm terrified that place has come down, too! I want to get the children." The shaking stopped for a few minutes as they slowly and meticulously began to maneuver around all the rubble that had landed in the streets. Part of the street had buckled, but they continued to drive around it. People had their hands out, begging to get on the bus. Juliann locked the door for fear someone might do something to hurt them. When they just about reached the school, the shaking began again, this time even stronger. Juliann watched, in panic, as the school building tumbled over onto the street. Without as much as a thought, she ran out of the bus and wildly began to look for a small crack or hole in the walls so she could get into the school to find the children.

Ricardo followed her. She managed to kick in a beautiful stained-glass window that was still intact. Bending down, she picked up a large rock and began to knock some of the glass off along the edge, then she slipped her leg over and climbed in. Ricardo followed.

Once inside, they tried to climb over parts of walls and ceilings that came down, but they were completely blocked off from the rest of the building. Children's screams could be heard from everywhere as the shaking began again. Juliann recognized some of them; and the pain of hearing those wails made her climb even higher, but her way was obstructed into the large room. The shaking subsided again, leaving her a chance to calm down and figure out how she was going to get to the kids.

She knew some were alive, so she backed out slowly and said to Ricardo, "Let's go around to the sides of the building to see if we can get in that way."

He nodded and followed her back out the window she had just crawled through. As she was coming down the stairs, she started to scream for help. "Please come help us get the children out of here!" she begged. She kept screaming even as she was running toward the back of the building.

A few men who were working and helping others came running over and followed her along the side of the building. Nothing looked safe. Some of the walls had come down and the rest had tremendous cracks running through them. She found a door that still looked pretty solid around the frame. She tried to get it open, but it was jammed. Ricardo came over and started kicking it in, but it didn't budge. Suddenly, two men came over with a large piece of wood and began to swing it back and forth, trying to dislodge the door. On the forth try, the door shattered into pieces and off of its hinges.

Juliann walked through the door, but Ricardo stopped her. "Let me go in and look around first."

The sound of crying children could be heard everywhere. It was breaking Juliann's heart, because she knew what she was going to be looking at. *Why did God do this to innocent children?* she asked herself. *They just began to live. Take the old people, if You must, who have enjoyed and are ready to go. Don't take the children! Not a precious, innocent child!*

Ricardo came out carrying a young boy. "There are more in there." He lowered his voice and grabbed her arm. "Please wait until we get most of them out..." he paused, "...before we cry for the ones we lost."

Juliann looked into his eyes. "That bad?"

He closed his eyes and nodded, hurt etched, starkly, across his face.

Juliann went through the door and what her eyes saw nearly brought her to her knees. This one room was in ruins. The walls had fallen on the children who were under their desks. Many were crushed and Juliann knew she couldn't help some of them—they were dead. She had seen this before in Haiti; and it drudged up a past she had hoped to forget. One by one, they brought out the children. Some alive and broken—others dead. Juliann was a doctor, and yet, she was not immune to death when she was forced to watch it. She got down next to the ones who were alive, some barely hanging on.

She yelled, "Ricardo, pull off some of the clothes from the dead. I need tourniquets right now to stop the flow of blood from their wounds. I need strips of cloth."

Ricardo and the men carefully took only little scraps of the torn dresses and ripped shirts. Then they went back into the building and slowly started bringing more out. Ricardo had tears in his eyes as he meticulously and lovingly carried out the ones he had lived with. Gently and carefully, he placed them on the ground and closed their eyes. He took off his shirt and ripped it into pieces and covered each face. There were five dead children, and four who had made it—so far from their home. Juliann didn't want to wait for another aftershock, so she followed Ricardo into the building and started moving the large pieces of debris to get to more children.

For hours they worked—moving stone-by-stone to get into the six rooms filled with children. In the fourth room, Ricardo cleared off a desk after minutes of lifting off the heavy debris. It was the look on his face and the tears in his eyes that Juliann knew something was desperately wrong. Gently, he lifted the desk off of a body. She carefully climbed over parts of the ceiling, and looked down to where Ricardo was standing. Unable to hold it in, she began to cry. Slowly, she sat down and laid her head on the chest of her friend and teacher, and began to sob uncontrollably. Unpredictably, Ricardo and the men moved her aside to pick up the body. Without warning, the building began to shake again. This time the loud rumble from the earth and the moaning of the building blended together…as it began to crumble on top of them....

CHAPTER 17

Sofia TURNED THE VAN AROUND AND HEADED BACK the other way for about a mile. Then she left the highway completely and they started to drive down a bumpy dirt road until she got to another paved lane she'd been looking for. Once they had started driving down that road, everything seemed to look a little better. At least the scenery wasn't sheer destruction. Sluggishly, the van began to climb a winding road that twisted and turned for miles as they gradually climbed into the mountains. There were only a few cars on the same road and all were going up. Nothing was coming down. Once they had to stop as two men got out of their vehicles and starting shoveling and pushing boulders out of the road. One man tied a rope around the boulder and around his trailer hitch on his truck and pulled it off the road.

Maggie had taken her phone out of her purse and tried it again. There had been no phone reception at all since they left the house. A few times she sighed in frustration as she tried to get ahold of Juliann or Damon.

She texted on her cellphone:

'WE HAVE FIVE BABIES. JULIANN?? HEADING TO THE MOUNTAINS.'

"It doesn't look like it went through. Damn it!"

"Sorry, Maggie. This car doesn't have a radio either."

"This is crazy, we don't have any communication with anybody, and we don't really know what is going on around here or anywhere. I know that first earthquake had to be at least an eight and the aftershocks have been in the high sixes or sevens!" Maggie muttered, annoyance apparent in her voice. "The one in Japan, that had that large tsunami, was a nine. I don't know if this was bigger or smaller. But whatever it is, if that shake was from the ocean floor, I'm glad we're up here!!"

"I am too. I'm very glad the windy road put the little ones to sleep. I'm really scared, Maggie."

Maggie patted her shoulder. "Don't be. We will be fine as long as you know where we are and where we are going. Somehow or someway, we will get in touch with someone. I'm worried about if Juliann and the others are okay and whether or not they made it through."

As they traveled up the mountainous road, the forest began to get denser. It was actually beautiful, with lots of trees, thick brush, and vines everywhere. Wild orchids were laced through the trees and attached to the vines, along with other beautiful tropical flowers. Maggie also noticed the different types of wild fruit trees. Lots of mangos and one avocado tree were meshed into the landscape. Parts of the road looked like they had fallen off and it was almost down to just one lane. They followed a car and truck at a distance and were vigilant not to lose sight of what Juliann had said earlier, 'Be careful of nice people, they are not your friends.'

After miles of driving up, they could finally feel the terrain leveling off. "We are almost to this safe spot I had found years ago when I was alone and on the streets. When things became too scary for me, I would come up here for weeks just to be alone. It overlooks the ocean and we will be able to see what is going on in Puerto Cortés and along the beach. There is also a good size creek with a small waterfall," Sofia said, as she concentrated on the road.

"I'm glad you know where you're going. You have helped me so much."

Unexpectedly, the forest began to thin a little and the blue sky was back. Maggie looked at the sun and smiled. "Are we close?"

"*Si.*"

They were both desperately scared and apprehensive as to what they were going to do after finding a safe place to be until the shaking slowed down. It had been years since Maggie had found herself in the middle of a catastrophic situation. She had already lived through the flood at Elizabeth's, but that was more going into a situation with your eyes open and knowing what you needed to do. She had gone to help her friend and had others who knew exactly what to do and how to do it. Randolph and Damon were well organized. She just tagged along to give full support to Elizabeth and William. This was a whole different ball game. She had absolutely no idea what needed to be done or how to do it. She had never been around little children for any length of time, except for Denise and Elizabeth's. Then that was just for a few days, if not hours. Now, she had five very small children and a teenager who probably was barely old enough to drive.

Sofia turned off the mountain highway and drove very carefully down a dirt road for about a half mile. Suddenly, they came to a small, secluded open field that overlooked the city, the bay area, and the complete shoreline below. Maggie was surprised by this little hideaway. It was almost perfect. There were no buildings that could fall on them, no chance of a tsunami reaching them, and it was sheltered enough to keep them safe.

Sofia stopped the car. "Do you think this is okay?" she asked.

Maggie smiled. "I think it's the best protection we could ever have right now. There is no way we can leave the country. We don't have money at our fingertips. And if we can ride out the earthquakes, without them taking down this mountain, we will be fine!"

Sofia grinned. "I took some money that Juliann stashed away in case we needed it."

Maggie bent over and hugged Sofia. "You are such a sweet young girl; you thought of everything and have been such a major help."

Sofia blushed and finally replied, "*Gracias*."

Maggie looked at Sofia and started to get her thoughts organized. "Okay, I say we get this area safe for the kids. We can build a fire to cook. Oh shit...."

"What?" Sofia's eyes opened wide in surprise.

"I don't have anything to start a fire. I should have thought it out better before we left. Damn!"

"Maggie, the box I went back for has a lot of things I threw into it, including a carton of matches. I lived on the streets for a few years, so I kind of grabbed some things we needed," she shyly looked away, exposing her past.

Maggie sighed and then grinned. "I owe you."

"All I want is to keep these little ones safe."

"Well, if I wasn't there, what would have you done?" Maggie asked with curiosity.

"The same thing we are doing now. I would have brought the children to a safe place." She opened the door and said, "Follow me."

Maggie looked surprised at the maturity of this child who thought of everything and put the children's needs in front of her own. She opened the door and slipped off of the seat and onto the ground. She stood there for a moment and Sofia came around and took her hand. She led her to the edge of the forest just before it opened up to the small field. There was a fire pit already made and huge logs from fallen trees moved to make a closed-off area. It was perfect; and Maggie surmised that Sofia had done this years back when she had nowhere else to go. Then they walked to the edge of the ragged cliff. Looking down, they could see the whole city of Puerto Cortés. Maggie was surprised at the size of the city and the enormity of the industrial, fishing, and transportation port.

It didn't resemble any of the smaller towns they had been through. It was more of a vast resort area mixed in with a whole other side filled with cargo and transportation ships. The large pods from the cargo ships looked like they had been tossed around in a hurricane—gathered into large piles. Huge ships were still docked at the port of call and hadn't received too much damage. Some of the smaller recreational fishing and sailboats dotted the water, others had washed ashore. The large hotels along the shoreline were heavily damaged. Cars were stacked in piles along the parking lots. Most of the buildings were destroyed and it was heavily flooded a half-mile in. Large waves continued to creep further and further inland from each aftershock. It was heartbreaking for Maggie, but extremely painful for Sofia. Maggie could see it in her face as a trembling hand reached up and wiped her tears.

She put her arms around Sofia and hugged her. "I'm so sorry. It's very difficult to watch when you've lived here all your life."

She looked at Maggie. "If I don't have My House, where am I going to go? What am I going to do?"

Maggie wiped her tears. "Don't worry about that right now. I know across the continent I have a very upset family who probably is very worried about all of us. So, let's just worry about the children, and hope Juliann and the older children made it out okay!" Maggie felt this need, and so she bent over and kissed Sofia's forehead and hugged her tight once again.

Then she heard a small voice next to her say, "I have to go to the bathroom, Miss Sofia!" Marco was standing there holding his crotch.

"Oh my God!" Maggie said, surprised at seeing him standing there, right next to the cliff area. "Come on, Marco. I don't want you falling off the mountain!" Maggie swung him into her arms and starting walking over to the van that was parked by the forest's edge. Sofia ran ahead and started to gather up the children.

When Maggie got to the car, she said to the bright-eyed children, "Okay, this is going to be a camping trip. We are going to cook over the fire and have a fun afternoon and then tonight we get to sleep in the van and pretend we're camping."

The children looked at her like she was talking a foreign language. "What is camping, Miss Maggie?" Elena asked.

Maggie smiled. "Well, let's see...it's where you take a trip from home and you get to do fun things like cook over a campfire, sleep in the car, and maybe take a hike to the waterfall to get water to cook our dinner tonight. Does that sound like fun?" Maggie asked with enthusiasm. She looked at Sofia. The worried look on her face was still there. "Come on, sweet one, don't worry. You are going to be okay. I will make sure of that!"

Sofia barely cracked a grin. "Okay, Miss Maggie."

Maggie walked over to the van and said, "Let's get out what we need and settle in. Let's give the *hijos* something to snack on. I'm a little hungry, too."

Sofia pulled out the big box and Maggie was surprised. She had packed a few pots and pans; matches; candles; some glassware; some dishes; toilet paper; and other necessitates they needed.

"You did a great job, Sofia. How bright of you to run back and gather these essentials!"

"I knew we needed certain things."

"You said there was a creek with running water, right?"

Sofia nodded.

"I say we give them each a banana and then we take a hike to the creek with the two pots and a large bag. We can gather plenty of old branches for extra firewood, and we can see what's up around here. Could you do me a favor and take Marco, to the bushes, to go to the bathroom?" Maggie smirked.

Sofia took Marco's hand and grinned back. "Sure. Anyone else have *que ir a orinar*?"

Maggie looked confused. "Does that mean 'to go pee'?"

Sofia nodded her head.

Maggie pulled out her phone. She turned it on and there was one bar. Immediately she knew she didn't have enough bars to call, so she typed out a quick text message. 'SOFIA, THE CHILDREN, AND I ARE SAFE IN THE MOUNTAINS.' She hit send and nothing happened. She looked down and the bar was gone, again. Now what was she going to do?

CHAPTER 18

DAMON WAS SITTING IN FIRST CLASS. THE SEVEN-hour flight had taken its toll on his nerves. With all that time to think, he was going crazy with worry. He barely managed to get a few hours of sleep, but he was definitely prepared to go look for the women. When he walked off the plane, the airport was filled with people trying to fly out of Guatemala. The earthquake had hit the northern part of Guatemala and Belize almost as hard as the coast of Honduras. Millions of people were swarming to get out of that area for fear of an even bigger one. Damon looked up and noticed the television. People were standing all around it in hopes of seeing what was going on with the earthquakes. After a moment of watching the worst-of-the-worst, he put on his sunglasses and started to walk forward. Just as he was rounding the seats filled with people, a hand grabbed his shoulder and swung him around. Damon was startled, but when he looked up, his face relaxed and the two men grabbed each other in a tight hug.

Randolph's eyes looked sad and he took a deep breath. "I landed an hour ago, and I have the plane packed with water and medical supplies they wanted shipped into the area. It was the only way the White House would sanction me into going. I'm more than happy to do that; and I offered my plane to the government to fly back for more supplies. Honduras has sustained a lot of damage. Looks like the area where the quake hit the hardest is in complete shambles and dealing with chaos and the inability to get anything done."

Damon clapped his friend on the back and said, "That's not a good thing. I'm really concerned that I haven't heard from Maggie. Have you heard from Juliann?"

Randolph shook his head. "They said the cell towers were down and they're trying desperately to get them back up. My pilot even had a hard time getting communication to land in the airport. That's why they closed it down for a while, along with a few others in the area. They're only giving us a small window of time to fly into San Pedro, Sula, so we need to get to my jet in a hurry!" They both slung their duffle bags over their shoulders and started to run.

Within minutes, they were taxing down a runway with the engines in full throttle. Damon pulled out his phone and tried to text and call again—no signal was found. Randolph did the same and had the pilot even try to get someone to call the number. Nothing worked.

"I bet we're the last flight out of here. Looks like that last aftershock is closing down the airport again. Thank God we got out in time."

They both sat down on the couch and an attendant came over with a tray. Each one took the glass filled with whisky and chugged it down. Damon asked for another shot. Then they both laid on the couch and closed their eyes. The flight was less than an hour and not soon enough for Randolph and Damon to hop off the plane and head toward the terminals. There were very few planes on the runways and it seemed like the baggage handlers were nonexistent. It looked very peaceful and quiet on the outside.

Once they opened the doors into the terminal, it was sheer chaos. People filled the airport in every inch of space. It was like a repeat of Guatemala an hour ago, with the exception that it was three times the pandemonium. People were screaming, and children were crying— everywhere. Their lives were nothing but confusion and the maddening act of having to wait. Randolph looked around with despair and then said to Damon, "Follow me."

Damon held his duffle bag close as they tried to push their way through the crowd and out the exit.

He yelled to Damon, as they tried to get through the mob of people. "I have a car waiting to drive us into the city."

Damon looked at all the distraught looking faces and stopped short. With emotions rising, he turned and grabbed Randolph with a desperate look in his face. "Do you really think we'll find them alive?" He wanted to hear something positive, because nothing but negative had been filling his head since he saw the pictures of all the destruction on television. The commentator had said that the death toll was rising and that whole towns had nearly perished by the third large aftershock. Damon needed to hear something encouraging.

Randolph covered his one hand over Damon's and said, "We are going to find them. And...I swear when we do...Maggie will never leave our sight!"

Damon clipped him on the head with his hand and they both turned with their small duffle bags and continued walking toward the exit. The chaos around them added to their anxiety. Once Damon walked outside, the morning sun hit him in the face like a splash of cold water. He followed Randolph down the walkway and over to a Hummer parked at the curb. Randolph opened the door and grabbed Damon's duffle bag and his own and threw it into the backseat. They both climbed in and the driver quickly took off.

Randolph smiled at Sam. "Damon, this is Sam. He knows his way all around these parts, and I've brought him along to help us. If we are going to find them, he knows every inch of all the cities."

Damon tapped Sam on the shoulder and said, "Thanks. We will need all the help we can get."

Their first destination was the orphanage. The highway was closed because of the buckled pavement and sink holes that had occurred during the last twenty-four hours. "We'll, take main roads to get there, not to worry, mister."

As they left the airport, and traveled down the road, hundreds and hundreds of people, with brown bags and suitcases, filled the sides of the roads. It was pitiful to see these people who had lost everything except for what little they were carrying in their hands or on their backs. Children were crying, and families that had been torn apart during this catastrophe had little left and no place to go. The shelters that were set up were very few and far apart and could not accommodate the exodus of people. Just the looks on their faces showed the defeat they had received at the earthquake's violent destruction of their only place of refuge. Watching them walk toward the airport was a tragic sight for anyone's eyes, let alone Damon and Randolph, who had never dealt with having to find a 'needle in a haystack.'

They traveled down roads, and went through small towns, seeing the same things over and over. Crumpled buildings and crushed spirits lined the streets of these composed and subservient people. They just walked, not knowing what was at the end of the road, or if that road would disappear like everything else, too.

After a long silence, Randolph quietly said, "I've seen this a few times. Every time it gets harder and harder for me to watch. Haiti's quake in 2010 killed three hundred thousand people and left more than a million homeless and without food, water, or shelter. It took months for the government to set up makeshift housing. It destroyed my faith in all our governments as I sat there with Sean Penn, waiting to see what kind of relief those people would get. The same with Indonesia's quake and tsunami that left over three thousand dead and a half-million homeless. Families broken apart, children left homeless, and life meaningless for people who really are very simple and peaceful."

Damon could see that Randolph was having a difficult time dealing with this. Damon didn't know what to do or what to say. Hordes of people were walking down the road with no place to go.

Then Damon said, "I hope Juliann and the children aren't amongst the crowds, walking toward nowhere. I've been trying to figure out where they are going and—" Unexpectedly, his cellphone beeped. That was the first time either one had heard the familiar sound they had anxiously been waiting for.

With the ease and actions of a panther, he slid it out of his shirt pocket and looked. His eyes opened wide and a slight smile filled his face as the breath he was holding was released slowly. Randolph grabbed the phone and looked at the screen. The two messages Maggie had sent almost a day earlier had finally made it to his phone. He sat there with tears welling in his eyes, not knowing what mountains she was in—just knowing she had messaged him, and that she was safe, he could feel his shoulders begin to drop down and relax. The next question he asked himself was…. *Where the hell were Juliann and the rest of the kids?*

CHAPTER 19

MAGGIE WAS SCARED BUT DIDN'T WANT TO SHOW IT to the kids. They were being so good and had no idea what was going on. They thought they were on a camping trip with the school. They had moved the van closer to the trees, at the edge of the tropical forest. They pulled out a large jug and decided to take the children for a walk down to the creek and small waterfall that Sofia had been to before. The children were delightful, Maggie thought, as they walked down the worn path. After a half-mile, they came to the end of the trail. In front of Maggie was a beautiful waterfall crashing into a big pond, and a stream continued on, twisting through the overgrown ground. The children were excited to see the waterfall and wanted to play in the water.

"Not today, guys! It's too late to let you go in."

The children started to get restless and so Maggie sat down with them, while Sofia filled the large jug with water. "We are going to come back tomorrow and play for a long time in the water. Does that sound fun?"

Cheers and laughter filled the small area. Sofia looked up and smiled. She looked tired. Maggie saw her downcast face and stood up and walked over to her. Sofia wrapped her arms around her and laid her head on Maggie's chest. For the first time ever, Maggie listened to Sofia weep. The children looked at Maggie with big round eyes and looks of confusion. Maggie turned to the children and said, "Sofia has had a hard day. I say we help her walk back to camp and we make some dinner for all of us."

Maggie kept her arm around Sofia. "I'm so scared. And I'm afraid for Chica, Juliann, Ricardo, and the kids. I wish I knew where they are and if they are okay. Those three big earthquakes were pretty big and that school is not a safe place."

"I thought we would wait it out here until it stops shaking. Bringing the kids down to a school reduced to rubble is not going to help. If your small town looks anything like the one below, we are all in a big heap of trouble!"

Sofia hiccupped. "I know."

"You lived up here, didn't you?" Maggie questioned.

Sofia nodded. "For over a year."

"Is this a safe place? Do others come up here? Is the waterfall a tourist attraction?"

"No, there are bigger ones about two miles down a small path. Most tourists can only get to them from the other side of the mountain. This place is very private and only an occasional hiker will stop by if they are lost."

"It good to know we won't be bothered, or fearful that someone might want to take our supplies. We must keep the van doors locked."

The children held hands as they walked back down the trail. A few times Maggie and Sofia stopped to pick some ripe mangos off the wild growing trees. Maggie also picked some wild blackberries and put them in small plastic bag she was carrying in her pocket. As they continued to walk, Maggie watched as silent tears slid down Sofia's face.

Maggie slid her arm around Sofia. "You're worried about Juliann and the kids?"

Sofia nodded her head. "And Ricardo...I hope they are okay."

Maggie smiled sadly. She knew what that was like, to lose the only friends you had. She lived in constant fear of losing her best friends when they were in the orphanage together. She constantly worried that someone would adopt them and then she would be all alone. But it never happened. Nobody wanted Maggie, Elizabeth, Lucy, or Randolph. They were too old, and the adoptive parents were only considering the babies.

They finally made it back to camp. Maggie sat down and started playing a game with the children while Sofia got out the supplies to make a simple dinner. First, Sofia made sure all the rocks were in a neat circle big enough to hold a campfire. Then she went to the nearby tropical forest and found some old dried twigs that would serve as the kindling for the fire. Sofia was well-versed in the art of camping and knew all of the 'do's and don'ts'. She went to the van and siphoned half of a cup of gas from the container and walked over to the fire pit. Maggie got the children up and moved them ten feet away as Sofia sprinkled it on the wood. With a quick reflex motion, she struck a match and threw it into the fire pit. Poooof...they now had a small fire. The children's faces lit up with eagerness to learn more about this interesting form of light.

Maggie got down on her heels and gathered the children. "This is very hot and can burn your little fingers, so do not touch. I don't want you to go near it, either; your clothes can catch on fire. We always have to be careful around fire. Sofia and I are going to make us dinner and we need the heat to cook it. So you must be careful, okay?"

The children all nodded their heads, even though their eyes were hypnotized by the flames—all except, Marco. He said, "My daddy had our food on these sticks." He made a motion of his hand across the stick and pretended to put it over the fire. "It was really yummy."

Maggie smiled. "I bet it was delicious. We are going to make some macaroni."

The kids started clapping their hands and cheering. Sofia took out a big pot and filled it with water and set it on top of the lug nut wrench she had found in the van. The wrench laid across the small circle of rocks, letting the pot sit six inches above the fire. It was a brilliant idea of Sofia's. She was a very resourceful young woman who knew how to improvise. As she rummaged through the van for something metal to place the pot on to keep it from smothering the kindling, Maggie watched in awe. When she finally came out holding the lug nut wrench, Maggie smiled as she walked to the fire pit and carefully placed it on top of the small circle of rocks. She even maneuvered the height and leveled it off with amazing skill. By adding more rocks to make it higher, and taking some away to lower it—changed the heat. Maggie watched Sofia as she boiled the water and put the macaroni into it. She was a wonderful help and knew just what to do. Maggie was thankful and so pleased she had her this very bright young girl.

Once the macaroni was cooked, Sofia added some powdered cheese mix. She cut up those mangos they got on their walk and handed a plate to each child. She had only brought five plates so Maggie, and she, waited until the children were content and then they ate. Everyone was sitting around the small fire now, appeased and content.

Maggie looked at Sofia, and said, "Not bad at all. Great job!"

Sofia smiled. "It was quick and easy. We have to be like that around the house. Too many children to feed, and they are all hungry at once!"

All of a sudden, there was another large earthquake. The ground began to shake and rumble and the van started swaying back and forth. The children got scared and huddled between Maggie and Sofia. They encircled them with their arms; and Maggie began to sing a lullaby. "Hush, little baby, don't say a word, Papa's going to buy you a mockingbird...."

The children cuddled closer and listened as Maggie sang the whole song very slowly. By the time she was finished, the shaking had stopped. The sun was just beginning to set; and Maggie wasn't sure as to what they should do as far as sleeping arrangements.

Maggie raised her voice so Sofia could hear her. She had just walked into the forest to dump the hot water. "What do you think, Sofia? Should we sleep inside the van or outside? You know this area better than me. Are there bugs or animals that can get us outside?" Maggie looked around as though she felt little animal eyes were watching her. She had never slept in the wilderness before, and her heart was pumping a mile a minute. It was bad enough she was terrified of her circumstances, but now she had the 'unknown' hitting her in the face like a glass of ice water.

Sofia finished dumping the hot water deep into the forest and was walking back toward Maggie. "I think we should all cuddle up in the van. We'll stack most of the stuff in the front seat. I'll tie the two ice chests to the roof, so there will be plenty of room. I'm not afraid to sleep outside, it's just...the children might get up and wander off in the middle of the night."

Maggie sighed in relief. "Great! I thought the same thing also."

Sofia looked at the little children sitting near the fire—tummies filled and tired. "None of us have a change of clothes, so it looks like we are going to have to go down to the creek tomorrow and wash. How long do you think we should stay up here?"

Maggie closed her eyes for a few seconds, not knowing what to say. "For a few days. Just until things calm down; and it gives everyone time to get help. Right now, we are safe here. I don't know how safe we are in the towns or villages. Someone may want the van, or the food, or the gas. I don't want to risk these children until we see the military come in to help. We can see that by looking at the town below."

Sofia agreed. She walked over to the van, rolled down the window and spread out the blanket in the back. When she was done, one-by-one, Maggie walked the children over to climb into the back. It was very tight quarters with five children and two adults, but nobody even noticed. Before Maggie closed her eyes, she pulled out her phone and texted another message. With one bar, and no reception, her only hope was that someone got it. Everyone was sleeping as Maggie closed her eyes and thought about what a traumatic day it had been. Never in her years had she ever felt such fear. She was very thankful that they had gotten out of the town and into a safe place. A small aftershock bounced the van, but no one noticed but Maggie—they were all asleep.

Rene D. Schultz

CHAPTER 20

MORE OF THE TOWNSPEOPLE HAD GATHERED AND were caring for the children that had been pulled out. The two men, who were with Juliann and Ricardo, had managed to get out of the building and waited for the shaking to subside. After the shaking had stopped, those two men went back inside. Ten minutes later, they came out carrying Ricardo's lifeless body. He was covered with blood. Gently, they placed him on the ground next to the others and went back in to find the woman. This time, they each came out with an injured child. They got a large pipe and went back into the building. A few minutes later, they came out with Juliann. Her still body was placed on the ground and gradually you could hear her moan. They wrapped a tight tourniquet around her badly broken leg to stop the bleeding. There were a few nuns, from the local church, now helping with the injured and one was praying over the dead. The men continued to bring out more children—mostly alive.

Although weak from loss of blood, Juliann knew what she had to do. She had a nun get the keys from Ricardo's pocket. "Let's get the injured on the bus and take them to the nearby hospital." She moaned, in tremendous pain.

They took out the seats of the bus and loaded it with the injured. When they had completely filled it with the more severe injuries, one of the men drove the bus to the next town that had a small hospital. Once they got there, Juliann could see that extra medical help had been sent in to that hospital by the government and Red Cross. The bus driver ran into the hospital, and came running out with two nurses and a gurney. Even with her protesting, they picked her up and laid her on the gurney and rolled her into the hospital.

Angry, she shouted, "I'm—" she gasped in pain and then yelled again, "...get the children first!"

"Calm down. We will get everyone. The government sent us medics. The old school collapsed on top; thank God most of the kids are injured, not dead."

One nurse looked at her and said, "You're leg is severely injured and if we don't do anything to stop the bleeding—you're going to lose it or your life."

Starting to feel a little woozy from loss of blood, she said, "I'm a doctor, I'll be okay! Please take care of the kids!"

The two nurses went and got the doctor. When the three of them came back, they leaned over Juliann. One of the nurses said, "I hope it isn't too late...she's lost too much blood!"

Juliann never heard the last word. Her mind was blurry as she drifted off on the thought that she really had lost too much.... She began to fade....

Rene D. Schultz

250

CHAPTER 21

DAMON TURNED BACK AND SAID, "OKAY, SHE MADE it out alive with a few children. How are they heading into the mountains, and what mountains are they going to?"

Randolph sighed and handed the phone back to Damon. Quietly, he sat for a moment, thinking. "Okay. We know she is safe and made it out of the building! Since we are real close to the orphanage, let's see if we can find Juliann? None of us have heard from her."

The driver headed a few miles down the road to the orphanage. The relief on their faces from just those two little, say-nothing messages was immeasurable. Knowing Maggie was safe made all the difference in their world. Now, they could see what was going on with Juliann and the rest of the children.

The Hummer pulled up to the orphanage and they were amazed that it was still in fairly decent shape, considering. Part of the walled fence had crumbled and it was just enough for the guys to climb into the front driveway. They both looked in shock and they noticed only one young lady sitting on the steps, weeping.

Randolph ran over, sat next to Chica, and put his arm around her. "What's going on, Chica?" he asked.

Chica continued to weep. Then, in a low whisper, she said, "I don't know where they are. The school is completely down and there are some dead bodies in there and I don't know about anything else." Big sobs came out of her chest as it continued to heave up and down. Randolph took her in his arms and began to rock her. "It's okay, sweetheart. We will find all of them. I promise." She nodded her head in his chest. He rocked her for a few minutes, while Damon took a look around the front and back of the building. There was nothing there other than some structural damage. No children—no Juliann—not a thing that would lead them to either.

When Damon was finished, he came back and looked at Randolph. "Let's head over to the school and see if we can find anything. I'll ask around and see if anyone knows anything."

Randolph nodded and he carefully lifted Chica up in his arms, and started to walk toward the car. Once she was seated, he asked Sam, "Can you take us to the school?"

They traveled to the next town. Near the middle of the plaza was the demolished building. Chica laid down on the seat, her sobs could be heard as the men started to walk toward the building. They didn't expect to find much, because the earthquakes had started twenty-four hours before. They attempted to get to the front portion of the building, but like Juliann, they had no success. Everything was closed off. They went around to the back and Randolph's stomach began to lurch as the smell and the disturbing visual brought up the bile in his throat. The bodies had been taken away. What remained was the massive amount of lost blood that had taken the lives of the dead—for all to see. Damon put his hand on Randolph's shoulder.

Damon squared his friend's shoulders and looked into his teary eyes. "Hey, if you're having a tough time, let me look around."

"I can do it. Give me a sec...."

They both continued to look around the outside. There were only a few areas they could enter into the inside. In one, they entered into a room, there was nothing there but broken and crumbled debris. Blood was everywhere, but that was expected. How much blood, and how many children were dead, was unknown to them. They went through the four rooms, the other two were unattainable. They both knew that there were bodies in those two rooms, but they had no idea whose.

When they came out of the last room, they could smell the stench of death all around. Slowly, an old man started walking toward them. His shirt and pants were filled with blood and he was exhausted and despondent looking. He started to walk past Damon and Randolph without any acknowledgement, as though he was in shock and really wasn't hearing or seeing.

Gently, Damon went up to him and said, "Where are the children? Where are the teachers?" He just looked up and didn't answer. Damon asked again, "*¿Dónde están los niños?*"

"They took them to the hospital. And some went to the burial ground. It is a sad day for our country and a painful day for our town. We lost many." He sighed and wiped his eyes. "I was the caretaker of this school and my *niños* are gone. Happy, smiling faces...all gone!"

Damon put his hand on his shoulder to show the old man he was grieving too. "Where can I find the hospital? Do you know if the lady from the orphanage, Juliann, was taken there?"

"When they pulled Ricardo out, I cried. When they pulled her out, I could cry no more."

Panic gripped Randolph's heart. "Where's the hospital?" Randolph begged.

The old man pointed. "The next town to the north. They have the hospital there. The bus took them."

Randolph's eyes opened wide. "The bus?"

Damon bent over and hugged the man, quietly he whispered, "God walks with you tonight for being here for the *niños*."

The old man wiped his eyes with his dirty, bloodstained sleeve and began to walk, listlessly, around the building. It was as though his job wasn't done, and he still was there to tend to the school and all the children.

Damon looked at Randolph and said, "He saw it all. You can tell in his eyes. Let's get the hell out of here and to that hospital."

They got back into the Hummer and by then Chica was sitting up. Her eyes were filled with agony and her hands were still shaking.

Damon asked Sam, "Do you know where the hospital is in the next town?"

"Yes, sir! I'll take you there!" And the car drove off, trying to miss all the debris in the streets, along with the people. Fifteen minutes later they pulled up in front of a red brick building that looked like it had made it through the quakes. There was a Red Cross flag flying outside and it looked like lots of nurses dressed in white were amongst the crowd. They sat in the car for a few moments, watching, as people were carrying their injured loved ones into the hospital. Others were sitting outside wailing and crying in pain at the loss they were forced to endure. Damon opened the door and the men jumped out. "You want to come in, Chica, and see if you can identify anyone from the school?"

Chica nodded and said, "I hope all our orphanage children made it through."

They gradually walked through the door and tried to maneuver around some of the loitering crowds of people. They finally approached an older woman dressed in white and taking names and asking for any identification. Randolph stepped forward and asked, "I'm an administrator of the school in Santa Bello. The school sustained a lot of damage and we hear the children and teachers were brought here. Do you have a list or can we see who is here?"

She pulled out her clipboard and said, "It just has their names if we have them. There are many here and some were released. You can take a quick look and see if you find any of them."

Randolph looked at her with confusion. "What do you mean some were released? They were just children! The ones from the orphanage had nowhere to go and no one to get them. That's why we are here."

She shrugged her shoulders and continued to talk to others that came up to question her. Damon looked at Chica and said, "You're going to have to help us identify the wounded. You're the only one who knows them. Okay?"

Room by room, they carefully walked through the first floor, looking for anyone Chica could recognize. The first one they found was Lydia. When Chica walked into a room filled with eight beds, she spotted Lydia and ran over to kiss and hug her. Lydia was beside herself and started crying. She was severely injured with a broken leg and several stitched contusions all over her body.

Randolph looked at Chica, tears running down her cheeks, and said, "Tell her not to worry; we will have a place for her when she is released."

They could see her body and face begin to relax. Chica then said, "We're going to look for others, so get better and we'll be back! Did you see anyone else from the house?"

Lydia shook her head.

They went to the next room and Chica found four more children from the school. Randolph and Damon took note of that and Chica's reunion with them was filled with joy. She also told them what she told Lydia—they'd have a place to go—no matter what. This went on until they had located twenty-two children from the orphanage and four of the eight teachers. Four of those twenty-two children were not injured but staying with their friends and sleeping on the floor. With that many accounted for, Chica had much to smile about— with the exception of where Juliann was. No one would let them go into the final small wing of the hospital. That was where the more severely injured patients were.

Unable to get past the steel doors, they waited until a doctor came out and immediately they stopped him with questions. "Doctor, I'm looking for a woman by the name of Juliann Martinique."

"I have a Julie, but that is all I know of her or her name."

"Juliann Martinique is a Pediatrician from the United States. She now runs a local orphanage near San Limo. She's part French and part Filipino, small and petite. Does this sound like the 'Julie' you are talking about?"

The doctor nodded and confirmed. "Yes, it does. I'm afraid you can't see her yet. It's touch and go with her stability. An hour ago we weren't sure she'd make it. Her leg was severed at the knee and her loss of blood was almost too much for her body."

"Is she awake or conscious of her surroundings?"

"No. We have her in an induced coma so that her body has time to deal with the trauma. Hang around and let's see if she makes it through."

Chica stepped forward and asked, "Do you know if Ricardo is here too?"

The doctor frowned. "I understand he threw his body over hers when the third quake hit. If he hadn't laid on top of her, she would be dead. His body took the blunt of the collapsed ceiling."

Chica slowly slipped down to the floor and her sobs could be heard bouncing off the small room they were standing in. Randolph bent down and picked her up in his arms and sat down in a nearby chair. He knew that Chica, Sofia, and Ricardo were good friends and this sudden loss was breaking her in two. Damon stood with the doctor to discuss the injuries and to see if there were any other teachers or children in ICU with Juliann. He found out there were two children and one teacher. The rest had perished in the earthquake and that if they wanted to claim the bodies; they would have to go to the makeshift morgue down the street where all the causalities from around the area were located—including Ricardo.

They stuck around the hospital for the next four hours; and then the doctor came back into the room with a saddened face.

CHAPTER 22

Everyone was so tired from the long day and the hike. The children went right to sleep and Maggie sat there listening to the odd sounds of the tropical jungle. It was the second day that Maggie and Sofia had been camping in the mountains. The aftershocks had started to calm down; and Maggie was beginning to finally feel some relief from the fear. The little ones had been really good and they were actually having a fun time. After sleeping soundly, as the sun started to rise in the morning, Marco opened his eyes and touched Maggie's face. "I have to go to the pee pee tree, Miss Maggie," he whispered.

Without saying a word, Maggie sat up, opened the door, picked up Marco and slipped out of the van. Together they walked over to the edge of the forest. By now, the little ones had become seasoned 'campers' and learned that when you didn't have a toilet, the forest worked fine. Maggie stood there with her head turned away to give him privacy. When he was done, he came out as he was pulling up his pants.

Maggie ruffled his hair. "Are we ready for another fun day, Marco?"

With childish exuberance, he said, "Yes, I want to play in the water today?"

Maggie smiled down at his cheerful face that was filled with so much trust. "I think that is a good idea. Maybe we can pick some wild berries, because I'm starting to get tired of mangos!"

By the time they made it to camp, the children were climbing out of the van, and Sofia was beginning to heat up the water.

Maggie walked over and asked, "What's for breakfast today?"

"Mango oatmeal!" she laughed.

Maggie laughed out loud. That was how the day started. While the children were enjoying their breakfast, Maggie and Sofia walked toward the cliff and looked over the edge to see what was going on in the city below. It looked like the military had been sent in to help. People were everywhere, some even sleeping along the roadside. It looked like a large truck was stopping to pick up the dead people wrapped in shrouds. Some help had come and they watched the military trucks delivering water and bags that looked like rice. Some of the buildings were crushed, while others stayed where they were and stood strong.

"Do you think we should go down there and have someone try to contact Juliann? Or better yet, I could call my fiancé, Damon. I bet him and Randolph are petrified with worry."

"I will do what you wish. I just think we should wait another day or two to make sure the area is cleared of death, and they have somewhere for us to take these little ones."

"That's a good idea. Besides, I feel safe up here. I'm getting used to the camping stuff!"

Sofia gathered the children and locked up the van. Sofia was very careful cleaning up and with putting everything back into the van. Maggie thought it must have come with the years of living on the street with little protection and people who were your friend one minute and stabbing you in the back for a lousy container of glue the next. Maggie knew only too well what Lucy had gone through those nineteen years of her life. Drugs, prostitution, vagrancy, and the final sword in her back was rape. For years, Lucy lived a life that Maggie or Elizabeth could not possibly fathom. They didn't know about shelters and what you had to go through just to find a place to sleep for the evening. They didn't know what it was like to have a relentless addiction, an empty stomach, or wake up each day with the all too real prospect of death curtailing each moment. Maggie became successful right out of college. Elizabeth went right into a marriage with a hardworking farmer. Randolph knew what street life was like. He lived on the streets for a few years after running away from the orphanage when the girls had all been pushed out on their own. He knew more than Maggie could ever imagine, yet he wasn't angry or filled with malice. He never talked about those four years he wandered around like a nomad. Maggie had heard a few stories, but they were just to appease her curiosity.

Maggie looked around, trying to get a grasp on reality. For the past several hours, she felt like a nomad. She knew nothing about the country she was in; had no clue as to where she was; didn't know where or how to find help; and here she was trying to survive in a forest with a young girl and five babies. One day—she had only been there one day before her life had begun to spin in circles. All she wanted to know was if Juliann had survived the earthquake, or if she was one of the misfortunate causalities.

Maggie and Sofia started down the trail to the small pond and waterfall. For the next few hours, they were going to let the children strip down and play in the water. Sofia washed their clothes with a bar of soap and laid them on the rocks to dry. Maggie sat on the bank of the creek and skipped rocks on the water. Maggie pulled out her phone to look at it. Suddenly her face lit up. Sitting on the screen was a text message from Damon. 'WE JUST LANDED IN HONDURAS.' She stood up and energetically ran over to Sofia. "He's here! My fiancé is here in Honduras! This message is from this morning."

Sofia looked at the text. Maggie looked at her face and, immediately, could tell she didn't know how to read. Her heart went out to the young girl, and she read it out loud with excitement. She knew he would come over mountains to find her. She could already feel his presence.

"He's going to find us! I know it!"

With sarcasm in her voice, Sofia said, "What does that mean? That you will go home and live your perfect life, while all of us have nowhere to go except to the streets again. Ricardo, Chica, and I will be alone and on the street again?"

Maggie had never given a thought to that. *What would happen when they got here? With a home that may not be safe, where would the children go? Who would take care the children?* She had so many unanswered questions to resolve and here Sofia was afraid she would be left alone again. Something needed to be done. Damon and Randolph would never let her stay in Honduras to find homes for the children.

Maggie put her cell in her bra, right over her heart. It was starting to get late, and the children were restless as they gathered berries and enjoyed their sweet flavor. They were dressed in their dry clothes and Sofia and Maggie gathered them up to head back to the van.

Rene D. Schultz
264

CHAPTER 23

THE DOCTOR CAME OUT AND SAID THEY HAD LOST another one of the children. Her head trauma was too severe and they had done everything they could. He then gave Damon and Randolph the thumbs up that Juliann had made it through the tough spot and he predicted she would now survive. Both made the decision to go look for Maggie. The quicker they found her and the faster they got out of the country and got the best medical care for Juliann—the better off they would all be. Her rehabilitation was going to take a while. The trauma she sustained was that of a military person with PTSD (Post-traumatic stress disorder). This was a woman who was used to being on the move and in control of her surroundings. That was soon going to stop while she gave herself time to heal. This was going to slow her down, and with the loss of the children, they had no idea what kind of mental instability they were going to see.

Randolph looked at Damon with sad eyes and said, "How are we going to tell her that she lost her leg?"

Damon looked straight at him. "We tell her...'that her life was spared.' God spared it for a reason, so that she can continue to take care of the children. I mean.... He must have spared her for a reason!"

They got out of their seats and started walking to the Hummer. They were determined to find Maggie and the babies. Chica followed silently. Once they got into the car, Randolph turned around to the backseat and asked Chica, "Do you have any idea what mountains Sofia could have taken Maggie too?"

Chica nodded her head. "I know exactly where they might be. Sofia and I would go up there once in a while to get away. When Sofia was homeless, she lived up there and lived off the land for a year."

Damon looked at her in surprise. "Really? How many miles?"

Chica remained silent. "I don't know. I never went to school. I know it will take us a few hours to get there if the roads are okay."

Sam listened to instructions from Chica and took the same back roads that Maggie had taken with Sofia.

"I hope this is the right place! If it's not, I don't know where they could be," Chica quietly said.

Damon took his phone out of his pocket and there was still no reception. He was so tired of pulling the phone out of his shirt pocket, he thought for sure he must have rubbed a hole in it.

The road was boring as they continued driving up into the mountains.

"Turn in here and drive down this muddy road for a minute." The light in her eyes started to shine as they got closer to their destination. When Chica saw the van, she started to scream, "That's our van! They are here! Thank you, God." She looked toward the sky and mumbled a few words.

They pulled up behind the van and stopped the car. Everyone got out and looked around. Damon and Randolph hugged each other. "This looks pretty empty. I'm a little nervous," Randolph said.

"Nah...they are fine. They cleaned up and locked everything in the car."

Chica smiled and said, "When Sofia was homeless, this was her hideout. They're probably down by the creek and watering hole."

They waited patiently for fifteen minutes. Then Damon couldn't stand it any longer. "Which way to the creek, Chica?"

She pointed. Damon was rolling up his sleeves when he looked up and from a distance he saw some movement. When he finally recognized Maggie, he took off in a dead run. Maggie had just looked up as she was answering Marco's question. What she saw brought immediate tears to her eyes and without notice she let go of Marco's hand and starting running toward Damon. When they both finally reached each other, tears were streaming down both their faces. Damon picked Maggie up and held her tight against him and swung her around. Damon looked up into Maggie's face and slowly she leaned down and sealed their excitement of finding each other with a kiss. Damon didn't want to let her down or let her go. He had a second chance and he didn't want to mess this up. He had been so terrified he'd never see her again, and here she was in his arms. Smiling her quirky little grin. Both her hands came up and framed his face. Her shaking hands drew her closer to his face and she whispered, "I love you! Don't you ever let me go wandering off into scary places like this again!"

A big grin crossed his face, "I'm going to have to find you other things to keep you busy and closer to home. I have been going out of my mind with worry." Maggie slid down his body until her feet hit the ground. At that same time, Chica noticed Sofia first. They ran towards each other and Chica started to sob. The gut-wrenching sobs were echoing off the mountains. But no one cared. The children just sat down silently and watched all the commotion. The reunion of the two friends reminded Maggie of a few years earlier, when she first found Elizabeth at the farm. After twenty years, when Maggie had stepped out of her car and slammed the door shut, the noise had generated interest from Elizabeth and her two small daughters playing in the front yard of their farm. Upon immediate recognition, they started running toward each other on the dirt driveway. They collided with a howl of agony from Maggie and a scream of pleasure from Elizabeth. Prancing in a circle, they wept and wailed and held onto each other with a power that washed away the years: two friends so immersed in that one solid moment that nothing else mattered. Slowly they had slipped to the ground—neither willing to let go. It was like Chica and Sofia, two friends so immersed in each other, they didn't notice what was going on around them.

Randolph cleared his throat. "Okay, enough is enough. Tell us what happened and how you wound up here."

"*Eres mi querida, amiga!*" Chica said to Sofia.

Sofia touched Chica's face and said, "I'm so glad to see you. How are the children and Juliann? And where is my Ricardo?"

Chica bent her head and burst into sobs again. Sofia cupped her face in her hands and looked into her eyes. "It was bad?"

Chica nodded her head. Slowly, she gained composure and told everyone what she could remember. When she got to the part of Ricardo, it became so difficult to look her friend in the eyes. She bowed her head and quietly said, "*Su novio* died saving the life of Juliann. I'm so sorry, Sofia!"

Sofia's body began to shake; and slowly she stood up and walked around the van where she could not be seen. She sat down and hugged her knees as her grief gripped her heart. Her moans of grief and heartache could be heard by everyone.

Chica looked up and said, "They were going to get married one day. They loved each other so much. They were two broken souls who finally had found such happiness."

The pain on Chica's face was more than Maggie could handle. She laid her head on

Damon's chest and began to weep. "Why?" she kept whispering. "Why these sweet children?"

Damon and Randolph could do nothing but watch and absorb the pain Sofia was feeling.

Finally, Maggie pulled her head up and asked quietly, "Where is Juliann? Where are the older children?"

Randolph sadly said, "Juliann is in a coma in the hospital. We were there until the doctor came out and said she would make it through. She's barely hanging on…and she lost a leg."

"Nooooo…." Maggie screamed as Damon held her tightly against him, not allowing her to completely fall apart.

He crooned, "She will be fine. We are taking her back to Randolph's ranch. We all have to get out of here, now! She needs better medical care. We needed to find you first. Now that we have found you, we need to get going as soon as possible. Rand has his plane in the airport. Time is very crucial for Juliann's recovery."

Maggie pulled away and looked at both the men with a fierce attitude that had completely taken over. "I don't care how we do it, but Sofia, Chica, and these babies have to come back with us! Take me to the embassy. I want them in Casa de Niño's!"

Damon and Randolph looked at her in surprise. Finally, Randolph said, "We can't possibly arrange that. They need visas and passports!"

Maggie was standing tall and straight with her hands crossing her chest. "I don't care. I'm not leaving without them. The little ones will love it there; and Sofia and Chica can become helpers. So, we can get them working visas. Besides, the fewer orphans this country has to deal with, the better off they are. What about the older ones? How many of them survived?"

Randolph put up his hand to stop her ranting. "We will find a place for them, here!"

Sofia came around the corner and was holding onto Chica. They both watched and Maggie stamped her foot and said adamantly, "No!"

Chica stepped forward and said the older children that had survived had already been taken somewhere by the military. Out of the twenty-six, only five had died, but no one knew where they were, either. She said, "Just take the babies. Sofia and I will be okay. We'll stay up here for a while, until things calm down."

Maggie's face turned bright red as her uncontrollable anger surfaced. "Stay here and what? Fucking live like vagrants? No!" She whipped her head around towards the men, and screamed, "Take me to the embassy, Damon!"

Randolph relented and said to Maggie, "Okay, let's get going and see what we can do."

The five little ones, Chica, Sophia, Randolph, Damon, and Maggie took what they needed out of the van and piled it into the Hummer. Randolph looked at Sam and said, "Remember where this place is, Sam. I want the van picked up and brought back to the orphanage. Just in case! Now you can take us to the military base. I need to make some phone calls and I think that may be the only place to use a phone."

They drove for a few hours and finally the sun was starting to set. They pulled over to the side of a road where a cart vendor was selling cooked meat and tortillas for a price to all the homeless and displaced people. They fed the children and proceeded to the base. Once they were there, Sofia and Chica stayed in the Hummer and put the babies to sleep. Randolph, Damon, and Maggie went in search of the officials they needed to talk to. Randolph was on the phone for hours as Maggie and Damon paced the offices waiting to see if they were going to get the seven children out of the country on visas. Or if they had to leave them there with strangers.

They also were trying to make arrangements for Juliann to be taken out of the country, permitting that her health was stable enough to get through the eight-hour flight. Randolph had to strategically plan this trip and possibly fly in private doctors to monitor Juliann during the flight. During the negotiations with the government officials and the embassy, they were putting restrictions on the children. They would only be allowed through customs and directly into Mexico. They could not cross the border into California where Maggie and Randolph lived. That was a big part of the negotiations that was constantly being debated. The government wanted these children to remain in Mexico and not be allowed to go into the United States. Then they required Randolph to produce documents to show his part of ownership in the orphanages—both in Honduras and Mexico. When he produced the statements showing his participation of funds, they were astonished. When they finally realized who he was and the power he had around the world, they relented and were giving it great consideration. Randolph knew this game all too well. He knew they were going to play him for a contribution to their government that was in desperate need of money and supplies due to the earthquake.

"I know this game, Maggie. We will get the children, but first I have to give them a pittance. Or what they will call a security agreement of the children. Fuck them, I'll give them the money. I just want those children! Period!"

Maggie looked angry. "But they are holding you hostage! How dare they!"

Randolph laughed. "Get over it, Maggie. They can do any damn thing they want. The sooner we get out of here—the faster I can get Juliann to the best hospital."

Within the next hour, Randolph had agreed to send in four large shipments of water and medical supplies into their country in exchange for the children's documents and passports. Maggie was beside herself with happiness. She truly wished she could have taken every orphan home and out of this struggling country. But life wasn't fair and she knew that, and getting the seven back to Mexico was enough to lighten her heart.

Rene D. Schultz
274

CHAPTER 24

MAGGIE WALKED TO THE ROOM WHERE THE military had placed the children, while waiting for Randolph to seal the deal. They fed them sandwiches and they were watching a small television. Only on rare occasions, at the orphanage, were they allowed to actually watch television. When Maggie opened the door, she saw the children were immersed into the children's show; they were laughing and clapping their hands. Maggie wondered how come children were so resilient to major trauma that could displace them for two days and yet they still had smiles on their faces. They had displayed such patience and trust in Sofia and Maggie. They weren't like some of the selfish, whiny, ill-behaved children in Los Angeles with parents who allowed such disturbing manners. How many times had she been face to face with a mother in a store who gave into the child's ransom, over a tantrum? Whether it was a toy or candy, the tantrum was rewarded for bad behavior. She looked at the children again and smiled.

Maggie felt like she had just adopted five little ones and two amazing teenagers. Sofia had gotten her through two days of hell. She knew what to do and where to go. She literally saved the lives of Maggie and the children with her quick thinking and responses. Then she received the shattering news about Ricardo, her boyfriend. You could see the tremendous pain cross her face, and yet, all she wanted to do was weep in private. Chica was a hard worker who did more than her share at the orphanage—never once displaying a frown. Early morning to late at night, she cleaned; did laundry; bathed; ran errands; and fed the children. And they were both about to receive news that was definitely about to change their lives forever. They would now live in an ideal environment, and under the wings of many remarkable people at Casa de Niños.

Marco had fallen asleep on Sofia's lap. Everyone was sitting on the long leather couch, laughing at the television. Maggie walked over and pulled a chair right in front of the couch. She leaned over and shut off the television with the remote and sat down. "Well, how are my babies this evening?"

Sofia said, "They have been angels!"

Chica nodded.

"Well I have some great news for you," Maggie stated.

Chica's eyes looked down. Fear on her face began to show. "Did they find another house for us? Or do they just want the babies?"

"Well, they found a new house for you. I'm sure you will enjoy it!" Maggie smiled.

Chica began to panic. "Can't we go back to our home? Don't let them put Sofia and I back on the streets. Don't take our babies away. Don't let them separate us!" she cried out in fear.

Maggie got up and sat down next to Chica, who was just starting to sob. All the children started to cry, and soon the room was filled with overwhelming noise. In a loud voice, Maggie hushed the children and wiped the tears away from Chica's cheeks. "I want you and Sofia to know we are not breaking you apart. We are not taking your babies away. You are coming on the plane with me and Juliann and we are taking you to our beautiful Mexican home!"

Sofia laid her head down on top of Marco's and began to cry. Chica kept hugging Maggie. The room was just filled with so many emotions and the sadness was now turning into happiness. "Thank you...thank you...Thank you..." Chica kept saying.

Maggie looked at Sofia. "Sofia...are you okay? You don't want to go? I'd thought you'd be happy." Maggie looked confused.

Sofia didn't answer or lift her head. She just cried and cried and cried.

Chica got up and went to her friend. "I know...I know exactly what you are crying for, my dear friend."

Maggie watched in silence.

"You're crying for Ricardo. Because his dream was that the both of you would leave Honduras and make a life together. Right?"

Sofia nodded her head, never lifting it.

"Well, my friend. I think 'your' Ricardo was a hero and saved Miss Juliann, so that we could go on this journey with her to another land. I think your Ricardo is sending us to this new place."

Sofia turned her head slightly to look at her friend. "You think so?"

Maggie touched Sofia's face. "God works in strange ways. Sometimes I can't figure him out. But there is always a reason. We may not know now, but we may find out later."

Sofia laid there for a few minutes with her eyes closed. Maggie thought it looked like she was praying. Maggie got up slowly and said, "We may have to stay a few days until Juliann is strong enough to make that eight-hour flight. But I know you're going to love Casa de Niños."

Sofia whispered to Maggie. "Where do they have Ricardo? Did he have a necklace on? Are they going to bury him?"

Maggie stood up and bent over and kissed Sofia's forehead. "I will see if we can find out."

Sofia covered her face again. She was grieving the only way she knew how and as private as she could; holding in the pain and not letting anyone see her weakness. Maggie understood that. She had done the same thing, until she left the orphanage at eighteen. She grieved for years over her lost childhood that sometimes came back to haunt her. Sofia had a lot of healing in the years ahead.

The children were tucked in the corner of the plane and sound asleep. The rest of the plane was filled with private doctors and nurses that Randolph had hired to take the flight with Juliann. The staff doctors at the small hospital didn't really think she should be moved, but then, their facilities were not equipped enough to deal with all her trauma. The massive number of injuries and the lack of medical help and supplies was overwhelming to that small town. Juliann was still in an induced coma and that was a big help on this flight. They were going to fly directly into Los Angeles and have her transported to one of the best hospitals in the nation. He wanted her in the best and he wanted her close to his home. He was torn between staying with Juliann and going back to get everyone situated in Mexico. Maggie could hear his sigh of relief when that impossible decision was taken out of his hands. The doctors at UCLA told him they wanted her isolated for seventy-two hours along with the self-induced coma. No friends, no family, no interruptions of any sort. They wanted to completely stabilize her body and keep her totally relaxed.

They had made it to Los Angeles and had a four hour layover to make sure she was safe within the state-of-the-art hospital. Once he was given clearance, with reassurance from the doctors, the plane's engines roared back to life again. Randolph was headed home to Mexico where he could re-evaluate his life and make some major decisions he had been putting off for a few years. So many of his emotions had changed when he was in Honduras. How many times had he found himself in the middle of a major disaster, and faced with hairsplitting choices that could leave him with life altering results? Where was his stability when he was constantly flying all over the world taking on everyone else's problems? Why was he afraid to settle down? What was creating this unbridled turmoil that kept him wandering? He wasn't sure how it happened, but Juliann had brought this reality to the surface. *'Do you only stop when you die, or do you figure out what this restlessness really is that makes us wander the world? If you find the answer to that question— would you let me know?'* she asked the last night she was in Mexico.

The plane took off and Maggie smiled when she saw the terrified faces of Chica and Sofia. They had never been on a plane before and for the second time, in just hours, they were speeding down the runway, heading for the unknown. Their lives had consisted of nothing except pain and suffering until the last year with Juliann. Even now, that had been taken from them and they were trusting these strangers—blindly—with their lives. Once the plane had leveled off, Maggie got up and sat down next to Chica and Sofia.

She put her arms around both of them and said very reassuringly, "I don't want you to be scared. You're going to love your new place. Trust me on this. Juliann was in charge of setting up this orphanage before she went to Honduras. I'm hoping we can get her back here to do her rehabilitation. She's got so much ahead of her. It's going to be difficult learning how to walk all over again, with one leg."

Chica's sad face reflected her feelings. "I hope she makes it her home. I've missed her." A tear slid down her cheek. "I miss all the innocent children and my heart is filled with such pain with our loss. Losing five of our friends, and Ricardo, hurts our hearts."

Maggie wiped the tears with her sleeve. "I know. Did I ever tell you that I was raised in an orphanage?"

Chica and Sofia shook their heads. "You were?" Sofia asked.

Maggie smiled. "Yes, I was. And so was Randolph!" She pointed to his sleeping form laying on the lounge chair. "So, I want you to know that you are not alone. You will have the same life you did in Honduras—only better. You will be with the babies, and Randolph is still working with the government to get the others here, too. Right now the government is being very mean, but Randolph will get them to give in. I would like both of you to get some rest, this is going to be a shorter flight then the last one and you've had a very traumatic few days."

The plane touched down on the private air strip, and slowly taxied to the waiting cars. Randolph was on the phone and Damon was just staring out the window. Maggie looked at his tired face and knew he needed some rest. She was grateful he was in her life. Randolph and he never stopped nor gave up on finding them. They had pulled it off, and brought those five little ones back to a better life. The little ones were watching out the windows as the plane taxied. Maggie watched Marco get off his seat and walk over to Damon. He said something, and Damon bent down to listen to him. With one quick motion, Damon scooped Marco up into his arms and placed him on his lap. Marco was excited and Damon was pointing out the window and talking to him. Maggie's heart melted when she saw the big man and the little boy enjoying such a simple moment. She couldn't help to wonder if it would have an impactful meaning to the two of them.

Damon never settled down enough to have children, nor did he want them. Maggie and Damon had talked late one night about the possibility of having their own child. Maggie knew she was getting older and her time had just about run out to have her own. She pictured herself as a mother. She also questioned her vulnerability that night to suggesting they adopt. Damon was stingingly honest, and said he didn't want any. He didn't think he would make a good father, and he definitely had no role model in his upbringing to fall back on. He liked picking up and traveling without the responsibility of taking care of another person. That sentence made Maggie wonder if she had become his 'responsibility' or 'albatross' around his neck.

She looked again at the man she loved, and wondered if he was cheating himself, or if she was going to let him cheat her? What did she want to do? And how important was it to her?

CHAPTER 25

THE CAR PULLED UP TO CASA DE NIÑOS AND THE gates opened. Chica and Sofia were looking out the window, wide-eyed and stunned. It looked like a resort—to someone who didn't know it was an orphanage. That's what Randolph tried to capture when he planned it. He wanted the children to feel happy and to make it their home. The car stopped and Maria opened the car door with a welcoming smile on her face.

She peeked her head into the car, and with excitement in her voice, she said, "Oh my, I can't wait to meet all my new friends. The kids are so excited to meet their new friends, too!"

The look on all their young faces showed their intimidation by her sudden burst of enthusiasm. Maggie knew this had to be a frightful moment for them and they all started to move closer to her. Except for Marco, he was still seated on Damon's lap. Marco whispered something into Damon's ear. The big smile on Damon's face and the hug he gave Marco was enough for Maggie to recognize that he underestimated himself at becoming 'father material.' Damon's face turned toward Maggie and their eyes met. Suddenly, a little pair of hands framed Damon's face and pulled it back, so that Marco could have all of his attention.

Marco said out loud, "I don't want to go."

Damon replied back, "I'm afraid, son, you are going to have to get out of this car. I know you will like it here."

Marco tightly wrapped his arms around Damon's neck and held on for dear life. Maggie, in turn, gave Sofia and Chica a big kiss on the cheek as she introduced them to Maria. Maria picked each little one up, lifted them out of the car, and gave them a big hug and kiss also. Except for Marco. He wasn't happy and his face showed it. Damon didn't know what to do, so he did the only thing he could—he held on to Marco and got out of the car. Maggie walked behind Damon and watched as he struggled with Marco's reactions. Sofia and Chica held on to each of Maggie's hands, terrified of their new surroundings.

"*Muy bueno*," Chica said under her breath.

"*Si*! And this is your new home." Maggie smiled.

Sofia got wide-eyed. "This is not Randolph's home? This is our new school? It's so big and beautiful!"

Maggie nodded her head and said, "*Muy bueno*."

The children from Casa came out to meet their new friends—Elena, Juan, Gitana, and Luz. Marco refused to let go of Damon. "Let go, Marco. Join your new friends." Damon begged.

"NO!" he raised his voice and pouted.

Damon did not know what to do or how to handle this. So he did what was the easiest, again. He held on to Marco and continued to walk.

Sofia and Chica were in awe as they were shown around and introduced to everyone. Then they were taken to their room that they shared with two other girls their age. The room was painted yellow and was bright and cheerful. They each had their own bed, dresser and a bathroom they shared. Chica was excited, but Sofia bent her head as tears dripped onto the floor. Maggie walked over and drew her into her arms. Sofia laid her head on Maggie's chest and said, "I wish Ricardo was here, too. He would have been the hardest worker and would have loved it here. Why did he die? Why did God take him?"

Maggie stroked her long black hair. "I think maybe God wanted him for those little ones he also took to heaven. We all miss him. But I can definitely feel his spirit surrounding us."

"No, his spirit is in Honduras, and I never got to say goodbye."

Chica came over and said, "He is here in spirit, I can feel it too, *hija*. Let's show him we can make it. We are survivors, remember?"

It was time for dinner and Maria let the others take charge of the new little ones. They all said their goodbyes.

"Tomorrow morning we are going to church. It's the prettiest church I've ever seen, and it's on Randolph's ranch. We would like you to join us," Maggie said to Sofia and Chica.

Chica spoke up first. "Yes, we will say our prayers for our friends left behind and our goodbyes to Ricardo. Thank you, Miss Maggie." Sofia remained silent.

Damon, Randolph and Maggie were totally exhausted by the time they got to the hacienda. Maggie took a hot bath and when she walked back into the room, Damon was passed out on the bed. His small snores were so endearing to Maggie and she wanted nothing more than to be held tonight. Looking at his relaxed face for the first time in days, she didn't have the heart to wake him, so she slipped into bed, shut off the light, and cuddled next to him. It had definitely been a long, grueling week and they still had Juliann's recovery to worry about.

Maggie woke up and the room was empty. She got dressed and went into the kitchen to find some coffee and to see how the plans were going. Lupe was in the kitchen making fresh tortillas. "Morning, Lupe." Maggie said, as she bent over to hug the small woman.

"*Buenos días*, Miss Maggie. Did you sleep well?"

"Better than the last few weeks." She snatched a fresh tortilla and buttered it. She took a bite and moaned.

A pair of arms came around her waist and Damon pulled close and whispered in her ear, "You know what your 'moans' do to me!"

Lupe laughed.

Maggie pushed Damon away. Then her face turned bright red. "Oh my God, it was just a 'tortilla'...moan. For cripes sake, it was not a 'I'm hot and bothered' moan!" Damon started to laugh and finally Maggie got over her embarrassment and laughed along with him.

Maggie leaned against the kitchen counter and sipped her coffee. "Is it all set up and ready? I can't believe Randolph did that. Juliann is going to be blown away, if she makes it out of intensive care and comes here to recover."

"I think it will bring a lot of closure to a lot of people." He sipped his coffee. "You pick up the girls. Randolph and I will meet you at the church." He put his empty cup on the counter and she slipped into his outstretched arms—still holding her coffee.

"Randolph is an amazing man," Maggie said out loud, as though confirming her thoughts.

"If I was a jealous person...."

She tapped his nose. "There's nothing to be jealous about! You are the one who holds the key to my heart!" She put her cup down and gave him a kiss. "I'll see you in a little while. Save a few seats for us. I'm not bringing the little ones."

Maggie pulled the Jeep into the small parking area of the church. It was the most charming church, and the first one built in the entire area hundreds of years ago. It was simple and plain, with the most unique stained-glass windows that let in all of the morning light. Many nights when they stayed at the ranch, Maggie had wandered down there to sit and watch the sunset as her life began to change. It was the perfect place for Maggie to retreat, when she felt the need to be alone, and reflect on all the changes that had taken place the past five years.

The church was surrounded by a large grass area, lush tropical gardens, and petite picket fencing. Maggie and the girls sat in the car for a moment and absorbed the little church. They watched as the people from the town gathered around their favorite place on this Sunday morning, to pay homage to God and the generations of their families who had been there before them. One-by-one, they walked into the church, removing their hats or putting on their simple lace coverings. Tradition meant a lot to these humble people and having a church where their fathers, grandfathers, and great-grandfathers had once prayed was a sacred enjoyment.

Maggie took a deep breath and exhaled slowly as she opened her car door. She knew what was coming and her hands started to shake. With eyes open wide, the girls got out of the car and waited to grasp Maggie's hands so she could walk them into the church.

Maggie had once given up on God. For years she hated him for putting her in the orphanage. What mother would leave her seven-year-old daughter sitting on the cement steps in the rain, with a note pinned to her coat? How could God do that—she wondered for years. It wasn't until she went to visit Elizabeth for the first time that she realized it really wasn't about her—it was about her young, selfish mother who chose her boyfriend over her daughter. That Sunday in North Bend, holding Elizabeth's hand after an absence of twenty years, she walked into the church to finally restore her faith in God. Today, she felt the need to restore the faith of these two young girls who had very little in life to reflect back on. Two broken girls, who were almost shattered into pieces days ago.

They passed the open gate, and walked up the pathway to the church entrance. On each side of the carved mahogany doors stood Randolph and Damon. Maggie gripped the girl's hands tighter. As they entered and walked down the middle aisle of the church, they noticed all the townspeople, simple and humble people, who knew what these children had gone through and the loss they have to live with. Maggie walked them to the front of the church. Sitting on top of two beautifully hand-carved posts was an open casket. Both the girls looked terrified and stopped. Maggie was shaking as she slowly drew them to the open flap. Sofia looked down and immediately started to sob. She framed both her hands around his face and kissed him on his lips for the last time. Then she laid her head on his cold chest and began to talk to him. The silence in the church was for a young woman who had lost her first *novio* and was filled with tremendous heartache. Chica bent over and put both of her arms around her friend. She knew how much this meant to her best friend. Silently, her tears flowed down her cheeks, never wavering as she let her friend purge the grief that had filled her heart for days.

Maggie whispered in her ear, "Ricardo is now here in body and spirit, forever—with you." Maggie knew that Sofia would be able to sleep a little more peacefully now, knowing he was so close.

Maggie could not believe how relentless Randolph was with the Honduran government. He refused to go anywhere, or do anything for them, unless they found Ricardo, so he could take him back and lay him to rest. He knew exactly what this would mean to those two young girls, especially Ricardo's *novia*, Sofia. So he spent an extra two hours negotiating and when they finally found Ricardo in the makeshift morgue, they packed him up, and put him in the cargo hatch. He wanted him buried in the front of the church, to let the people know that this honorable and brave young man had thrown himself across Juliann's body to save her life. He had taken the brunt of the cave-in. Juliann knew this. That is why the doctors kept her in the drug-induced coma. They thought the emotional trauma far surpassed her physical need to heal. They didn't want her to know about the deaths of the children along with the loss of a leg. She needed time for the leg to heal without any emotional setbacks. At that time, it was life or death.

Maggie saw a glimmer of metal sparkle around Ricardo's neck. She bent over with Sofia and gently she took it off and put it around Sofia's neck.

Maggie whispered, "I know he'd want you to have it."

Sofia hugged Maggie. She didn't have to grieve alone anymore. She had a whole town full of people who watched her pain and knew what she was going through. Finally, Maggie took the girls to the front pew and they sat down while they had a special service for Ricardo. When it was over, Randolph, Damon, and six men from town stepped forward and carried the casket down the aisle and out the door. They followed a path to the small garden in the corner of the yard where all the flowers were blooming and an old oak tree shaded the large hole that had been dug. Carefully, they lowered the casket and put Ricardo to rest. There wasn't a dry eye in the crowd. That emotional morning would have an everlasting effect on everyone. Not only on these two young girls. Here they were, humbled by kindness, not only from Randolph, Damon, and Maggie, but by a whole town full of people who shared in their grief.

Rene D. Schultz

292

CHAPTER 26

FOR TWO DAYS, MAGGIE AND MARIA WORKED HARD at getting the children settled in. Maggie, Damon, and Randolph had to fly back to Los Angeles to lend support to Juliann while she was recovering. It was hard having to say goodbye to the children, especially for Maggie. Elena and Juan could not understand why she had to leave, and although they liked Maria, it wasn't the same kind of bond and they played out their anger as little ones always did. Chica and Sofia understood the circumstances and wanted Maggie to be instrumental in getting Juliann back on both feet and back to Mexico. Although they would miss her, they were happy to have Maria in their lives and the little ones around them. Marco was another story. He cried and cried when Damon went to leave. He pounded his hands on Damon's chest and kicked his feet—over and over, leaving Damon in a big ponder as to how to handle it. Maggie finally took the crying child out of Damon's arms. Immediately, she noticed the disappointment on Damon's face. Somehow he was becoming attached to that small, arrogant, and dramatic little boy without even knowing it. Randolph dropped Maggie and Damon off at home and then he took off for the hospital.

The last night Maggie was in Mexico, she picked up Sofia and took her to the little church. Together, they sat outside watching the sunset on the old stone bench Randolph had placed next to Ricardo's grave.

"Will you be okay when I leave?" Maggie asked.

She looked away. "I think so. This place is more than I ever dreamed of. For once in my life I feel a calm that has given me hope for my future. I only wish that awful earthquake had not taken my Ricardo. I wish we could enjoy this together."

Maggie brushed the hair from her eyes and bent over and kissed Sofia's forehead. "Did I ever tell you how much you mean to me? How if it wasn't for you, I might not be here today. You were the guiding light in Honduras that saved the little ones and me." Maggie bent over and kissed her again. Then she whispered, "If I had a child, I would have wanted her to be just like you!" Tears came to Maggie's eyes as her only regret in life resurfaced.

Together, they slowly walked into that small church that held so much meaning within its walls. They each walked over to a pew, sat down and bent their heads.

When the plane took off, Maggie felt like half of her was left behind. It was only a week ago she had left for a quick four-day trip to Honduras to see her friend and the orphanage. After the earthquake, and separation from Juliann, her only goal was to get home. She had come back a totally different person—she could tell. In those seven days, her mind had become attached to so many memories. Not bad memories—a lifetime of memories that she could place into a photo album. She wanted to get back to Los Angeles and try to resume the normalcy she had left behind. Everything that once was meaningful in her life was changing so rapidly. Her need for writing was becoming a distant priority; her relationship with Damon had deepened; and suddenly there was a deep void she had never felt before.

It took them a few days to settle into Los Angeles. The first night home she remembered crying on the phone with Elizabeth, as she told her story. Hours later, Lucy and Denise came over just to make sure Maggie was okay. They wanted to hear her story and how she stayed alive with all the death and destruction surrounding those days. They both thought Maggie was so naïve, and yet she had survived.

Denise sipped her hot coffee. Then she said, "I can't imagine what you went through."

Maggie looked solemn when she said, "No, you couldn't. Nobody could. I was there with Juliann, and yet we both went through completely different life-changing experiences."

Both the women had commented on how quiet Maggie had been since she came home. Maggie sloughed it off, saying, "I'm just tired and trying to catch up with the reality of what happened."

Lucy looked at Maggie, "I truly get that!"

"I know! I think a lot of this has to do with missing Chica and Sofia."

"How is Juliann doing?" Lucy asked.

"Rand hasn't left her side since he's been back. He spends some of his days there and most of his evenings. They set up a sofa in her room. Yesterday they finally brought her out of the coma. I go there to visit a few hours a day."

"Do you think she will go back to Honduras?" Denise questioned.

Maggie closed her eyes. "I don't know. She needs some time. Rand wants to bring her to Mexico to do rehab, I don't know if she'll go there either. I know she gets these enormous flower arrangements every day and she sends them down to the oncology ward. I assume they are from her parents, but she never mentions them— not ever!"

"When she's ready, she will talk. It took Lucy a while to open up after we found her. I didn't want her to tell me until she was ready." Maggie put her arm around Lucy who was sitting next to her on the couch.

Lucy turned and looked directly at Maggie's sad face. "I talked to Elizabeth today. She said, William and her were getting ready to come out next month for Christmas. I was thinking maybe we should have Christmas at Randolph's hacienda this year. It will be a break from our tradition, but I think it will hold a different meaning."

Maggie smiled. "Really? Can we do that? Have everyone in Mexico?"

Lucy patted Maggie's hand. "That seemed to perk you up a little! I think it would be nice to let our kids met the children in Casa de Niños. Besides, I know you want to see how Chica, Sofia, and the kids are doing."

Maggie put her hand over her heart and beamed. "I certainly do...."

Denise stood up and grabbed her purse. "I'm sorry, I want my grumpy, mopey Maggie back!"

A week later, the family agreed to spend the holiday season at Randolph's hacienda. Maggie couldn't be happier. She couldn't wait to go tell Juliann. For the past few weeks, she had kept Juliann up to date on the progress of everything going on. Delight and excitement filled her voice when she told Juliann about Sofia, Chica, and the small children and how happy they were. She told her how ruthless Randolph was with negotiations with the Honduran government until the embassy finally gave in—in exchange for money and favors. Randolph didn't care. He worked his hardest to get the children out of there.

When Juliann had come out of the coma, she was emotionally too weak to let her know everything that went on during that shattering week. Each day as she began to get stronger, slowly Maggie brought her up to date—including Ricardo. Juliann had cried for days at the loss of her dear friend and helper. She actually remembered those moments just before she was injured. Those memories, and the pain, constantly floated around in her nightmares. She recalled picking some debris off a young child when the ground began to shake again. Ricardo moved as quickly as he could, and pushed her down to the ground, laying his body across her. Abruptly, everything began to fall from the ceiling. The weight was insurmountable, and the pain was past excruciating. Just before she passed out, she remembered seeing out of the corner of her eye—the sky.

She didn't know if that meant she was looking at heaven—or if the building was lying on her chest. She didn't know what happened to Ricardo, everything after that moment ceased to exist. She was told by Randolph that he gave his life in exchange for hers. He was that kind of kid. He watched out for the children and the ones he loved, after all, he had had nothing in his short life until Juliann found him on the streets and offered him a safe haven. Juliann was devastated at his loss. The ache of losing him would not allow her to speak his name.

Until one day, while Maggie was visiting, she finally needed to talk about him. She was very quiet and somber as she laid in bed. Maggie sometimes didn't know what to do or how to help. She would bring in her cellphone with pictures of the kids at Casa, to see if it would spark any interest back into her life—it didn't. Then, one morning Maggie showed her a recent picture of Sofia sitting in the corner of the play yard writing in her journal. Maria had taken that picture without her knowing.

Juliann looked at it and said, "I'm so glad they had each other."

Maggie looked at Juliann and questioned, "Who is 'they'?"

Juliann suddenly smiled. "Sofia and Ricardo. No one knew but me, for the longest time. They had fallen in love. Sofia had come to me one night to ask if she was allowed to see Ricardo. Imagine that...."

"She is such a dear young woman, and I think she respects you immensely—enough to ask you."

Juliann's eyes glassed over. "I said to her, 'My little bird...spread your wings and fly. Love who you will, and never let anyone in life stop you.' Oh Maggie, I miss my babies."

Tears welled in Maggie's eyes as she listened to the words of her friend. "Sofia is dealing with a lot of grief. She told me her story of Ricardo and how much she loved him. We have been helping her deal with it and she's doing a little better. The little ones are thriving in the new environment."

Juliann wiped her tears and said, "I want to see and hold my children again. I want to be there during Christmas. I think, I will work real hard in the next few weeks, and make that my goal!"

Maggie bent over and gave Juliann a hug. "It would be my honor to personally carry you out of this hospital and onto that plane!"

Juliann grinned, "Deal!"

From that morning forward, Randolph and Maggie began to see the light come back into Juliann's eyes. Something had changed. She had won the fight with grieving and generated a new fight on her hands—to leave that hospital and walk again. The doctors were amazed at the transition and the new patient they were dealing with. She began to get aggressive with her rehabilitation and every day she accomplished some goal she had set. There was no stopping her and Randolph was not surprised by her tenacity. The old Juliann was back and kicking stronger than before.

Later that week, when Maggie was visiting, she pulled out her cellphone and showed her some more pictures that Maria had sent. All the children, from both orphanages, were playing and there were smiles galore. The picture that drew Juliann's attention, and brought a big smile to her face, was of Damon and Marco. Damon had Marco on his shoulders. They were both laughing; and Marco had pulled Damon's hair out on both sides to make it look like horns. Damon was walking toward his car.

"Well, well, well…. Looks like Damon might have a lifetime buddy!" Juliann said, pointing to the picture.

Maggie grinned. "I didn't show him the picture Maria took. I know he's stopped overnight, once or twice, at Randolph's on his way home from a case. I didn't know why, until Maria sent me this picture on the QT. I think he's become attached to that little guy! Or that the little guy has slowly whittled his way into Damon's heart. Whichever one, he hasn't said much to me."

She tapped Maggie's hand. "It's not hard with any one of those sweet children. They are so willing to give their love to anyone who wants it. Looks like Marco was a good picker!"

Both the women laughed. Then Maggie had a serious look on her face. "Do you think I'm too old to have babies?"

Juliann looked overjoyed at this question. "That depends. Do you want one of your own with Damon? Or would you want to adopt?"

Maggie looked confused. "I don't know. I would love to have one of Damon's children, but we aren't even married. And you're a doctor…my body might be too old to have children of my own, especially because my reproductive parts were never used!"

Juliann started to laugh. "Sometimes your choice of words gets me hysterical. 'Reproductive parts?' I think that is something you should talk to Damon about. Does he even want children or that heavy responsibility? I mean—it's a lifetime commitment."

Maggie looked sad. "But what if I want a child, and he doesn't? Where do we go from there? I remember questioning myself when I was almost forty. I asked myself, *'Would I miss out in life if I didn't have children? Would I be richer if I married and had a child of my own? Did I limit myself emotionally, afraid of failure like my mother? Did fear close the door on my heart?'* Here I am at forty-five, and I'm questioning myself again. "

Juliann was lying in bed and Maggie was sitting next to her. She held out her open arms. "Come here, crazy lady! Bend down and give me a hug." Juliann watched as a single tear floated down Maggie's cheek. "I think you need to talk to Damon, tell him how you feel and go from there. And always remember, that life is filled with choices. You just don't want to live with regrets!"

Maggie looked at Juliann. She had withdrawn and looked like she was pulling up a sad memory. "Do you have regrets?"

Juliann looked away. "A few...."

"So you speak from experience?"

"Enough experience to last me a lifetime! I've had the past few months to sit in bed and reflect on my life. I've made some big mistakes that I chose not to repeat." She sighed. "So, please, my dear friend, if you want to do something, think deeply and once that decision is made—just do it or those regrets will forever come back to haunt you—trust me!"

Maggie thought to herself, '*Do I give up the idea of having children, if Damon doesn't want them? Or do I give up Damon and have a child? How can this be a fair decision?'*

CHAPTER 27

ANOTHER MONTH HAD PASSED QUICKLY AND Christmas was just around the corner. Elizabeth, William, and all their children were so excited to fly down to Mexico. They had been there for a few short trips over the years, but nothing like a full Christmas break. With all the work that needed to be done to restore the farm after the flood, even William could not wait to rest and relax.

Lucy was almost reluctant to come and was going to send Mary Jane with Maggie. She had been dating Bradley Lane for close to a year. Ever since the shooting at Safe House. As an investigative reporter that traveled around the world in hopes for the next big story, his job sometimes took him away for weeks at a time. This had given Lucy plenty of space to gradually adjust to their slow-moving relationship, and the emotional changes it brought into her life.

Bradley was a hard-shelled loner who had been through a tumultuous marriage that ended in divorce ten years earlier. His wife was an alcoholic who had left him for an old schoolmate after seven years of marriage. They had one beautiful son who Bradley adored. Soon after his wife had left him, his only child accidentally drowned, at the age of six, in the backyard swimming pool. It happened one night when his wife had passed out after a full day of drinking. His son and a friend were diving into the pool at the shallow end, when unexpectedly he hit his head and drowned. Bradley was beyond consolable over the loss and it became a crucial turning point in his life. For the next ten years, he had submerged himself into his job, leaving him no desire, nor time, to indulge in any kind of meaningful relationship.

That night he met Lucy, he was very impressed with her quick thinking and actions to save the lives of her coworkers. He thought she was a very interesting lady and for the first time in a long time, he actually wanted to learn more about someone. His intentions were more protective than developing a relationship. Lucy was very upfront and honest with him about her sobriety. She also let him know about her years living on the streets, the part of her dark past that followed her. The first few months they communicated on the phone, or through text messages. With his constant traveling, it also left less pressure to fit in time for him into everything else she had going on; her challenging job that she worked so hard at maintaining and her daughter, Mary Jane. Lucy had never dated, and was a very private person. Her main concern was about Mary Jane and what kind of bond she would have with any man that Lucy brought into her life. He loved children and he got along incredibly well with Mary Jane. It was just that she had had only two men in her life over the past five years, and she adored Randolph and Damon.

Mary Jane had only been with Lucy for the past five years. When Lucy was living on the streets, and without any means of supporting her child, social services stepped in and placed her in foster care. Mary Jane was conceived from rape, and she was barely two years old when the state pushed her in its broken foster care system. Those early years had been so lonely and hard on Mary Jane—being shuffled from one foster home to the next. It was like being a piece of luggage that was frequently passed around. Many of the social workers didn't care, most of the time they just placed her in houses filled with strangers. Just as she would settle in, the system would pull her out and repeat that ugly cycle. This went on for years, leaving Mary Jane emotionally distraught and introverted.

Once Maggie found Lucy and helped her to become clean and sober, she went after full-custody for Mary Jane. By then, she was almost eight years old, and grateful to finally have a permanent home. The dramatic changes, and solid stability, had been a highpoint of her relationship with her mom and Maggie. It was also the stability that kept Lucy working hard at sobriety. Mary Jane was happy, well-adjusted, and adored her mother and all the family that now surrounded her, including her best friend, Briana—Denise's daughter.

Lucy called Maggie one afternoon. "Hello."

"Aren't you getting excited about going to Mexico for Christmas? It's only a week away!"

"I'm so torn, Maggie. Bradley has the week off and I was hoping to spend some time with him. You know we've been seeing each other for nearly a year and it would be our first Christmas together. He wanted me to meet his family." There was a silent pause.

"Are you okay with that?" Maggie asked.

"That's really scary for me, to even consider meeting someone's family. This is where his family has a chance to judge me. I really don't care if they like me or not. It's the turning point that will probably deepen this relationship...or end it. I don't know if I'm really ready or know how to handle this."

"The same way you handled it when you told him about your sordid past of being homeless, the 'johns,' and being raped on the street. You sit down and be honest with your feelings."

"I know. But then, he's an investigative reporter like Becca, and probably knew everything before I told him."

"When you did tell him about your homeless past, did it stop him from wanting to be around you, Lucy?"

"No."

"Then he accepts your past and who you are now. Listen, Lucy, everyone has a past—everyone! You can't change it, but you can learn from it. I did a lot of soul searching this past year with all that I went through. I've come to the conclusion that I now have to concentrate on me—and what makes me happy!"

"Well, I want to be with my family and I don't think that will make him happy. From what he tells me, he has a big, loving family. Four sisters, nieces and nephews, and two great parents. How can I compete with that? That is what scares me! What if they judge me? What if they don't like me?"

"YOU don't compete. But you go to meet them and give them a chance. It's only fair to him."

"How can I do that?"

Maggie replied, "I'd do three days in Mexico. Come home and do time with Bradley and his family. Then you've given everyone some of your holiday time. Does that sound fair?"

Lucy was silent for a moment. "Yes, what a perfect solution. I will talk with Bradley."

"Why don't you invite Bradley for the days with us? I'm sure everyone would love to get to know him better! I've only met him a few times. Let him come hang with the family and kids."

"Really? You don't think anyone would mind? That would be great. Thank you, Maggie. I knew you would come up with something that worked."

"I love you, Lucy, I want you to be happy."

The private jet was flying from Los Angeles to Mexico. Maggie, Damon, Lucy, Mary Jane, Bradley, Randall, and Meg were on board. Randolph was already at the hacienda, along with Elizabeth and William. They had arrived one day earlier, and were already enjoying Lupe's authentic Mexican meals and hospitality, along with beautiful balmy sunsets. This had been a tumultuous year—from the summer of unpredictable weather; from flooding to tornados, and now ice storms that had besieged their state in the past week. For once, William actually acknowledged his anticipation in this end of the year holiday reprieve from the farm. Elizabeth was just eager to see the whole family and finally spend some quality time together. Her year had been emotionally challenging, with Randall gone and in school, and now with Meg in Los Angeles, too.

It had been one of the hardest, but most emotional years they had experienced together. There were so many changes, and so much had taken place, with the shooting at Safe House, Meg nearly losing her life in the flood, Juliann losing a leg in the earthquake, and William and Elizabeth nearly losing their small town. Looking back, the small stuff, now, almost seemed insignificant to the reality that everyone had made it through. This was going to be healing and a new beginning to a new year they were all looking forward to. It was going to be a fun-filled ten days of sheer bliss and relaxation. Randolph had planned events and excursions to keep everyone busy and happy. But, most of all, he was hoping Juliann would get out of the hospital earlier than the doctors predicted, so she could join them at the hacienda.

The roar of the jet engines nearly lulled Maggie to sleep. She was sipping on her wine and snuggled up next to Damon on the couch. He was texting on his phone.

She tapped his phone with her finger. "I'm taking everyone's phone away when we get to the hacienda. Yours included!"

"Oh yeah?" He raised his eyebrows. Then he winked.

"We're on an official vacation, remember?"

Damon bent over and whispered something into Maggie's ear and suddenly her face turned bright red. Feeling the heat of her flush, she looked around and was thankful that no one had noticed her reaction to his words. Damon tapped her nose and winked.

Bradley was playing a game on the iPad with Mary Jane. Lucy was watching, with amazement on her face, as her daughter beat Bradley and was filled with laughter. Randall and Meg were tucked in the corner at Randolph's desk, using the computer. Meg was showing him some of her projects from school.

The plane began to descend as the engines thundered in the sky. The pilot came into the room to announce that they would be landing in ten minutes. They all buckled up and were waiting with great anticipation.

Once the plane came to a complete stop, the steward came over and opened the door for their departure. Meg and Randall were the first ones down the steps and into the arms of their mother. Lucy, Bradley, and Mary Jane were next. Mary Jane was running toward Randolph and jumped into his open arms. He swung her round and round, making her so dizzy he had to hold her tight until her head quit spinning. Damon slowly walked down with Maggie as they watched everyone gathered on the tarmac. The four orphans were once again back together; their ties deeper than when they had spent the twelve years in the orphanage. Everyone gradually filled the three

Jeeps that were waiting to take them to the hacienda. Randolph rode with Damon and Maggie.

This was a new experience for Bradley. He had been learning a lot about the reclusive and tough CEO of Compsoft. Everything he had heard and all that was written about Randolph was far from the man he was beginning to know. Known as a ruthless opponent in the boardroom that would cut you to shreds in a blink; this was not the sensitive and loving man in front of him. Bradley was completely surprised by his attentive, caring relationships with his family.

Once they pulled into the hacienda, pandemonium broke out and the kids disappeared as though they all knew where to go and how to get there. And they did! Randolph led the adults along the path around the house, along the edge of the cliff overlooking the ocean. The sun was just setting over the horizon and the dramatic hues of the sky reminded Maggie of the first time she was here.

Walking between Damon and Randolph, Maggie said, "This place always seems to amaze me. Every sunset is more beautiful than the next. I can still remember the first one. From the moment we walked around this corner, I knew why you fell in love with this place."

Randolph squeezed her hand. "That was the best day of my life."

Maggie stopped and looked up at Randolph. With eyes glistening, she proudly said, "Mine, too!"

They turned and started to walk again, leading the adults across the patio and by the free-formed pool that blended in with the landscape. Carefully, they stepped around the large formations of rocks and plants that gave it a natural exotic ambience.

Maggie watched Bradley's face as he took in the world of Randolph Parker and his family. It was an unassuming but deeply extraordinary world of simplicity, mixed with natural beauty and art. His eyes opened wide as he looked around.

Maggie touched his shoulder. "It's beauty at its finest. Don't you think?"

Bradley nodded his head, looking to absorb his surroundings and the family he was with. "This is beautiful. My family has an estate on Cape Cod and this reminds me of it. Where the ocean meets the land and it becomes surreal."

"Cape Cod! I love that area on the east coast. The town of Nantucket stole my heart." Maggie smiled.

He laughed. "That was my summer playground! I could find more mischief on that little island than my parents ever thought possible. I would sail over there all the time."

Randolph turned around and said, "I met your father at some charity event. He's a very nice man and he adores his children. You have four sisters, right?"

Bradley smiled. "I guess you probably knew who my father was from the minute I introduced myself?"

Randolph clapped Bradley on the back and said, "Come on. Damon and I knew practically the minute you said a word at Safe House. Damon is an investigator of people, and you're an investigative reporter—one in the same. Don't you think? Besides, in my private world, it doesn't really matter who you are."

Lucy's face turned red and she got angry. "You checked him out?"

Bradley took ahold of Lucy's shaking shoulders and turned her gently toward him. "I didn't expect any different, sweetheart! I'm just as cautious and protective over my four sisters. Come on, it's done! We all finally laid our cards on the table. Let's enjoy this beautiful sunset."

Lucy still looked stunned. "You knew all about me before I confessed about my past, didn't you?"

He brought her hand up to his mouth and kissed it. "We all have a past. It's really about living in today—it's not the past or the future. That first night, I was in awe of that unselfish person that risked her life for others. If I let your past bother me, I wouldn't be here right now."

Damon clapped Bradley on the back. "You know—I'm beginning to like this guy!"

For the next few hours, they enjoyed the wonderful balmy evening as the moon rose over the ocean and cast its shimmering light. The children put on their swimsuits and splashed in the pool as the adults sat back and relaxed.

Damon looked at Bradley and suggested, "Why don't you take a walk along the beach. It's a beautiful evening. Maggie and I do that every chance we get. I think it's only fair that we share!"

"Great idea!" Bradley stood up and pulled out Lucy's chair. Bradley took her hand and they walked over to the stairs. Lucy took off her sandals and Bradley took his off and rolled up his jeans. Carefully, they disappeared down the stairs.

Maggie looked at everyone sitting around the table and then she took her finger and pointed it at Randolph and Damon. "I should smack you both right here and right now. Leave poor Lucy and Bradley alone. You are not their social directors!"

Damon stood up and grabbed Maggie's hand, and pulled her up. "Say good night to everyone. I may not be their social director, but tonight I am yours!" He planted a kiss on her lips and pulled her toward the house. Maggie started to laugh and suddenly Damon swung down and scooped her up and carried her into the house. Maggie could hear everyone laughing.

CHAPTER 28

THE FIRST THING IN THE MORNING AFTER BREAKFAST, they piled into the Jeeps and drove to the orphanage. Maggie was excited to see the kids and to see Chica and Sofia. Barely able to get her breakfast down, she kept nudging Damon to hurry up.

"Slow down, you little hussy!" He swatted her ass.

Maggie's face turned red and she looked around to see if anyone was paying attention to his brazen words. "I'm just anxious to see the children. Take your coffee with you and let's go!" She tugged at his hand and he laughed as she dragged him to the Jeep.

Randolph was laughing as he yelled out to Damon, "She might as well put that damn leash around your neck, now!"

Damon looked at all the kids that were getting into the cars and held on to what he was going to say. He slid into the driver's seat and started the Jeep. Within minutes, they were pulling up to the gate. The gates automatically opened and the cars pulled in and parked. Standing in front of the complex, all of the children were waiting anxiously for their guests.

As Damon was getting out of the car, Marco came running over with his hands out. Without as much as a blink, Damon bent down and lifted him up into his arms. "Hey, buddy, what's up? Are you happy to see me?"

At three years old, he had never had a male role model in his short life. His fourteen-year-old mother had died on the streets inhaling the glue that killed most of the younger ones in Honduras. Juliann had found him in a group of children on the streets. Terrified he was too young to survive; she snatched him up and brought him to the orphanage. Now, he was in Damon's strong arms, jumping up and down with happiness. Once he calmed down, Maggie watched as Marco took his small little hands and rubbed Damon's face. To Maggie it looked like a father and son type of relationship starting, and yet, Damon didn't want the responsibility of children.

Maggie made a decision she was going to talk to Damon on this trip. She wanted to let him know that this maternal part of her was starting to surface. She didn't necessarily want her own, but there was no reason why with all these little ones, they couldn't adopt. She didn't want to force his hand, but she knew she didn't want to deal with regrets later on in life, either.

Maria showed the adults around, the children blended in with the others. Damon went to the playground with Marco, and Maggie went in search of Chica and Sofia. Chica found Maggie and they walked around looking at some of the changes.

"How do you like it here?" Maggie asked.

"There's no comparing to Puerto Cortés. I love this place, the town, and the people. They let me take one day off a week, and sometimes Sofia and I just go into town to window shop and talk with the people. It's fun."

Maggie hugged Chica. "That's what life is about—having a fun time."

Chica suddenly looked sad. "I wish you would tell Sofia that. She's been moping around a lot."

Maria found them and asked Chica if she would go clean and dress Pablo's skinned knee. "Seems he was jumping off the slide with Juan and they both got scraped up. I would really appreciate the help."

Chica smiled. "Those two little boys are like a ball of fast moving fire when they are together!"

Chica took off in a run to see what she could do for the little ones. Maria sat there for a moment and said to Maggie, "Maybe you should take Sofia for a walk and see if she'll talk to you. She's been very moody and depressed lately."

Maggie looked at Maria and said, "I heard the same thing from Chica. Let me go look for her."

Maggie walked around until she found Sofia in the corner of the yard—sleeping on a patch of grass. Maggie sat down and tickled her with a blade of grass. Sofia took her hand and swatted the pesky intruder away. Maggie did it again, this time with a big smile on her face. Sofia swatted again, only this time she opened her eyes. With a gasp of air, she sat up and threw herself at Maggie, hugging her with all her might.

Reluctant to let her go, Maggie finally backed away and asked, "I heard you were having a tough time. What's wrong? I told you to call me and gave you my phone number. How come you didn't call?"

Sofia looked away, with tears starting to accumulate. "Too scared."

Maggie drew her brows together. "Of what? Me?"

Sofia shook her head.

"Let's walk." Maggie stood up and helped Sofia. For the first time, she took a good look at her standing there. She had gained a little weight and her face was fuller. That would have been normal and Maggie would not have noticed if she hadn't got to know her better when they were stranded with the children in Honduras. Maggie took her young face between her hands and made her look directly at her. "Are you okay?"

Sofia looked away. "Can we go to the church? Just for a few minutes. I'd like to see Ricardo."

Maggie took her hand and they walked to the Jeep. She saw Damon and explained, "Sofia wants to go to the church for a few minutes. We'll be right back."

Once they got to the church, they got out of the car and walked over to the bench in front of the grave. They sat down in silence as the breeze blew across the garden.

"You miss him, don't you?" Maggie broke the silence.

"*Si.*"

"What's wrong, *hija*?" Maggie asked.

Tears started to slide down both cheeks and they turned into sobs. Maggie moved closer and put her arms around the young child. When her sobs were reduced to hiccups, Sofia finally said, "I'm so scared, Miss Maggie."

"Why?"

She took her hand and started to rub her stomach. Maggie inhaled deeply and let out her breath slowly. "You're going to have Ricardo's, baby?"

Sofia nodded as the tears began again.

Maggie quietly asked, "Does anybody know?"

"No…."

"I don't want you to be scared. There is no reason. I don't want you to tell anyone for a few days. Let me think about this and see what we should do. I just don't want you to be frightened—there is no need. You've got a lot of people who love you and we will find a way to see what we can do."

"Okay."

Maggie put her finger under her chin and tilted her head up. "Hold your head high. There is nothing to be ashamed of. Ricardo is the father and was a brave young man. He saved Juliann's life."

Sofia nodded.

"Do you want to keep the baby?"

"I don't know if I can take care of it by myself."

"Well, I don't want you to worry. We will figure something out." Maggie hugged her.

That night at dinner, Damon could tell Maggie had something on her mind. She was one of the most transparent women he'd ever known. "You okay, Maggie? What's up?"

Maggie shook her head. "Nothing, just tired after a very long day. Boy, those kids just wore me out!"

Damon's eyes opened wide. "Really? I thought you were thinking about having children? Can't keep up with them?"

"Of course I can! Just not thirty-five all in my face—at once!"

Damon laughed. "I have good news. Randolph is going to pick up Juliann tomorrow and bring her back here. She's excited to see Chica, Sofia, and the little ones. It's been months, and she has missed them so much. I think Randolph is hoping to talk her into staying and settling down in Mexico."

"I'm so happy she's going to spend the holidays with us. I've missed her tremendously. I can't wait to see her!"

That night after a family dinner, filled with noise and chaos, everyone sat around the patio talking about the next few days and all the activities Randolph had planned. They were going to spend the next day at the ranch and do some serious horseback riding, barbequing, and have some of his ranch hands and their families enjoy it with them. He planned piñatas for the younger kids, a mini-rodeo for the older ones, and in the evening, a group of Mariachi's walking and strumming through the crowd. Everyone went to bed early to prepare for the next day.

Maggie had wrapped a towel around her body when she walked into the bedroom. Her eyes scanned the room, looking for Damon. Out of the corner of her eye, she saw a movement on the patio, so with her bare feet sliding across the tile, she targeted what she was looking for. Damon was lying on the large lounge chair in the moonlight, slowly sipping a short glass of whiskey. She could tell he was concentrating deeply about something. With the sleekness of a panther, she slid in next to him on the lounge, stretching her entire body alongside of his.

He looked down at her and she could see the slight creases around his eyes as he grinned. "Long day?"

Maggie nodded her head. Then she laid her hand on his chest and started playing with the button of his shirt. "I watched you today with Marco. He sure has attached himself to your hipbone!"

He placed his hand over hers on his chest. "He's a cute little critter!"

"I don't know if it's such a good idea to let him depend on you so much. I'd hate to see his heart broken. He's such a young little boy and when we leave next week, it could be devastating to him."

"Why don't you just tell me what you want to discuss with me, instead of beating around the bush?" Damon said, grinning.

Damon knew her like a book. He always hit the target when it came to Maggie. She pushed herself up into a sitting position so she could see his eyes when they were talking. She had a way of distracting him when she knew the conversation was going to get intense. "You know how we were talking a while ago about how time was running out with me having my own children, but leaving the door open to maybe adopting a child?"

Damon looked down at his glass and swirled the amber liquid. "Uh huh."

Maggie slipped the glass out of his hand and took a small sip and handed it back. She hated the taste of hard liquor and she scrunched up her face as it slid down her throat. "Well, I have been doing a lot of thinking lately."

"As you always do...." He tapped her nose with his finger.

"Yes! And it left me with a lot of questions I've had to ask myself. One afternoon Juliann and I had a long talk at the hospital, she said regrets are hard to live with. She told me a few of hers."

"Yeah?"

"I don't want to live with regrets because I was too selfish to see the whole picture."

Damon lifted her chin up and looked her directly in the eyes. His concern was beginning to show. "What kind of regrets are we talking about?"

"I've been alone all my life. My mother left me to fend for myself and then I had closed myself off from everything and everyone. When I finally went to find Elizabeth, and stayed at her house for that week, I began to feel like I never gave myself a chance to let anyone get close to me. Then you came along and it terrified the hell out of me!"

He smiled. "Am I that scary?"

"No...I...."

"Why don't you just come out and tell me what you're really thinking."

"I love you with all my heart, but I want to share that—"

He cut her off. "Oh? You want a *ménage á trois*?" Damon smiled. She could tell he was just playing with her.

"No, I want a child. I want a little Maggie or Damon running around my house! I'm not getting any younger and I don't want to regret it later in life that I didn't take that chance."

Damon started to laugh out loud. "Oh...this is the serious talk you've been wanting to have? Well, how can we have a child if we aren't even married yet?"

Maggie sat straight up and her nostrils began to flair. "I don't give a shit if we are married or not! I want to have a baby! Even if it's not my own, but adopted. After spending that time in Honduras and here, I know now, this is what I want!"

Damon had a serious look on his face. "And what about me? Does it matter if I do or I don't?"

Maggie bent over and wrapped her hands around his face, just like Marco had done. "I was hoping you would consider it at least." She bent down and kissed him.

When she finally pulled away, he said, "Do you need an answer tonight? Or can I have a few days to absorb what you are asking of me?"

Maggie tapped his nose, this time. "You can think about it. I just wanted to put it out there. I've been giving this a lot of thought."

Damon took a sip of his whiskey and pulled her back down to lay next to him. "Okay."

Rene D. Schultz

CHAPTER 29

MAGGIE WAS REALLY EXCITED. JULIANN WAS FLYING in early and Maggie got up to greet her at the plane with Randolph. Damon stayed back at the hacienda to sleep in. Maggie watched with great anticipation. When the plane finally stopped and the doors opened, Maggie stood on the tarmac, giving Randolph time to bring her out. Within seconds, Randolph was carefully carrying her down the stairs with a big smile on his face. Maggie hadn't seen him that happy in a long time.

Juliann had her arms around his neck and her head on his shoulder. When they reached the bottom, he walked over to Maggie. She kissed Juliann on the cheek and was jumping up and down. "*La bienvenida, a mi amigo.*"

Juliann started to giggle. "Oh, Maggie, it's so good to see you! And it's so nice to be back here. I can't wait to see everyone."

Randolph placed her in the wheelchair that had been sitting on the tarmac. Then they all began to stroll to the nearby Jeep. With all the energy of a young kid, Randolph lifted Juliann up and positioned her into the front seat. "Are you okay?"

"Of course, silly! I'm going to be okay, now! I'm so excited to be here today. I feel like I'm finally home! I hate hospitals and now I can take a breath of fresh air." Randolph helped Maggie into the Jeep, kissed Juliann on the cheek, and shut the door. When they got to the hacienda, exhilaration was everywhere. Everyone came out to welcome Juliann and then the festivities began.

Lupe had made a big buffet breakfast and large tables were set up on the patio to accommodate everyone. Lights were being strung up and the big party was coming together for Juliann's homecoming. Maggie was thrilled and everyone was in a partying mood, even William.

The children and the family were having a great morning. They had just finished breakfast when Damon leaned over and whispered to Maggie. "You promised me that we would spend the day together. I wanted to go into the nearby town and enjoy some private time, just the two of us. I promise we will be back way before it gets dark so that we can hang and enjoy this fiesta!"

Maggie looked around her and frowned. Then she looked at Damon with his pleading eyes as they focused on her. "I would really like just the two of us, right now."

They got up and said their goodbyes. Randolph looked at Damon and clapped him on the back.

Juliann was sitting down and Maggie bent down and hugged her. "I think Randolph has a few surprises for you."

"What? Tell me...."

"I wouldn't be much of a friend if I ruined it now, would I?" Maggie stood up and waved goodbye.

Damon and Maggie got into the Jeep and drove off as the gathering of friends continued. Randolph let the rest of the helpers organize the patio. Then he turned to Juliann and said, "Are you ready to go see all the children? YOU have so many kids who are waiting patiently for you! Come on...let's go!"

When they pulled up in front of Casa de Niño's, the gate opened and Randolph drove in. Standing eagerly in the courtyard were all the children. Screams and laughter filled the air when Juliann was carried out of the car and seated in the wheelchair. Maria was the first to impatiently come over and give her a hug. Then the children gathered around. But it was Sofia and Chica who brought the tears to her eyes as she placed her hand over her pounding heart.

They both bent down and wiped the tears from Juliann's face and their own. "Let's go someplace where we can talk."

The two young women took her to the corner of the yard where Sofia would always go to hide. The girls sat down on the grass and they talked about the whole tribulation they had gone through in Honduras that finally got them here to Mexico. Each had their own story, and each was healing the best they could. Many tears, lots of laughter, and acknowledgements of the past floated around as the pain continued to purge. All except for Ricardo. Sofia had asked Chica earlier if she could show Juliann his grave by herself. Chica agreed.

HOUSE OF STONE

Elena, Juan, Gitana, Luz, and Marco were so excited about her visit, but they were also very apprehensive. "You aren't going to make us go back, Miss Juliann, are you?" Marco asked, almost in tears.

Juliann looked dumbstruck at his question. Then she looked around at the four other little faces and could tell they were just as worried. Wanting to appease their fears, she answered. "This is your home now. Nobody is going to make you go back. This is where you will be, unless someone wants to adopt you."

Marco started to pout. "I want Mr. Damon to adopt me!"

Juliann looked surprised and then started to laugh. "Oh...really? Has he been around to see you?"

Marco pushed his lips out more in his pout and nodded.

"Well, let me see what I can do." Juliann remarked.

Marco began to jump up and down and clapping his hands.

By late afternoon, Juliann had nearly spent all of her energy and Sofia asked Randolph if he could take Juliann and her to the ranch. He agreed. When they got there, the place was swarming with lots of people setting up the area for the activities that evening. Lots of flowers and lights were being strung everywhere. The area was being filled with personal, meaningful, and spiritual beauty.

Juliann sat in the seat of the car and asked, "Does she know?"

Randolph grinned. "No! We were all sworn to secrecy."

Juliann smiled. "I'm so excited for her."

They got out of the car and Randolph gave Sofia the handles of the wheelchair. "I'll see you ladies, later!"

Juliann looked confused as Sofia quietly began to wheel her up the path and came upon the big oak tree and the bench. "I've been here many times, but I never have seen this bench. What a beautiful little area Randolph has made in this corner."

Juliann turned and saw the tears streaming down Sofia's face. She wanted to hold her in her arms, but she was stuck in the wheelchair. She held out her open arms. "Come here, sweet one. Why are you crying so?"

Sofia moved her closer to the bench and sat down on it. "Randolph would not leave Honduras without Ricardo."

Juliann's tears began to fill her eyes. "But he died, didn't he?"

Sofia got off the bench and laid down on the grass on her side, as though she were cuddling with someone. Her hand slowly stroked the grass. "We stayed two hours longer in Honduras, while Randolph pleaded with the government to release Ricardo's body. I did not know that then, not until we came back and he had a beautiful funeral for the whole town. We buried him right here."

Juliann gasped. "My Ricardo is here in Mexico with us? My sweet young boy who had laid his body over mine to save my life was brought back by Randolph?" Juliann began to sob. "Oh my God...."

Sofia sat up and took hold of Juliann's hand, as if it was not enough to give her this amazing gift. Sofia placed her hand on her small belly and rubbed her hand on it. Juliann gasped again, "Oh dear God, you're carrying his baby?"

They were both sobbing as the reality of death and life came in a bright light. Randolph watched from a distance and let the tears roll down his face. He would have done it over and over again with that nasty government if it meant making these two women as happy as they were.

When the tears had finally subsided, Juliann asked, "What are you going to do with the baby?"

Sofia smiled. "I'm giving Ricardo's baby to you. I know Ricardo would want you to raise the baby."

Juliann looked at Sofia and whispered, "It would be my honor...." She smiled and brushed the hair out of Sofia's face. "I will make Ricardo and you proud of your baby."

They sat there under the tree and talked as everything around them continued to become chaotic.

It was starting to get late. As they were walking through town, Damon stopped and looked at the most beautiful dress in the window of a fashionable dress store. It was a high-end shop that catered to tourists.

He stopped and looked at Maggie, then at his watch. "I think we had too much fun and now we are running late. Why don't you slip into the store and try on that beautiful white dress in the window. I love the off the shoulder look and it's so traditional for Mexico."

Maggie started to laugh as he pushed her into the store. "I think it's a traditional wedding dress. I can't wear that! I have a dress already for the party. Besides, it's quite expensive," she said, looking at the price tag.

"Damn it, Maggie, I don't think you will have time to change when we get back. In fact, I bet the party is in full swing. Put the dress on and see if it fits! I feel awful I kept you out so long. Please, babe...."

Maggie laughed. "Really...?"

Damon shoved her toward the dressing room. The he asked the sales lady to pick out some pretty white sandals to match it.

When she came out of the dressing room, Damon's eyes opened wide. "Wow! You look beautiful!"

Maggie blushed. "Thank you. Just take me back and I will change very quickly."

"We just don't have time!" He turned toward the sales lady and handed her his credit card. Maggie looked confused. They left the store, got in the Jeep, and headed toward the ranch.

"Where are you going? The party is at the hacienda."

"I know. I promised Randolph I would pick something up at the ranch before we came home. Holy crap! Hurry up, we're running so late!"

CHAPTER 30

WHEN DAMON AND MAGGIE PULLED UP TO THE ranch, the place was bursting at the seams with all their friends, family, and townspeople. Strands of light were hung across the space and it was overflowing with the most beautiful exotic flowers. He pulled up to the church and parked the car. He came around the car door and opened it. As Maggie stepped out of the car, she felt her fingers go numb. Standing to the side of the walkway that led to the church were Elizabeth, Lucy, and Meg dressed in authentic Mexican dresses, holding bouquets. On the other side of the walkway were Randolph, William, and Bradley. The church was filled to capacity as the sun was beginning to set over the horizon.

Maggie looked at Damon. Confusion was written all over her face. "What is going on here?"

He bent over and said, "You asked me if I wanted to adopt kids. I said I would think about it. I also think I said...we would have to be married...right?"

The light went on, and Maggie was standing there with shock written all over her face. At that moment, Damon plucked a flower from one of the large arrangements and slipped it behind her left ear. Then he got down on one knee and said, "Miss Maggie Gray, will you marry me tonight in front of God and all our friends, family, and townspeople?"

Amongst all the cheering and screams of anticipation, Damon stood up, tucked her hand in his elbow, and slowly walked Maggie down the aisle of her beloved church....

IF YOU'VE FINISHED
READING THIS BOOK,
PLEASE LEAVE AN
HONEST REVIEW ON
AMAZON.
THANK YOU!

I LOVE TO GARDEN, TRY NEW RECIPES, TAKE LOTS OF pictures and occasionally I enjoy a glass of wine with dear friends. I've never jumped out of a plane, climbed Mt. Everest, or seen the Northern Lights of Alaska. But, I have danced in the rain, sent a message in a bottle and I've rode my motorcycle down the Pacific Coast Highway on sunny California days!

My passion of writing has led me on the most amazing journey. I thrive on developing strong storylines that showcase today's contemporary lifestyles. Rags to riches, Robin Hood, and surviving the odds, seems to be my one common denominator that showcases my fascinating and diverse characters.

Bishop Street is an emotional, gut-wrenching journey of survival, friendship, and second chances... After twenty years, Maggie makes a life changing decision to find her three best friends from the orphanage. From the small towns in North Dakota, across the exotic beaches in Mexico, and searching the streets of homeless shelters in Los Angeles... will she find more than just her friends?

Done Deal is an inspiring book about a woman who doesn't understand why the pharmaceuticals are holding back 'orphan' drugs that can save lives. Why insurance companies won't pay to keep people alive. And why the government is closing its 'blind eyes.' Cissy goes on a quest to find these answers and what she discovers is shocking. With an anger that leaves her cynical, and with time running out, she sets out to 'right a wrong.' She forfeits her integrity and leaves a legacy that will crush the greedy pharmaceuticals and the corrupt insurance companies!

With the new age of technology, hackers become a reality and new Robin Hoods emerge.

Women are constantly pressured with the overwhelming message that achieving 'perfect beauty' is mandatory to be accepted and successful. Mercedes survived a childhood with a hateful and mentally ill mother who constantly called her an 'ugly duckling.' She knew she was not beautiful, or stunning, or even close to either. She was plain, simple, and ordinary. Take this journey with Mercedes and her four friends, who live in a city that judges a woman solely by her outside, and not her inside. Will the pressure to obtain beauty become her downfall, or will reality raise its ugly head and teach her the biggest lesson of her life? **'Beauty is only skin deep!'**

FOLLOW ME:
RENEDSCHULTZ
AMAZON – BARNES & NOBLE - GOODREADS